THE JAMMED

JUDGES

A Doro Banyon Cozy Historical
Mystery–BookThree

D.S. Lang

Ebook ISBN: 978-1-962039-08-6

Paperback ISBN: 978-1-962039-09-3

Editor: Alyssa B. Colton

Cover Designer: Karen Phillips

This is a work of fiction. The story, all names, characters, and incidents portrayed in this book are fictitious. No identification with actual persons (living or dead), places, buildings, and/or products is intended or should be inferred. Real locations are used fictitiously.

Chapter One

As she walked across Campus Commons, Dorothea Banyon savored the sunshine. The towering trees—elms, maples, and oaks—were sprouting green leaves, while daffodils and tulips budded in the beds lining the front of College Hall. After the winter's wrath was spent and before summer's roasting began, spring offered a tender transition. As Doro walked along, she was reminded of the season's brevity, which made her cherish it even more. Spring was a time when all things seemed possible.

"Good afternoon," Mrs. Jones, secretary to the college president, greeted Doro as they crossed paths. "You look happy."

"Who isn't happy on such a lovely day?" Doro stopped next to the older woman. As usual, Mrs. Jones was clad in a neat suit with a skirt that fell below her knees. Today's ensemble gave a nod to the warmer weather, since she wore a lavender linen blouse beneath the gray serge jacket. A bouquet of lilacs peeked out of the brown bag cradled in her arms. "The flowers are beautiful, and I love the scent." Doro took an appreciative whiff.

Mrs. Jones smiled. "My bushes are laden with blooms this year. Stop any time and pick as many as you like. I'm taking these to the office, in hope they brighten spirits and lessen complaints."

"How can anyone's spirits be low with such glorious weather?" Doro asked. Her mood soared as high as the birds in the cobalt blue sky.

"You know how it is at the end of a term. Students are anxious about examinations, and professors are trying to get everything done ahead of the summer closing. Then, there's the May Days festival this weekend. Committee work is keeping me busy after office hours. Folks have this and that they want handled. I enjoy it, though."

Sympathy filled Doro. "Taking over as committee chairwoman has added to your tasks." The previous head of Michaw's community events committee had been murdered in December. Sadly, few people missed the domineering matron, so Violet Jones was a much better choice due to her organizational skills and easy-going personality. Still, as a widow who worked full-time, she was shouldering a lot of responsibilities.

"I don't mind. It's such a fun event, and I enjoy welcoming spring after a long winter." Mrs. Jones chuckled. "As you get older, the cold weather and snow are harder to take."

Doro grimaced. "I'm not fond of winter now." Frigid winds sweeping across the farmland outside the town of Michaw often made for misery while out-and-about. Although the campus was compact, going from building to building meant a lot of walking. In winter, tramping through snow and ice was not unusual. But the inclement conditions were behind them for another season, and Doro was glad. "I'm looking forward to the cooking contest."

Mrs. Jones adjusted her spectacles, as if to get a better view of Doro. "Are you planning to enter?" A note of surprise was in her voice.

A chuckle escaped Doro. "No, I'm a mediocre cook, at best. Besides, my apartment only has a kitchenette, which doesn't provide enough space for a culinary project."

"Wheaton Hall has an enormous kitchen on the first floor. Some of the residents use it for cooking and baking large quantities," Mrs. Jones observed.

While the Hall, where Doro and other female professors lived, boasted modern appliances in the expansive kitchen, the domestic arts did not interest her. They never had and never would. Her career as a librarian came first and foremost. Mrs. Jones already knew that, so Doro grinned at the veiled suggestion, but it did not move her. "Many do, and it's already reserved by several women who plan to enter one of the contests. My friend Aggie is one of them. She's excited, and so am I. Aggie is a wonderful baker."

A smile curved Mrs. Jones' lips. "I sampled her fare at the spring luncheon last week. She brought cupcakes, and they were heavenly."

Pleasure spread through Doro. Her friend was talented in many ways, but Aggie lacked confidence. Winning the baking contest might increase her self-assurance. "She makes luscious desserts."

Mrs. Jones' shoulders rose and fell. "Even though I'm not a judge, I can't pick sides."

"Of course not," Doro agreed. "Luckily, I'll only be a bystander, so I can cheer Aggie on."

"As a best friend should. All the individual competitions are blind taste tests. In the baking portion, each entrant is making a jam roll, and we won't know who baked which one until the winner is named." She pushed her spectacles up. "I've asked Constable Lammers and Officer Mallow to be judges. Both said they've never had a jam roll baked by Aggie or the other ladies. I take them at their word."

Uneasiness crept through Doro as she wondered if everyone would feel the same way. "Wade and Ev are both honest." She had known Wade Lammers, the town constable, all her life, and he was trustworthy to the bone. Although Everett Mallow had only come to Michaw College the previous October, he'd also proven to be above reproach. As campus security officer, Ev had plenty on his plate, but he'd taken on the role of deputy constable, as well. Now, the two lawmen were friends.

"I didn't think they'd lie, but I want to ensure we're fair." The brunette sighed. "With Wade and Aggie stepping out, some folks could get upset. Most likely, a few of the participants will wonder."

"Wade's been a judge every year that I can recall. He used to take time off from his railroad job to be home for the big bake-off."

"True," Mrs. Jones agreed. "But I don't want to create extra scrutiny on him and Aggie."

Since her friend and Wade Lammers had been stepping out for several months, Doro was well aware of the speculation about the pair. Some folks disapproved because the constable was fifteen years older than her friend. On top of that, two unmarried ladies, a widow and a spinster who were closer to Wade's age, were not subtle in their displeasure. Or their pursuit of the man. "Neither do I. They aren't actually courting yet, and I'm afraid gossip is part of the reason." The line between stepping out and courtship was blurry at best, but the pair only attended events together sporadically.

"The town constable is already in the spotlight. Wade gets more attention because he worked on the railroad for years. Some folks don't believe that was enough experience for his current position."

"He was a security officer," Doro pointed out. "That seems similar to me."

"To me, too, but a handful of people find fault with him for small matters. One is his children needing attention." A soft sigh left Mrs.

Jones. "His mother helps, but Wade takes them to school and tries to get home for supper every night. As you know, the previous two constables were married, and their wives handled home matters."

"You'd think the critics would want him to go courting," Doro commented.

A look of resignation crossed the older woman's face. "Part of the issue is where Wade's interest seemed to be engaged."

The comment solidified Doro's suppositions. "Because of the age gap between Wade and Aggie being so wide."

"That's a big reason, especially for Betty Stanley and Lila Billings. They both took food after Wade's wife died a few years back. In return, he and the boys raked leaves for Betty and Lila. The boys also shoveled snow. Kind gestures, but the women took them as more than friendly help." Mrs. Jones grimaced. "Betty has been dropping off treats at the constable's office ever since Wade took over."

The information was not new to Doro. "Wade is polite, sometimes to a fault. Betty Stanley and Lila Billings are still inviting him and his children to dinner, according to what he's told Aggie. As for returning the baskets, Wade ends up staying for a cup of tea because Betty complained about being lonely. As for Lila, she frequently asks about safety for a woman living alone. Wade thinks she's really afraid, although Michaw is nearly crime-free."

"She can be dramatic," Mrs. Jones said. "Wade and Lila were in the same class, and I hear she was sweet on him back then. That was before my husband and I came to town."

"And before my time," Doro replied, "but I've heard the same thing. I've also heard Lila was terribly disappointed when Wade started courting his wife. They were all young then, so it stands to reason she saw an opening after he became a widower."

The older woman nodded. "She's been subtly, and not so subtly, pursuing him ever since they were kids. And he gave her a little en-couragement when his mourning period was over."

"By buying her basket at the May Days festivals."

"Yes. I'm afraid she took his kindness as interest. Lila isn't much of a cook. She focuses on quantity instead of quality. Her uncle was the only one who ever bid on her offerings. Now, she isn't happy about Wade and Aggie," Mrs. Jones said in a somber tone. "Not at all."

Like Doro, Lila Billings was an only child. Her mother had died when Lila was born, and her father had perished during the Spanish flu epidemic a decade earlier. Her uncle still lived in the area, and Lila had stayed with him for a time. If she was truly fearful, why not go back to his home? The question spun through Doro's mind, but she kept it to herself. "I understand her feelings to some degree. Looking ahead to being all alone can't be easy." Would that be her eventual fate?

"It isn't," Mrs. Jones agreed, "but Lila doesn't do herself any favors by criticizing Aggie. Although she's subtle, Lila often mentions Aggie having a career and wanting to work after marriage. Some folks agree married women should stay home."

Not just some. Many felt that way. "The college has a longstanding policy against employing married women, let alone mothers." Al-though the rule was under discussion, nothing had changed yet.

"At present, yes," Mrs. Jones replied, "but the board of trustees only fell one vote short of allowing female employees to be married."

"I know, but one of the *nays* would have to leave the board before the policy could be altered. Right now, all of them have several years remaining in their tenure." Although the Great War had wrought many changes in American society, only one-quarter of women were employed. Working married mothers were even scarcer. And Aggie would be a parent to Wade's youngsters, if they wed.

"President Adams is quietly lobbying a couple to change their votes at this year's annual meeting. Michaw has always been a progressive school, so that's his principal argument. That and times are changing. Many more women work now than did a decade ago. In another ten years, I'm sure even more will."

Doro's pulse raced. "Do you think it could happen as soon as this fall?"

"I'm not sure, but he's trying hard," she told Doro. "As for working mothers, that's likely to take more time."

More time. Doro had heard the phrase used frequently about the role of women. The Nineteenth Amendment gave ladies the right to vote, but only after generations of suffragettes had marched and lobbied. Despite that step forward, daily roles had changed little. Few girls went to college, and of the women who held jobs, most were widows, like Mrs. Jones, or spinsters, like Doro. "So, if Aggie married Wade, she would lose her job."

"Unfortunately, that's what would happen right now." Mrs. Jones shifted from one foot to the other. "Aggie wants a home and family of her own. At least, she's said as much to me. But most young women expect to marry."

The comment seemed benign, but Doro heard the question. Although she wanted to brush it off, Violet Jones was an old and dear friend of her mother, so Doro forced a smile. "That's true."

The older woman's gaze narrowed. "You and Officer Mallow are still sharing ownership of Tee, aren't you?"

Tee, named after Agatha Christie, was a stray puppy found on campus the previous fall. Mostly, the pup lived with Ev, although Doro took the little furball whenever necessary. "Of course, but I've been busy lately. Like you said, the end of a term is hectic. That means Ev is shouldering most of Tee's care right now. I'll pitch in and do more before I leave for Colorado."

Mrs. Jones' frown deepened. "Are you spending the entire summer with your parents?"

The question surprised Doro. "That's what I've been doing, since Dad took a job at Colorado College three years ago. Before that, both he and I went when classes were over here." When Doro was in high school, her mother had contracted consumption. The illness had lingered and worsened until doctors suggested Julia Banyon go to a sanatorium in Colorado Springs. With her brother, Doro's uncle, already living in the city, Doro's mother finally agreed, although she had hated leaving her husband, daughter, and mother. For several summers, Doro and Professor Ebediah Banyon had traveled west, so they could spend summer vacation as a family. Finally, he had taken the other job. Doro had thought long and hard about going but, with her maternal grandmother living in nearby Sylvania, she had not wanted to leave the elderly woman alone, and Rose McClaren had resisted forsaking her hometown and her lovely house. Her roots went deep in the northwest Ohio soil.

"I know, but I thought you might stay in Michaw this summer. Or part of it." A rueful smile tugged at Mrs. Jones' lips. "I'm not prying, dear, although I am curious. You and Officer Mallow seem to get along well, and he's a fine young man. I noticed the two of you enjoying each other's company at the town Christmas party."

Heat rushed into Doro's cheeks as she recalled dancing with Ev. Dancing and slipping outside to where boughs of mistletoe had hung from every arbor. They had only stayed moments, but had they been seen? One hand went to her lips, and her heart raced. "We danced a couple of times and chatted with each other."

"And enjoyed doing it," Mrs. Jones suggested, her eyes sparkling.

The comment was vague enough to make Doro uneasy. She and Ev had only been under the kissing bough for moments. A soft sigh left

Doro. "Ev and I have become friends."

The other woman's eyebrows rose a fraction. "Young women and young men generally aren't friends, Doro. You know that." Mrs. Jones glanced around them before speaking again. "You've evidently told folks you and he aren't stepping out, but you're often seen together. I hear plenty of gossip and try to rein it in..." Her voice trailed off.

Anxiety gripped Doro. "Are people talking about Ev and me?" She detested being the subject of tittle-tattle. Although she loved her hometown, news traveled far and fast in the village. While Violet Jones did not gossip, others did.

"A few," Mrs. Jones replied. "Most think you make a lovely couple. Some wonder why you don't court openly. Both of you are of an age where that's expected. You're almost twenty-six, and he's nearly twenty-seven. Most young people are married with a family by those ages. I'm not saying I agree. Whether or not you court is up to you. You and Ev."

Her mother's friend knew about Doro's dream to be the head librarian at the college, and the obstacles in her way, so Doro issued a reminder. "I've never planned to marry, because I always wanted a career. People found that odd when I was a little girl, but times have changed." Unfortunately, not as much as Doro would like, as gossip about her relationship with Ev showed.

Mrs. Jones studied Doro for several moments. "In the future, the college will change its policy about employing married women. Eventually, we'll see ladies with children being hired. If you want to step out with some young man, you should."

Suspicion evoked Doro's next statement. "My mother has mentioned a similar notion in her last few letters. I don't suppose the two of you corresponded about the idea."

A light flush rose in the other woman's face. "Your mother and I are

old, dear friends. We write about a number of things, you included."
Mrs. Jones paused before continuing. "We want you to be happy, my
dear, and so does your father. They like what they've heard about
Officer Mallow, mostly from you."

For a moment, Doro mulled over what she had written about Ev.
"He's a good security officer and a dependable deputy constable," she
replied. After being hired by the college, Ev had been confronted by
a murder on campus. Wade would have headed the investigation, but
his mother had been rushed to a Toledo hospital after a heart attack.
While her life had hung in the balance, Ev was named as a deputy.
Since then, he had continued in the role, which worked well for the
town, the college, and both lawmen. "He likes dogs and mysteries. As
I said, he's good at his jobs and gets along well with folks. I haven't
written much else about him." So, why did her parents think she and
Ev could, or should, be more than friends? Her mother and father had
never pressed the idea of courtship and marriage in the past. Not that
they were openly doing so now.

The older woman smiled. "Nevertheless, they think highly of him,
and so do I."

Doro's anxiety did not lessen. Although she could sway her parents' viewpoint by emphasizing that her relationship with Ev revolved
around Tee, what about stopping town gossip? That would be more
challenging. "I do, too, but that's all." Even as she spoke, Doro knew
her comment was not the complete truth. At Christmas, Ev had mentioned the two of them stepping out, and Doro had cited her focus on
her career. Since then, there had been no kissing, or dancing, or flirting.
As it should be. But they were in each other's company at times. With
Tee and as colleagues. Should Doro limit those interactions to avoid
further speculation? Uncertainty plagued her. She liked Ev a lot. Why
couldn't they simply be friends? "Now, I should get going."

"Before you do, I wondered if you might assist with the cakewalk this weekend. The cakewalk will precede the cooking competitions. Of course, we'll have the traditional May baskets for sale before the cakewalk, too." Mrs. Jones sighed, as a wistful expression softened her features. "My husband brought me a flower basket every May first from the time we were young. It was a tradition in our town."

"Here, as well," Doro agreed.

A smile brightened Mrs. Jones' face. "After my husband died, someone else started leaving a May basket on my porch every year. Someone still puts a beautiful one by my door."

Warmth hit Doro's cheeks, but she didn't admit to being the donor. "May baskets are surprises, so you're never sure who left them. That's part of the fun. Although you knew it was Professor Jones after a while, most givers remain anonymous."

"Knowing the benefactor doesn't lessen the joy." Mrs. Jones paused for a moment. "I have an inkling you make lovely baskets."

Doro avoided a direct reply. Instead, she offered her assistance. "I'll be at the auditorium for the cakewalk. If you need extra help for anything else this weekend, I'm happy to pitch in."

"As far as the cakewalk, I need someone to oversee the prizes. Donors will drop them off in the auditorium on Saturday morning, so you'd be arranging them on the table. If you could also man the victrola, that'd be wonderful."

"Of course. The cakewalk is a fun event. I looked forward to it when I was little. My dad almost always won a beautiful cake," Doro replied, "but the real excitement was seeing who got eliminated and who was on the winning number. Will I pull those, too?"

"If you would, I'd appreciate it," Mrs. Jones said. "Setting up the table shouldn't take too long, and it'll be before the contest begins. As for the actual contest, you know to lift the needle and stop the music.

Other committeewomen and I will oversee putting numbers on the floor and checking to identify those who aren't on a number before you pull one out of the hat."

Doro nodded. The cakewalk was contested much like musical chairs, except participants did not sit down. Instead, they needed to be standing on a numbered paper to continue. A number was drawn from a hat, and the person on that number got to choose a dessert from the table. Not all prizes were cakes, but all were mouth-watering sweet treats. "That will be fun. Aggie is bringing a fudge cake, and I'm baking shortbread cookies, which is about the only thing I do well."

"Cooking and baking are like everything else. The more you do of them, the better you get." Mrs. Jones let that thought linger before continuing. "Most folks will head over to the judging tent following the cakewalk. I hope Aggie is bringing extra jam or jelly. Judges often like to add some."

"She will, and she'll put her extra jam in her basket." Doro smacked her lips. "She put it up last fall, and it's delicious. Both of us have eaten it on toast all winter."

"Sounds tempting, but I need to watch what I eat nowadays. It's easy to pick up pounds as we grow older."

Doro's lips twitched. Violet Jones was as slender as she had been two decades earlier when she and her husband had moved to town. Only threads of gray in her brown hair and a few lines around her eyes gave evidence of time passing. "As busy as you are, I doubt if that will ever be a problem. Aggie would be happy to give a jar to you. A dab on toast never hurt anyone."

"I may have to take you up on the offer. I'm sure the presence of jam in her auction basket will increase interest," Mrs. Jones said. "In any case, it's always fun to watch the bidding."

"It is," Doro agreed. The sale of picnic baskets would take place after the baking contest concluded, and she knew Wade would outbid every other man for Aggie's contribution. The tasty blackberry jam would be a bonus.

"Are you planning to do more than watch this year? You don't often provide a basket to auction, and it's for a good cause. All proceeds benefit the grade school music program."

Uneasiness spilled through Doro. The subject of her participating had arisen in the past couple of years, and she had cited her hectic schedule. She still could, but Aggie was equally busy, and she planned to take part. With that in mind, Doro offered another excuse. "Like I said, I'm a mediocre cook. Back when Mother was here, she helped me put something together a few times. Of course, we had a housekeeper who made wonderful meals, and she pitched in."

"Your mother has many talents, but cooking isn't one of them," Mrs. Jones observed.

A rueful smile came to Doro's lips. "It isn't one of my grandmother's strong points, either. They can both make soups and stews, and they have several wonderful cookie recipes, but they always relied on household help for major meals. Without Mrs. Grover to supervise my baskets, my efforts have met with little enthusiasm." Actually, they had garnered no enthusiasm.

A chuckle left Mrs. Jones. "You seldom cook, but I've had your sugar cookies and your shortbread. All you'd need to add are sandwiches. Buy bread at the bakery and cold cuts at the grocer. You'll be able to get punch and lemonade at the celebration."

"Most women have heartier meals," Doro said.

"Not all do. Baskets don't need to provide a big dinner or fancy food. Remember, it's for a worthy cause."

Since Doro could not argue that point, she nodded. "I'll put something together but, once bidders know it's mine, I doubt if it'll get many bids." The first year Doro had made a basket alone, one of her high school classmates purchased it. Unfortunately, her fried chicken and coleslaw were nearly inedible, news he shared with everyone in town. The next year, she had tried again with a simpler menu—hard-boiled eggs, store-bought pickles, bakery rolls, and apples from the previous fall. One bidder, an old friend of her father, had saved Doro from complete humiliation by placing an offer. Since then, she had not offered an entry.

Mrs. Jones laid a hand on Doro's arm. "I'm sure there will be at least one avid bidder." She winked. "Plan to be at the auditorium around nine-fifteen on Saturday morning. The cakewalk will be at ten, and the cooking contest commences at eleven-thirty. Fried chicken is first up, followed by bread. The cakes will come last, so we should stay on schedule for a two o'clock basket auction."

"That's a full day," Doro commented, "since the grade school children have their choir concert in the evening."

"I love to hear them sing, but I don't need to do anything except enjoy listening. Their teacher handles that part of the weekend." After providing the details about Sunday's activities—a potluck and parade after church—Mrs. Jones expressed her gratitude to Doro and said goodbye. "I'll see you on Saturday."

"See you then." After a moment, Doro went on her way but troubling thoughts followed her. She did not like people judging her best friend for stepping out with Wade Lammers, but Doro was just as upset about folks conjecturing about her and Ev Mallow. As much as she loved Michaw—town and college—Doro disliked how nosey some folks were.

Chapter Two

Saturday dawned sunny and warm. Doro rose and dressed in short order. Before leaving her apartment, she stopped in front of the mirror near the door. Her pink cotton sateen dress boasted a white collar with a black-and-white polka-dot bow at the neck. The dropped waist bodice ended in a tiered skirt with matching polka dot trim. T-strap black shoes with a medium heel would make covering bare ground easy while looking stylish. She pulled the gold locket out from beneath her collar. The jewelry was an important family keepsake from her mother. For a moment, nostalgia overcame Doro as she studied her reflection. The pendant reminded her of Julia Banyon, but so did her reflection because Doro and her mother had the same blue eyes. With a smile, Doro retrieved a black cloche, boasting more polka dots in the form of a floppy flower, from the hat rack. After helping her friend in the downstairs kitchen, she would slide it over her sleek brunette bob.

Briefly, she wondered if she had made too much effort in dressing. Then, Doro brushed the idea aside and toted the hat, her food basket, and her pocketbook downstairs. The May Days festival was a major celebration in Michaw, and folks always spruced up for it. Despite May first falling on Wednesday, in the middle of final examinations, students and townsfolk would keep the celebration going through the dance, which was a week away. One custom was to dress up through-out the entire time, so Doro was in step.

When she reached the kitchen, Doro set everything on the coun-tertop. "Good morning, Aggie."

"Morning," her friend replied. With the back of one hand, Aggie brushed her auburn hair off her forehead before carefully placing her fudge cake in a decorated box. She looked up with a grin on her flushed face. "It's been a hectic morning, since I baked both jam rolls first thing. One for the contest and for my auction basket. I made the fudge cake last night. There's coffee. I'm too nervous to eat although I might have a shortbread, if there's enough."

Doro had baked shortbread late on Friday night and, to her relief, the batch turned out well, so well that she had to keep her fellow female faculty members from eating every cookie. Luckily, she had made several dozen. "We can each have a couple, and coffee sounds great." Doro set her basket on the big table. "I thought I'd put my sandwiches in the refrigerator, so the meat doesn't spoil." Giving someone food poisoning was something she wanted to avoid. Whoever was kind enough to bid on her basket did not deserve to become ill.

"There's plenty of room, and we can come back and get our auction baskets after the baking contest," Aggie said.

Some of Doro's enthusiasm ebbed as she reviewed Aggie's offer-ings. "Your fried chicken is as good as Mrs. Farmer's, and you've got side dishes, too. Potato salad and baked beans." She did not contin-ue by saying her sandwiches and cookies hardly measured up to her friend's feast.

"Mrs. Farmer is an extraordinary cook, and the girls who live in the dormitory are lucky to have her," Aggie replied. "In any case, I hope my extra jam roll will top my meal off."

"I'm sure it will." Doro sighed. "I have ham sandwiches and a couple of apples from last fall. They've been stored in the general store's root cellar since late October. They look fine."

"That's just over six months, so I'm sure the apples are still good or they wouldn't be for sale. And you made shortbread, which is delicious, so stop selling yourself short." Aggie's voice took on a sterner tone before she winked. "Your basket will garner interest."

In an effort to stop Aggie from mentioning Ev, as she all too often did, Doro turned toward the door. "I've promised to help organize the cakewalk, and I don't want to be late."

"All right. I can leave one jam roll and a jar of jam on the judge's table and then, help you out. I've got the fudge cake for the walk. You made enough shortbread, didn't you?"

Doro lifted the lid of the box in her tote bag. "Yes, but my cookies hardly measure up to a fancy cake, so I expect they'll be taken last." Once again, she felt deficient in domestic skills. Normally, Doro took her lack of homemaking expertise in stride. Today, it bothered her.

Aggie undid her voluminous apron to reveal a stylish navy dress. She brushed at the fabric. "I hope I didn't mess up my outfit." She peeked into the small mirror at the end of the kitchen and patted her hair. "I don't have time to fuss."

"Your hair is fine, and the dress looks perfect." Doro had encouraged her friend to buy the frock, which complimented Aggie's slightly rounded figure and pale coloring. "You look perfect."

Color crept into Aggie's face. "You were right about not buying such a straight-lined dress. Something with more forgiving lines is better for me." She gestured at Doro. "As slender as you are, you can wear the flapper styles."

Doro glanced down at her gown. "This isn't a flapper outfit. I wore one to the costume party last fall, but it's not something for the town May Days celebration." The flapper ensemble would set tongues to wagging, again.

"That was a stunning getup," Aggie remarked, "and it earned attention. Of course, so did your holiday outfit."

Heat flamed in Doro's face. "Stop teasing me." Ev's appreciative glance had lingered on her at the Halloween party and at the Christmas dance. His touch had lingered when they danced, too.

"All right," her friend said a giggle.

A new voice broke into the conversation. "You girls aren't usually up so early. At least you weren't when I lived here."

Doro turned to see Trudy Carstairs, a lanky blonde in her late forties, entering the kitchen. "Aggie baked this morning, since she's in the contest. She's also donating a sweet to the cakewalk, and so am I."

Trudy adjusted her spectacles and glanced at the table, where two boxes sat alongside the picnic baskets. "You're both participating in the auction, too, I suppose."

"We are," Aggie replied.

"We're involved in several of the weekend activities," Doro added.

A slight smile moved the woman's thin lips. "I remember you being enthusiastic about May Days when you were one of my students. In fact, you took part in all the Michaw celebrations, as I recall. Aggie did, too, when she was in college."

Both Doro and Aggie had been students of the science professor during their undergraduate days. "We did, but I don't remember you attending many toward the end of our schooling," Doro observed.

Trudy waved one hand in the air. "When you two were first students, I didn't have tenure, which meant taking on any extra task that might make me look good to the men in charge. After I got it, I didn't have to jump to the men's tune."

"Not all the male faculty members are against women," Doro pointed out.

A shrug moved Trudy's shoulders. "No, but I was lucky to be hired, since female faculty members were few and far-between. Your father was on the hiring committee, and he was a forceful advocate for employing women."

Pride swelled Doro's heart. "He was and still is."

"It was especially hard for those of us who chose science. The field is still filled with men," Trudy remarked. "Majoring in it wasn't easy, since I was one woman among many fellows. For the first two years of my undergraduate work, I held two part-time jobs. That made school even harder. Then, I got a scholarship. What a blessing." She glanced at Aggie. "You had to rely on outside help, too."

"I did," Aggie agreed. "Both Doro and I were fortunate when we applied to teach here, because you and other women professors supported us."

Pleasure filled the woman's gaze. "It's one of my top goals to get and keep more women among the faculty." A bleak expression crossed the science professor's face. "In the last year, we've lost two wonderful colleagues to marriage. As hard as I fought to hire women to replace them, I didn't succeed. I fear that happening again and again, since we have several young ladies like you two, who may go courting."

The observations gave Doro pause, and she saw a look of dismay cross her friend's face. Was Trudy asking if Aggie planned to move from stepping out with Wade to a more serious relationship? Or did she think Doro and Ev were? After several seconds of silence passed, Doro spoke. "I won't be stepping out or courting, so you don't have to worry about a man replacing me."

Trudy's angular face softened. "Good. I know you want to replace

Floyd Quartine when he retires. You'll need tenure for the position of head librarian."

"I'm working hard toward that," Doro assured her.

"Then, don't spend too much time on local events," Trudy said. "You grew up here, so townsfolk may expect you to do so, but be careful about shirking your work duties."

Although voiced in a friendly tone, the comment rang with criticism. "Most women in town donate a basket, since the money raised goes to the church for building maintenance. The same is true of funds from the cakewalk, only they're given to the grade school music program," Doro said.

"Naturally, local people are interested in such goings-on," Trudy said.

"President Adams supports college employees taking part, too," Aggie put in.

"He certainly does. He encouraged Mrs. Jones to take over as chairwoman of the town events planning committee," Doro added.

"Miles is back on a temporary basis, and who knows what the next president will be like." Trudy's pale eyebrows rose a fraction. "Except that it will be a man. Then, taking part in domestic events won't benefit women professors, especially those without tenure. You'll be compared to your male counterparts, who will devote themselves to the college."

President Adams was only back at the helm of Michaw College on an interim basis, but Doro figured the next top administrator would be equally progressive. Was she wrong? Uncertainty assailed her. In an effort to change the subject, Doro asked the older woman a question. "What brings you here so early on Saturday? We haven't seen you at this time of day on a weekend since you moved out last year."

Trudy lifted one hand and waved it in the air. "I'm having breakfast with Gladys Hollingsworth, as we do many Saturdays. Lately, she's come to my cottage or we've met at the diner. She'll be down soon."

"Do you miss the camaraderie of Wheaton Hall?" Aggie asked.

"Sometimes, but there's a garden at my place, and I was able to plant last year," Trudy replied. "I'll do more this spring. We'll use some specimens in our botany courses."

The response jogged Doro's memory. "Some of the women were talking about you starting plants inside over these last few months. What kinds do you have?"

Trudy waved one hand in the air. "This and that. Now, I'll go up, since Gladys can be tardy."

"We should be on our way." Aggie gathered her goods.

"Enjoy your little celebration," Trudy said before disappearing.

"We will," Doro murmured. Then, she and Aggie put the auction items away and left by the back exit. When they were outside, Doro brought up the older professor's attitude. "I'm never sure how to take Trudy when she talks about local customs."

"She isn't a fun-loving person. Even back when we were coeds, she spent all her free time in her laboratory working on extra projects. Science is everything to her. That and having tenure. Despite your dad's support, it couldn't have been easy for her. I'm sure she's right about the field of science. She and Gladys are the only women in the department now that Laura Downes got married." A long sigh left Aggie. "Although Wanda Placette left for the same reason, she taught history. In any case, it had to be a terrible disappointment when men took both positions. Trudy said as much. Plenty of women teach youngsters, but few are college professors. When I was a student, I figured on being a schoolteacher before marrying. At least I did when Rudyard and I were stepping out."

Doro noted no emotion in her friend's voice or expression. Rudyard Ingram and Aggie had been classmates. After he had helped save Aggie's scholarship, Rudyard had become a fixture in her life. At least he had until after his graduation. Then, he had gone on to medical school before returning to his hometown to practice with his father. Over the years, Rudyard's communication with Aggie had dwindled and dwindled. Five years earlier, Aggie had stopped writing to him, too. By that time, she had been pursuing a Master's degree in English, and her goals had changed. Or maybe they hadn't entirely. After all, she and Wade were involved. As Mrs. Jones had observed, Aggie wanted a family. As the young women crossed the campus, Doro took a sidelong glance at her friend. "You haven't mentioned Rudyard in a long time."

A rueful smile tugged at one corner of Aggie's mouth. "There's no reason to. We've gone our own ways, which is for the best."

After a heartbeat, Doro made an observation. "Because you like Wade much better."

Laughter left Aggie. "I do, and that's all I want to say right now."

CHAPTER THREE

After depositing Aggie's entry in the tent, where the judging would take place, the two young women headed to the auditorium. Mrs. Jones greeted them as soon as they entered the main room.

"Good morning, girls. Put your baked goods on the table, if you will. We'll have about twenty prizes and many more participants, so not everyone can win, but that's part of the fun," the older woman said with a chuckle. "If each person got a prize, it wouldn't be a contest."

"I suppose so," Doro murmured before setting her box down. She lifted the lid and put it aside. Her cookies were not as fancy as some of the items.

"I wish I could take part," Mrs. Jones said. "I love that shortbread."

"See," Aggie put in, as she placed her fudge cake next to Doro's cookies. "I bet the shortbread is snatched up quickly."

Although Doro figured Mrs. Jones and Aggie were being kind, she nodded. "Maybe so. But what can we do to get ready?"

"I have two boys who will put numbers on the floor, but some of us will ensure the papers are spaced correctly. The victrola is at the end of the table, and one of you could take charge of that. The other can handle giving out the prizes. You already know how it goes. When the music stops, each contestant needs to be on a number to continue. Of course, the person on the number drawn gets to choose a prize."

"Those who aren't on a number are eliminated," Doro supplied to confirm the rules.

Mrs. Jones nodded. "Yes. Unfortunately, they're out of the running for the rest of the cakewalk."

"But it's fun to see who's lucky," Aggie added. "I'd be happy to hand out the prizes. Should I make a list of winners?"

"Please do. The newspaper usually runs the names. Before we begin, the editor will take photographs of the table," Mrs. Jones said.

"It looks pretty." Aggie turned her attention to where the goods were accumulating as the other ladies arrived.

"It does," Doro agreed as she surveyed the long line of cakes, cookies, brownies, and pies. Most of the baked goods were displayed on pretty plates, often with a lacy cloth beneath them. A few items were highlighted by a vase of spring flowers. Briefly, Doro wished she had picked some of Mrs. Jones' lilacs, since her shortbread had nothing adorning it. Next to the other offerings, the cookies were on a pitifully plain plate. When she got her picnic basket, Doro would use some of the ribbons and lace left by other Wheaton Hall residents to fancy it up.

Since a crowd was gathering, Mrs. Jones joined the other committeewomen. Doro glanced through the records next to the phonograph. "There are a few choices here. *The Cakewalk Lindy* is an old favorite. Most are ragtime tunes."

"Those are great for the contest," Aggie said with a smile.

A new voice interrupted. "Dorothea Banyon and Agatha Darwine, why are you both behind the table?"

Doro turned to see Lila Billings, an elaborate box in her arms, scowling. Small and thin, with graying hair pulled into an old-fashioned bun, the woman exuded disapproval. "Mrs. Jones asked us to help."

A harrumph left Lila. "She's your mother's best friend, so that figures. Controlling the music means you can influence who wins." She turned her pale gaze on Aggie. "And you can convince the first winner to take your cake, so you win. That way, the judges will be predisposed to favor you in the contest. I saw you already put your jam roll in the tent, a fancy plate with lace under the cake. Men's heads get turned by something pretty."

Aggie stared at Lila in apparent disbelief. Momentarily, Doro also stood stunned by the outburst. When she found her voice, Doro sidestepped defending Aggie, who would only be more upset by additional attention. "Surely, you aren't insinuating the judges won't be fair. Two are town councilmen, one is a pastor, and the others are our local lawmen."

Lila put her box down. "I'm not saying that," she huffed. "They'll all be fair."

"And I'll let the cakewalk winners choose their prizes without influence. As far as stopping the music to help someone win, how would Doro know what number will be drawn? The slips of paper are folded up," Aggie pointed out.

A flush climbed into Lila's gaunt cheeks. "Of course." Hastily, she opened her box to reveal a three-tier spice cake. Scents of cinnamon, nutmeg, ginger, and cloves filled the air. Creamy frosting covered the concoction.

While the baked good looked attractive, Doro was reminded of Mrs. Jones' assessment of Lila's cooking—quantity over quality. *How much spice has the woman used?* The aroma of cloves was particularly pungent. Since using too much could cause an unpleasant taste, Doro wondered if the cake was edible.

After adjusting the doily under her offering, Lila spoke again. "I want to tell the committeewomen what a wonderful job they've done."

After Lila rushed off, Doro turned to Aggie. "How awful to say such things."

"She doesn't like me." Aggie bit her lower lip, as if fighting back a rising tide of emotion. "In fact, she seems to detest me."

"Impossible." A male voice, belonging to the town constable, broke into the conversation.

Doro looked past her friend's shoulder to see Wade and Ev approaching. "I agree," she said with a smile before glancing from one man to the other. Wade, two inches shorter and twenty pounds heavier than Ev, brushed a lock of straight dark hair off his forehead. While not as objectively handsome as the campus security officer, the constable had a pleasant countenance. His affable manner increased his appeal, so Doro understood her friend's feelings for the man. Ev Mallow, tall and lean, boasted a striking appearance. His square jaw, silver-gray eyes, ebony brows and lashes, and slightly wavy brown hair all drew feminine attention. Like now. Aware that several young women had turned to study Ev, Doro focused on Wade and tried to recall why he had said *impossible*. What had she and Aggie been discussing?

Wade's attention went to Aggie. "Don't let Lila Billings bother you. I don't know what she said, but I saw her talking to you two. I assume she was being snide."

"She was," Doro agreed.

A long breath left Wade. "She's an unhappy, lonely person. I've tried being nice to her, but I'm about at the end of my rope."

The admission revealed his new attitude, which heartened Doro.

She agreed with what Mrs. Jones had said earlier about Wade being too kind. Evidently, he was aware of the issue. Civility should be enough toward someone like Lila Billings.

Aggie shrugged. "You'd never hurt anyone's feelings, and I'm glad of that."

He turned his hat in his big hands. "No, but I don't want her hurting yours."

"She didn't," Aggie assured him, although her tone lacked certitude. "I'm handing out prizes and Doro is in charge of the music. Lila didn't like that."

"Is she afraid you'll choose the wrong music?" Ev, the lilt of laughter in his deep voice, addressed his question to Doro.

Doro couldn't withhold a chuckle. "No. She thinks I can control who wins, but I won't know who is on what number when I stop the music. Or what number will be drawn. She just wanted to complain." Her gaze went to a point across the room. "Looks like someone else is issuing a grievance."

When Ev and the others looked in the same direction, Wade groaned. "Betty Stanley is pointing this way."

"While she talks with Mrs. Jones," Ev added. "I wonder what that's about."

Doro didn't need to hear the conversation to know Mrs. Stanley disapproved of Doro and Aggie conversing with Ev and Wade. Her supposition was confirmed when Mrs. Jones joined the quartet a few minutes later.

"Good morning, gentlemen," Mrs. Jones said. After the men responded in kind, she continued. "I'm sure the four of you have plenty to discuss, but perhaps later. Judges of the baking contest would be wise not to converse with contestants."

Both her tone and expression were pleasant, but Doro did not miss the clear warning, and she doubted if the other three did, either. Even so, she shot a quelling glare at Mrs. Stanley, who had sashayed up to the group. "Ev and Wade won't be swayed."

"No, we won't," Ev agreed. "Besides, we won't know who baked which jam roll."

A snort left Mrs. Stanley. "That information wouldn't be hard to uncover."

A hesitation preceded Wade's response. "We aren't trying to find out, and we'll be unbiased, no matter what."

"Just as I expect you to be," Aggie put in with a smile. "I will not be upset if I don't win."

The constable's expression softened. "I know you won't."

Doro wanted to say Aggie's jam roll was spectacular, but she withheld the comment. Additional conversation meant Betty Stanley was apt to dally.

"We should move on," Ev said. "We don't want to create gossip."

Wade nodded. "We'll see you ladies later." The statement addressed all four women, but his gaze stayed on Aggie, as hers did on him.

When Doro glanced at Ev, she noted an expression of something akin to envy on his face. Bits and pieces of conversations spun through her mind. One had come from him at the town Christmas party: *We get along well, and we share Tee. Maybe we could step out from time-to-time.* His countenance had been similar then, right up until she had turned down the idea. Earlier in the week, Mrs. Jones had observed that most young women and young men wanted to court and marry. Plenty of females would love to step out with Everett Mallow. How would she feel when he chose someone else? Dismay grabbed Doro's heart and squeezed hard before she chastised herself. She'd made her choice between career and marriage long ago. But a tiny voice in the back of her mind whispered that choices could be changed.

After the men walked away, so did Betty Stanley, who was now all smiles as she chattered at Ev and Wade. Annoyance flickered through Doro. "Mrs. Stanley doesn't seem to take her own advice."

Mrs. Jones chuckled. "No, but that's not surprising. She likes to judge others, but she doesn't care to follow her own rules."

"She's very pretty," Aggie observed.

"Pretty is as pretty does, according to my grandmother," Doro replied, but denying the assertion was impossible. Unlike Lila Billings, who was plain and small, Betty Stanley was a stunning, statuesque blue-eyed brunette. The widow of a local lawyer, she had come to Michaw as a bride and stayed on after her husband's death a few years earlier.

Mrs. Jones' lips twitched. "That's true, but Betty is a lovely woman, as are both of you."

"She's considerably older than we are," Doro observed.

"Around forty, I believe," Mrs. Jones said, "which isn't so very aged."

Warmth rose in Doro's face. "Of course not." Violet Jones was, like Doro's mother, nearer to fifty, but she remained attractive and vibrant.

"That puts her close to Wade's age," Aggie said. She wrapped her arms around her waist. "And they've both lost spouses. Plus, Mrs. Stanley has a son. He's in the same class as Davey, Wade's youngest."

Doro laid a reassuring hand on her friend's arm. "Betty hasn't been stepping out with Wade."

Aggie glanced from Doro to Mrs. Jones. "They did right after Wade came back to town. At least that's what I've heard. I haven't asked him, because it's not really my business."

"They sat together in church some Sundays," the older woman agreed, "but I think that was mostly her doing. Same with being seen at other town events. Betty and her boy joined Wade and his children, not vice versa. Now, it's almost time for the cakewalk to begin, so let's take our places."

Doro and Aggie easily settled into their roles. Everyone was pleasant, which eased Doro's mind, especially when her friend relaxed. Aggie's fudge cake was the second item to be snatched up, while the shortbread went fourth. The winner, a local farmer's wife, handed a cookie to each of her three children, who gobbled them down and asked for more. After the family walked away, Aggie grinned. "See. Your offering was popular. You should bake more often. Not only do people enjoy wonderful treats, baking is a fun hobby."

Undeniable pleasure spread through Doro at the compliment. Realization followed. "I actually enjoyed making the shortbread. I didn't think about my classes, the library, or anything else for the entire time." Concentrating on making the cookies correctly had been her only concern.

A chuckle left Aggie. "You're a thinker, and so am I. Baking involves focusing on what's right in front of you. It's good for me, which is part of why I do it. And creating treats that people enjoy is nice, too."

"Excellent points," Doro murmured. "I get wrapped up in work, but I enjoyed baking when I was growing up. My mom and I often made special treats for holidays. She didn't like ordinary meal preparation, though."

"And neither do you," Aggie observed.

"No, I don't," Doro admitted. "And I'm not good at it, either."

"It's not difficult."

"Maybe not, but we have meals provided several nights per week," Doro pointed out, "and I don't mind sandwiches the rest of the time."

Aggie's forehead furrowed. "You won't always live in Wheaton Hall."

The topic rarely came up and, when it did, Doro dismissed it quickly. As she did now. "Maybe, maybe not. In any case, we need to get to the tent for the contest."

"We do."

On the way to the baking contest, Aggie's demeanor changed and her steps slowed. "I'm so nervous," she murmured as they drew closer to the tent.

"You shouldn't be," Doro replied. "All your baking is delicious. I know you'll win."

"That could cause problems," Aggie said in a troubled tone.

Doro paused and turned to face her friend. "The taste test is blind. We know that, and so does everyone else."

A frown formed on Aggie's face. "Some will say differently. Some already have, and that creates gossip. A constable doesn't need to be the subject of tittle-tattle."

"Wade didn't seem concerned."

Aggie sighed. "He isn't. At least, he says he isn't."

Dismay filled Doro. "You don't believe him? Wade has always been honest and open in all his dealings."

"It's not that." Aggie bowed her head. "He doesn't want me upset, so he downplays the criticism, but you and I have both heard it. Wade has, too."

Since Doro could not deny the assertion, she replied with caution. "You have a sensitive soul, which is part of what makes you a wonderful poet and person. But you take things to heart and fret when you shouldn't."

Aggie met Doro's gaze. "I suppose so, but I don't want Wade or his family hurt." She ran one hand over her face.

"You get along fine with the children, Wade's mother, his aunt, and his cousins, don't you?"

Aggie nodded. "I do. They're all wonderful."

When her friend did not continue, Doro filled in. "You still aren't sure about courting, and you don't want Wade to be subjected to ridicule if you stop stepping out."

A slight smile played across Aggie's lips. "You know me very well." She shifted from one foot to the other. "I've thought about talking it over with you, but I'm so uncertain."

"You can tell me anything, and I'll never share it with anyone," Doro promised.

"I know, but I'm having trouble sorting out my feelings," Aggie admitted.

The confession did not surprise Doro but, before she could respond, a man—nearly as wide as he was tall—stopped beside them. "Shouldn't you be in the contest tent, Miss Darwine? Or should I say Professor Darwine?" A snide note was in his tone.

"Good day, Mr. Hooper," Doro said.

The man's dark eyes briefly lit on her before he turned back to Aggie. "Maybe you don't think you need to make any effort, since your sweetheart and his friend are judges."

Color swept into Aggie's face as her eyes went wide. Because her friend appeared to be on the verge of tears, Doro spoke. "Sir, since you were a judge in the past, you know it's a blind taste test. As far back as I can recall, only one incident of hanky-panky took place. The entrant and the judge involved were banned from participating."

Hooper's round face went beet red. "You're repeating gossip, Dorothea. Malicious gossip."

Annoyance prodded Doro to push her point. "I'm repeating what everyone in town knows. You've been part of a whisper campaign to embarrass Aggie and Wade, while you were ruled out as a judge for your chicanery a few years back."

His nostrils flared with a sharp intake of breath. "How dare you speak so rudely to your elder? You should be ashamed."

As anger got the better of her, Doro lifted her chin. "You should be, but you're shameless."

"Doro..." Aggie began before she was cut off.

The older man's face went purple. "The both of you are brazen hussies. Instead of taking men's jobs and wanting men's rights, you should have husbands and children to keep you busy." He spun toward Aggie. "Wade Lammers ought to know better than to dally with a flapper." His gaze went from her auburn locks, cut in a stylish bob and set off with a silk hairband, to her fashionable dress, and on to her t-strap navy shoes. "Of course, it's more that you're dallying with him and making him look like a fool. You'll get your comeuppance, Miss Darwine. Mark my words." Then, he rushed off.

"Awful man," Doro muttered.

"This is exactly what I've been afraid of," Aggie murmured.

Doro turned toward her friend. All color had left Aggie's face, leaving her freckles to stand out in stark contrast to her pallor. "Mr. Hooper is a nasty curmudgeon. He was removed as a judge after trying to help Lila Billings win a dozen years ago."

Aggie gasped in surprise. "I never heard that."

"It happened before you came to Michaw, and few folks still discuss it. But they were both banned from future participation."

"Was he sweet on her?" Aggie asked. "He has to be twenty years older."

Doro shook her head. "He's her uncle. Her mother's brother."

"I never knew that," Aggie mumbled, "but we seldom cross paths."

"Luckily, I see little of him myself. He lives outside town and never visits campus. He undoubtedly wants to break you and Wade apart, so Lila has a chance. Not that she does. If Wade was interested, he could've courted and married her long before now." Another glance at Aggie's troubled expression revealed continuing discomfort. "Let's forget about Mr. Hooper, Lila, and everything except the contest. We can talk later. That'll help you put things into perspective."

Aggie seemed to shake off the negativity as she nodded. "You're right. I don't want to be late and hold things up."

Although the confrontation bothered Doro, mostly because she had not held her tongue, she smiled and hurried to the tent with Aggie. Once there, the two young women were caught up in the crowd and the enthusiasm. The previous competition had just wrapped up, and the winner was gripping her blue ribbon and smiling to all around her. Once she left, Aggie and Doro stepped inside.

After exchanging greetings with the other contestants, the judges, and the committee members, Aggie and Doro took seats on the side designated for participants and their families. Their exchanges with Ev and Wade were brief but friendly. No one could accuse either young woman of misbehavior, although, as Doro glanced around, she saw Mr. Hooper with Lila. Uncle and niece both stared back, but Doro did not look away. Not until a feminine voice addressed her.

"This area is for contestants and their relatives, Dorothea."

She looked up to see Betty Stanley, her red lips pursed, scrutinizing Doro from slitted eyes. Since the older woman probably wanted to sit beside Aggie and fill her ears with snide comments, Doro had no intention of relinquishing her seat. She gestured down the row. "Mr. Miller is with his wife. Mrs. Arnold is with her daughter. The Rollins are with her mother."

Betty's frown intensified. "They're related."

Doro smiled. "Aggie doesn't have family here, but we're as close as any sisters." She gestured toward an empty chair at the end of the row. "You could sit over there."

At that point, Mrs. Jones called for the crowd to settle down, which gave Betty little choice except to move away and take a seat. After the judges were introduced and each entry was pointed out, the five contestants stood to be recognized. Aggie was the youngest, and Seraphina Miller was the oldest at seventy-five. Petula Arnold, Bonnie Marlon, and Betty Stanley were all in their forties. Four of the ladies wore dresses appropriate for the spring picnic that would follow, and they each had some version of a cloche on their heads. Only Mrs. Stanley sported a lacy apron over her Sunday best attire, which included a wide-brimmed hat with a taffeta ribbon around it. Doro's earlier concern about being overdressed went away. Betty had far outdone her, and everyone else. Evidently, she had gone home to spruce up after the cakewalk. Doro withheld a grimace. The woman clearly wanted to stand out, and she did.

The judging began in short order. Although each contestant had entered the same sort of cake, Doro recognized Aggie's submission and watched as the men partook of it. Ev, Wade, and Councilman Connors all put extra jam on, which seemed like a good sign to Doro. But was it? A glance at her friend revealed Aggie felt anxious, too. The sampling was followed by the judges filling out cards. Since Doro had seen them in the past, she knew each had a space to rank the cakes, which had been lettered A through E. Only the top two would receive ribbons. Try as she might, Doro could not glean any signs of who won. By the time Mrs. Jones collected the cards and pulled the committeewomen aside, the excitement in the tent had become a palpable force. When she caught Aggie's eye, Doro offered a reassuring smile. Her friend's lips trembled as she tried to return it.

After what seemed like an hour, but could have been only ten minutes, Mrs. Jones again stepped to the middle of the judging table. She thanked the judges, the contestants, her committee, and the crowd before picking up the ribbons. "We got wonderful comments on all the entries, so our panel had a hard time choosing the winners. I know you're all eager to find out who they are, so let me begin with the red ribbon winner, Mrs. Seraphina Miller." An enthusiastic round of applause followed as the older lady accepted her second place award and returned to her seat.

Doro clapped along with the others, but she held her breath until the winner was announced. When Aggie's name was called, Doro joined in the applause. With pride and joy, Doro watched her friend receive congratulations on nabbing first place. Although Aggie was a fine instructor and talented poet, she got far too little recognition. Besides, being acclaimed as an excellent cook might mollify some of the disapproval about Aggie and Wade stepping out. Not that it was anyone else's concern, but in a small town, some folks thought everything was their business. And some wanted to interfere for personal reasons. Doro's attention moved to Betty Stanley, who had a fake smile pasted on her face. The other contestants all hurried to congratulate Aggie, as did the panel of judges. Both Ev and Wade looked impassive, but Aggie glowed with pleasure. Lila Billings and her uncle slipping out as Aggie accepted the blue ribbon only increased Doro's lightheartedness. Perhaps the pair would temper their criticism and carping. They should.

Mrs. Jones came to stand next to Doro. "Aggie seems pleased, and Wade looks to be fighting a proud grin."

"True on both counts," Doro replied.

The older woman turned back to Doro. "Since some of the local objection to their friendship is that Aggie won't make a good wife and mother, winning the bake-off might help quell the notion."

"I hope so," Doro agreed, since she'd had the same thought. "Now, if Wade wins the May basket with her wonderful meal, it would be perfect."

Low laughter left the older woman. "I was thinking the same thing, but he's likely to outbid everyone else, so winning shouldn't be difficult. The basket donors aren't a secret."

"True, and I'm sure he will offer whatever is required," Doro replied, but pleasure for her friend was tempered by wondering about her own donation. "There won't be a bidding war for my basket."

Mrs. Jones winked. "You never know."

Doro shook her head. "Mrs. Jones, I took your advice. I have ham sandwiches, apples, and shortbread. Others cooked up a storm, I'm sure. I know Aggie did. I bought ham and bread, since I've never made either. The apples are from the general store. Everything is refrigerated, not hot."

Mrs. Jones smiled. "Most of the baskets are in the cool house, so those meals are not hot at this point. Only a few ladies will go home and bring food right from the oven."

"Aggie and I put our meals in the refrigerator at Wheaton Hall, but fried chicken is fine cold. Same with her biscuits, potato salad, and baked beans. Everyone expects something more than a sandwich, an apple, and cookies, and everyone knows I can't provide more." For once in her life, Doro wished she possessed more homemaking skills.

Mrs. Jones patted Doro's shoulder. "You could if you set your mind to it, but your interest never rested in the kitchen. More in the library and classroom. Nevertheless, your basket will garner a respectable bid. I'm sure of that."

While Doro did not agree, she avoided further discussion by nodding. "We're supposed to retrieve our baskets and take them to the church."

"Go ahead, dear. I'll see you there soon."

CHAPTER FOUR

On their way to the awards ceremony, the two young women bumped into a pair of college students outside the judging tent. One, tall and blonde, snorted with laughter. His ice-blue eyes narrowed and a contemptuous sneer curved his thin lips as he stared straight at Aggie. "No wonder you don't have time to properly grade papers. You're too busy cooking."

The other, a few inches shorter and several pounds heavier, guffawed. "Because she knows she won't get tenure, so marrying the constable is her new goal."

Aggie, her face flushed, froze in place while Doro glared at the pair of miscreants, who she knew far too well. She addressed the tall boy first. "Parker Matthews, your lack of manners and decorum are showing." She turned to his buddy. "Harland Cain, the same is true for you. Michaw College has rules governing student behavior on campus and in town. Unless you're prepared to apologize to Professor Darwine right now, I'll be reporting you to Dr. Adams."

Parker's snide expression hardened. "Since he and your old man were buddies, Adams will jump to do your bidding."

Harland nodded his red head. "That's for sure."

Although she wanted to argue that the college president was fair, Doro knew it would be a waste of time. "I'll speak with him on Monday, since neither of you knows how to apologize. Dr. Adams may want to speak with your uncle, Parker." Some of the bluster left the young men, as she figured it would. Both boys were close to expulsion, and a negative report about behavior would seal their fates.

"Not necessary," Parker muttered. His gaze went to Aggie. "Sorry. Just kidding." Neither his tone nor his expression held a shred of sincerity.

"Yep," Harland readily agreed with a matching lack of authenticity. "Being funny is all."

Although both young men were dissembling, pressing her point would further upset Aggie, so Doro reluctantly relented. "All right, but I don't want to hear any similar comments ever again. Come on, Aggie." Doro took her friend's arm and moved forward. A backward glance caught the boys, sour expressions on their faces, standing in the same place. Uneasiness hit her, but she had no chance to scrutinize it. Instead, Doro focused on Aggie. "Don't let those bullies get to you."

"I've had trouble with Parker because he doesn't care about poetry, and his writing shows it. He's earned low grades on two previous essays. If his last one isn't significantly better, he'll barely pass, which will keep him off the Dean's List. He's threatened to go to his uncle. As a trustee, I suppose the man could keep me from getting tenure—or have me fired." Fear threaded through Aggie's voice.

"The uncle is as obnoxious as Parker, but Dr. Adams won't do his bidding," Doro commented. "Parker and his uncle are against women in colleges, as students or instructors."

"True, and Parker is only interested in what he refers to as *real subjects*, like science and math, and he only respects *real professors*, meaning men."

Doro frowned. "Do you know what his grades are in other courses?"

"All top scores in the sciences and mathematics. Mine is his first humanities course. He'll have to take others before he graduates, though."

"Does he want to be a doctor like his father and uncle?"

Aggie nodded. "He does. I hope he develops more compassion than he has now."

Her friend's anxiety made Doro offer reassurance. "Forget about them and enjoy your win. We need to get to the bandstand, so you can officially accept your blue ribbon."

"You're right."

Doro and Aggie went to the bandstand where the local newspaper photographer was set up. Since two other cooking contests had preceded the bake-off, those winners were included. Doro enjoyed seeing her friend's pleasure, and she was delighted so many people offered sincere congratulations.

When the crowd dispersed some twenty minutes later, Doro turned to Aggie. "We should get the rest of your jam. Then, we can pick up our picnic baskets and head to the church."

"Yes, we need to be on our way," Aggie agreed.

As they drew near the judging area, Doro saw an older couple emerging and paused. "I wonder why the Fultons are coming out of the tent now. They weren't there earlier."

"Maybe they wanted to sit down out of the sun. No one is currently using the tent, and it's a cool, quiet place."

"It is," Doro agreed, "but I'm surprised they came to May Days. Ever since they moved to the cottage outside town, they rarely make an appearance." The pair had worked for a wealthy widow, someone rumored to be in the rumrunning business. Mr. Fulton had often done errands for her in the city, so he had fallen under suspicion, too.

"I wonder if he still goes into Toledo often."

"It's hard to say, since they live outside town," Doro said. "I wonder why they remained in the area. Their employer has been gone for months."

Aggie glanced at Doro. "It seems odd."

"I agree. What do they do for money?" Doro asked. "Being hired help couldn't have paid well."

Her friend's gaze narrowed. "You think they're working with bootleggers? Wade hasn't said anything about it. Has Ev?"

"Ev and I don't talk in depth often," Doro said, her tone defensive. "Besides, if he knows anything about rumrunning in the area, it would be from his old boss at the Prohibition Bureau. He'd tell Wade, but neither of them would pass the information on to us."

"Probably true," Aggie said. "Since we can't figure out that mystery, let's get my jam and go."

When the two young women approached the older couple, they offered greetings, which were only returned in the most perfunctory manner.

"We must be on our way," Mrs. Fulton said.

"Yes, we can't dally," her husband concurred.

The pair was out of earshot before Doro formed another statement. "They didn't want to chit-chat."

"Evidently not," Aggie said.

As Doro stared at the retreating figures, she shook her head. "I wonder why."

"They don't want you grilling them about bootlegging is my guess. Come on. I want to get the jam and go."

Doro was still thinking about the Fultons, and their hasty depar-
ture, as she and Aggie went to the judging table. "The cake is all gone,
but the jar of jam is here. Looks like plenty is left, but it's a big jar."

"Only three of the judges had extra." Aggie put the jar in her satchel
and headed out of the tent. "I'll put this in my auction basket, along
with a fresh jar."

The mention of baskets moved Doro's thoughts away from the
competition and to the auction. Her offerings might not be as delicious as some others, but she could enhance the presentation. "Let's
hurry. I want to embellish mine a little. Some lace and ribbon."

Aggie's gaze widened and her jaw dropped before she carefully
composed her expression. "A lovely idea."

A short time later, Doro placed her picnic basket on the long table
outside the church. Even though her offering looked as appealing as
the others, Doro felt increasing anxiety. What if no one bid on hers?
As she scanned the crowd, Doro saw her boss, Floyd Quartine, who
waved. Some of her anxiety drained away. A long-time widower and
an old friend of her family, he knew her domestic skills were sorely
lacking. When she had told him about putting only sandwiches, apples, and cookies in her basket, Floyd had reassured her that many folks
would enjoy such food. Even if no one else took interest, he would—if
only to save her embarrassment. Feeling more confident, Doro joined
Aggie to wait for the sale.

Aggie's basket was among the first to be offered and, as predicted,
Wade outbid several others to snag it. Wade, his eyes sparkling, picked
up his prize before coming to stand by Aggie.

"You've gotten a wonderful meal, Constable," Doro observed.

A blush rose in Aggie's face, but Wade grinned. "I know. Her jam roll was extraordinary."

"The blackberry jam was delicious by itself," Ev said as he joined the group. "I could eat it by the spoonful."

"Thank you," Aggie murmured. "Both of you."

After peeking into the basket, Wade smiled again. "There's plenty of food here, enough for all four of us."

The comment reminded Doro of how paltry her own contribution was, but she had no time to fret because the mayor was lifting up her basket and asking for bids. Several endless moments passed before the first one came from her boss. The second offer came more quickly and from the man standing next to her. Surprise made Doro turn toward Ev, whose attention was focused on the auctioneer. Both he and Floyd made three more offers before the bidding came to a halt, and Ev went forward to get his reward. Although Doro did not think she imagined the buzz going through the crowd, she ignored it. What would people say about the two of them now?

As soon as Ev returned, he addressed the group in a low murmur. "Maybe we can all find a quiet place to eat."

"Good idea," Wade agreed.

Since the women concurred, the group headed to the far side of the church where a copse of tall elms stood. Several couples had already taken some spaces, so the quartet staked out a shady spot twenty feet away from the others. After exchanging greetings with folks, they got settled. For a time, passersby continued to congratulate Aggie. A few suggested the town constable was a lucky man, and he wholeheartedly agreed. Others gave Doro and Ev speculative glances. She ignored those, as best she could. Ev had no outward reaction. While Doro and Aggie laid out the food, the men commented on their hunger.

"It all looks so good," Wade said. "I love ham sandwiches and fried chicken, so maybe we can share the baskets."

Although she felt sure Aggie had put him up to the suggestion, Doro agreed. "That sounds fine, if Ev agrees." And why wouldn't he when he'd have a better meal that way?

"Sure. Doro has enough sandwiches for all of us," Ev chimed in. "And plenty of shortbread, too. It's a favorite of mine."

"It is?" she asked.

He nodded. "Yep. My mother often made it for special occasions. She always had a big jar of jam to go with the cookies."

"Really? You put it on them?" Doro asked.

Ev nodded. "I love to smear a big gob on each one."

After extracting the leftover jam from Aggie's basket, Wade set it in the middle of the blanket. "Luckily, there's plenty left. Since it's so tasty, I'd like to try your suggestion and put it on the shortbread."

A chuckle left Aggie. "You sound like little boys. We need to eat some of the proper food first."

Both Ev and Wade ate heartily before availing themselves of a piece of cake apiece, and Ev ate a cookie.

"This is a great jam roll," Wade said, "and I loved you providing an extra jar of jam. Not that you didn't put plenty in the cake. But more is welcome."

"It sure is," Ev agreed, after he picked up two shortbreads and put dollops of jam on them. After eating both, he grinned. "My mom got her recipe from a neighbor who was Scots. Those were almost as good as these are."

Tension drained out of Doro who had feared Ev's plastering her cookies with jam meant he didn't like them. But he did. And he had eaten two ham sandwiches with pleasure. When Wade offered him some of Aggie's fried chicken, Ev shook his head and exclaimed how ham was his favorite. Just having Ev bid on her basket was a pleasant change. This was the first time her basket fetched a respectable price and had two bidders. "You said your mother made shortbread for special occasions."

Ev nodded. "Our neighbor baked them more often, and she always had jam to make cookie sandwiches. I got used to eating them that way." He took two more of the concoctions and slathered them with the sweet spread. "So good."

Wade patted his stomach. "It was a wonderful meal." His gaze went to Aggie. "With lovely company."

She smiled. "It's been fun." A yawn escaped her. "Sorry."

"I bet you were up early getting things ready," Wade observed.

"She was," Doro interjected. "I went downstairs at seven-thirty, and she had already baked the jam rolls and biscuits, fried the chicken, and cooked potatoes for the salad. She made baked beans and the fudge cake yesterday."

"You were busy, too," Aggie pointed out. "You baked last night, and you took on duties with the cakewalk."

Doro put one hand over her mouth to stifle her own yawn. "It's been a full day," she admitted.

Both men chuckled, and Wade rose to his feet. "It's not over, since there's the concert later. I hate to rush off, but we need to talk with the mayor about tomorrow's parade. It'll be after the church potluck, and my kids are real excited because all three are in it."

"The concert and parade are big events for the children. I always looked forward to them," Doro said. "That and taking May baskets to people without being caught." Happy memories filled her mind. She needed to make at least one offering before Wednesday, which was the first of May.

"That's such a fun tradition," Aggie said. "We never did it when I was growing up in the city."

"It's more of a small-town custom," Wade said. "Most guys on the railroad never heard of the idea when I talked about it."

"I hadn't until I came here," Ev agreed. "But it's not just children who take baskets to folks, right?" He focused on Doro.

"No, some fellows take a May basket to their sweethearts. Or to ladies they hope to have as a sweetheart." Doro felt warmth creep into her cheeks as she replied. "Mrs. Jones told me that's how her husband started courting her. They were young, and it took a couple of years for her to figure out who was leaving the beautiful baskets on May Day. He continued putting one by their door right up until he died."

"How sweet," Aggie said.

"Very much so," Wade agreed. "The custom was to make the basket yourself but, with the festival came selling fancy ones. A bunch of them were lined up in the auditorium before the cakewalk. Plenty of men bought one for a wife or sweetheart, so I'm guessing some ladies will get them tomorrow morning instead of Wednesday."

Doro figured Wade had one for Aggie and wondered how many baskets would be by Wheaton Hall's front door in the morning and in the days that followed. Not that she planned to search for one with her name. Ev was being friendly, nothing more. "I didn't see any when we got to the auditorium this morning."

"They sold out by eight-thirty," Ev put in.

"You were there that early?" Doro asked.

Color crept into his lean cheeks. "Sure. I had to unlock the doors at eight o'clock." He cleared his throat. "There were some real pretty ones donated by your sister professors."

"Really?" Doro asked. "I saw Gladys Hollingsworth taking a big bouquet to her place late yesterday."

"She brought a basket," Ev said.

"Ev really liked it," Wade added with a grin.

Before the constable could say more, Ev interrupted. "Anyhow, I opened the place for everyone."

When he repeated his reason for being at the basket sale and cake-walk early, Doro's hopes plummeted. For a moment, Doro had wondered if she'd be getting her first May basket. Well, the first one that had not come from her parents. How unpardonably foolish, she was. Hadn't she informed Ev about her not stepping out with gentlemen because her career was her focus? "Of course, you did."

Ev jumped to his feet. "We can help you ladies pick up before we go to the meeting."

"There's not much to do," Aggie said, "so go ahead. We'll see you at the concert."

"I'm glad you're coming," Wade said. "Ma took the kids home to feed them and play with their cousins for a while, but I'll pick the bunch up later. Maybe you'll save a seat for me."

"Certainly. I wouldn't miss your children and the others singing," Aggie assured him. She looked at her watch. "We can go home, freshen up, and be back in plenty of time." Her attention went to Ev. "You're coming to the concert, too, aren't you?"

"He sure is," Wade put in. "My kids would be terribly disappointed if he didn't."

"After the meeting, I want to walk and feed Tee, but I'll be there," Ev said.

"I could walk her, if you're pressed for time," Doro replied. "You've taken over most of the responsibilities for the last two weeks, and I'll be gone most of the summer."

Some emotion darkened his silver gaze before it disappeared. "It's not a problem. I'll have more free time after classes are over, and Tee is good company." He glanced at Wade. "We better get going."

"Some food is left in both baskets," Aggie said. "Why don't you take them? We can get the baskets themselves in a day or two."

"Sounds like a good idea to me," Wade said.

Ev glanced at Doro. "If you don't mind, I'd love to have the leftover sandwich and a few of the shortbreads."

"You can take all of them," Doro replied.

"Since you like jam on the cookies, take the jar," Wade offered. "Aggie put an unopened one in the basket, so the kids and I will enjoy that."

"If you're sure." Ev looked from Doro to Wade and back.

Both nodded before the group said their farewells.

Doro watched as the two lawmen strode away. After they were out of sight, she turned to Aggie. "We should go, too."

"We should," Aggie agreed. "It's been a wonderful day, and the concert will cap it off."

For a moment, Doro considered her friend's comment. It had been a great day, far better than she had dared to hope.

Chapter Five

A few hours later, the young women headed to the sunset concert. The potluck and the parade would highlight Sunday. Each event represented a pleasant memory from childhood for Doro. The spring dance, scheduled for the following weekend, was strictly for grown-ups. Again, bittersweet emotions filled Doro. As usual, she would go alone, or tag along with Aggie and Wade. She pushed her disappointment aside as she and Aggie entered the park, where a crowd had already assembled.

"Ev and Wade are over there." Aggie gestured to some trees about fifty feet from the white clapboard bandstand, which now held boys and girls between six and ten.

When her friend headed in that direction, Doro followed. Concern hit her when she saw Ev's pallor. As she got closer, Doro felt more and more worried. Not only was he snow white, sweat beaded his brow, and he was hunched against a tree, as if in pain. What had happened since they parted? She hurried to his side. "What's wrong?"

His silver gaze, dark with discomfort, met hers. "Not sure. I started feeling nauseous a half-hour or so ago. It's gotten worse. Now, I'm hot and cold and..." He put one hand against his abdomen.

"Maybe it's something you ate," she murmured. Surely not her food. Guilt joined apprehension. "I hope it wasn't something from my basket."

He shook his head. "Maybe I ate too much, since I had several more cookies with jam after walking Tee. The shortbread is delicious." Somehow, he managed a weak smile. "Besides, Wade says he feels off-kilter, too, so we might've consumed too many treats. You don't feel sick, do you?" Anxiety filled his gaze.

"No," she replied. "I feel fine."

"You ate a ham sandwich, so it wasn't that. We all had some short-bread, so it wasn't that, either." One hand went to his mouth as his eyelids shut and opened again. "It's got to be my overeating."

The reassurance didn't ease her mind. Ev looked ghastly. Doro turned to Wade and Aggie, who stood a few feet away. While the constable looked pale, he wasn't as overtly ailing as Ev.

"Do you feel sick, too?" Doro asked.

Wade nodded. "A little, but Ev is worse. A lot worse. I want to hear my kids sing, but Ev ought to get home. He could've caught something."

"Good idea," Doro murmured before turning to Ev. "Can you walk to your place?"

After a long breath, he opened his mouth but, before a single word came out, he crumpled to the ground. His eyes shuttered before briefly opening to rivet on Doro. "Take care of Tee." Then, his dark lashes drooped, and he went still.

Shock and horror hit Doro, who dropped to her knees next to him and clasped his hand. "Ev. Ev." He had no reaction to her voice or her touch. Her pulse pounded in her ears as she looked at Aggie and Wade for help.

The next few minutes passed in a blur. Dr. and Mrs. Silven, who were seated nearby, hurried over. After a brief examination of Ev, the physician turned to his wife. "You stay and listen to the children. I'm not sure what's wrong, but I'll get him into our automobile and to our place." He looked at Wade. "What about you? Should I take you along?"

"I'd like to hear my kids, but I'll probably come after the concert," Wade said in an unusually weak and wavering voice.

"We can bring Wade," Doro replied, her own voice barely audible, even to herself. She glanced at the constable. "You may both have the same issue, so don't delay. We don't want our other local lawman down for the count." She tried to inject a humorous note, but fear plagued her as her gaze went back to Ev. If she did not know better, Doro would have sworn he was dead.

Doro watched Doc and a couple of other men cart Ev to the Silven vehicle. Since they were not in direct view of the audience or singers, no ruckus was created. No outward ruckus, at least. Inside Doro, a tempest of fear raged. Whatever ailed Ev was serious. Very serious.

After taking a seat at the back of the audience near Wade's mother and aunt, Doro tried to enjoy the concert. Usually, she found the children's performances charming. Usually, she was swept back in time to when she had been on the bandstand, and her proud parents were in the crowd. Now, Ev tumbling to the ground replayed over and over in her mind and, when the singing ended, she jumped to her feet. At the same time, Mrs. Lammers also stood up.

"Son, you don't look well," his mother said to Wade.

"Don't worry, Ma." His reassurance lacked strength.

Aggie clasped Wade's arm. "We need to get you to Doc's place before you end up like Ev." She glanced at Mrs. Lammers. "Ev fell ill before the concert, so he's already there."

Color fled from the older woman's face. "My automobile is close by." She gestured toward the edge of the park. "Can you make it that far, son?"

"Sure," he replied, although his tone held no conviction. "But I don't want the kids to be alarmed."

"I'll meet them when they come off the stage," his aunt, Nola Islington, assured him. "Luckily, they're used to you being called away. We'll go to my place for cookies and cocoa. If necessary, they can spend the night." Mrs. Islington, who was a few years younger than Wade's mother, offered a smile with her assurances.

Wade mumbled his gratitude, while his mother had a brief exchange with her sister before turning to the two young women. "Maybe you could help him along."

"Of course," Aggie replied.

Doro and Aggie exchanged anxious glances as they each took one of Wade's arms and led him to his mother's Winton Touring car. After a couple of false starts, he tumbled into the passenger seat. As soon as all three women were in the vehicle, Mrs. Lammers drove out of the parking area.

When they got to the Silven home, Wade nearly fell on his face getting out. "Sorry," he muttered.

"Let's get you into the house." Aggie, alarm lining her fine features, turned to Mrs. Lammers. "Maybe you should let Doc know we're here."

"I will," Wade's mother said before hurrying up the front walk and to the door.

The two friends and Wade followed more methodically. He stumbled several times but, after the first two, he quit apologizing, probably because he was getting out of breath. Doro released a sigh when Doc Silven descended the porch stairs to help.

He put an arm around Wade's waist. "Lean on me, and we'll get you inside."

Even with Doc's assistance, Wade struggled to mount the steps. Eventually, he was seated in the doctor's office, which was just off the home's foyer.

As Doro glanced around the room, she could not help but worry. "How is Ev?" Her heart thundered in her ears. And where was Ev?

Doc's expression remained grim. "He regained consciousness, but he's quite ill. Chills, sweats, vomiting. I've got him in a patient room down here. I don't want to leave him alone for long. It'll be easier when Magenta gets back from the concert."

"I could sit with him," Doro said without forethought.

A slight smile played across Doc's lips. "He didn't want me in the room, so I doubt if he'll want you witnessing his current state." His mouth flattened as concern darkened his gaze. "Besides, I don't know what's wrong yet. If it's contagious, I'd rather not have others get sick."

Disappointment and dismay warred within Doro. "I understand."

"When he's better, you can visit," the physician assured her before glancing at Aggie and Mrs. Lammers. "You three stay here, while I examine Wade. I'll return with a report."

With little choice, the women sat down and waited. Off-and-on, they engaged in casual conversation, but long spells of silence fell. When Doc reentered the office, his face was set in solemn lines. Doro clasped her hands in her lap and braced for the news.

"Wade is nauseous, too, but he hasn't vomited. Yet," Doc Silven said.

"What's wrong with them?" Aggie asked. "Do you have any ideas?"

"It doesn't sound like Spanish flu," Mrs. Lammers put in. "I had that myself, and the symptoms were different."

"I also had it, and you're right," Aggie agreed.

"As I said, I can't be sure at this point," Silven replied. "I'm sorry. I wish I knew more."

Uneasiness mushroomed inside Doro as she once again worried that her food had made the men sick. All four of them had eaten the ham and the shortbread, but neither she nor Aggie was ill. Even so, she put forth a plausible scenario. "When I was little, some folks got sick after the Fourth of July picnic. Doc Frotis said a big bowl of potato salad must've gone bad."

"Food poisoning has similar symptoms, but the baskets were all kept cool," Aggie observed. "Except the hot meals brought right from home."

"Keeping the auction food in the icehouse started after the potato salad problem," Doro said.

"A wise practice," Doc replied. "Allowing food to sit outside for hours during warm weather can cause problems."

The comments might, or might not, connect to Ev and Wade falling ill. While Doro understood the physician's caution, she wanted an answer. Waiting, especially for a diagnosis, was one of life's worst frustrations.

"We don't know how ladies handled their concoctions prior to taking them to the event," Mrs. Lammers said.

"True," Doro agreed, "but Ev and Wade only ate food from our baskets."

"Ev and Wade also consumed cake at the contest, which the other judges did." Aggie's brow furrowed, as if she was deep in thought. "All four of us had my potato salad and baked beans. Doro and I both had a couple of bites of cake."

"And my shortbread and ham sandwiches," Doro added. "Only Ev ate an apple."

"Spoiled fruit can cause problems, but you would've seen it was bad," the physician said.

"It looked fine," Doro replied, but what about her other offerings? Shaking her anxiety was impossible.

Doc looked from one young woman to the other. "Both of you appear fine. Do you feel all right?" After they answered in the affirmative, Doc continued. "Then, we can rule out those foods. What about quantities? I'm guessing the men consumed more than either of you did."

"Definitely," Aggie responded. "Ev mentioned being especially hungry, so he ate more than usual."

Doro clapped on to her friend's lead. "He thought it might be indigestion from eating too much food, in general, or too many sweets, in particular."

Doc drummed his fingers on the desk. "He's too sick for the cause to be overeating, which could create some abdominal discomfort, but not severe pain, vomiting, nausea, and diarrhea."

The list of symptoms made Doro swallow hard over the sudden queasiness rising inside her. A glance at Aggie revealed her friend was experiencing similar feelings. "How terrible."

"It's not nice," the physician replied in a somber tone. "Ev is in much worse shape than Wade, so did he consume a lot more of any item?"

"Ev had a few of the shortbread cookies, but Wade only had a couple," Doro replied, but worry still stalked her. "I had one, and so did Aggie."

Several seconds passed before Aggie made an observation. "Ev suggested putting jam on the shortbread, so Wade tried it," Aggie added. She wrapped her arms around her waist. "They ate a lot of jam."

"They did, especially Ev," Doro agreed. "Ev told us about always putting lots on shortbread when he was a boy, and he had shortbread with jam after he walked Tee."

A pensive expression blanketed the physician's face. "And this jam was yours, Aggie?"

She nodded. "I had an open jar on the judges' table, so they could add some to the cake, if they liked. My dad and brother always did that." Her lips trembled as she spoke.

"You mentioned Ev and Wade using extra jam at the picnic," Doc observed.

Because her friend seemed shaken, Doro responded. "Three judges, including Ev and Wade, put an extra scoop on the jam roll during the contest. Since the jar was almost full, Aggie put it in her auction basket, and Ev took it home with him after consuming a fair amount."

"You put the jar in your basket right after the competition?" the physician asked.

Aggie shook her head. "No. The prizewinners were photographed at the bandstand on the other side of the park. When we all walked over there, I left the jam jar on the table in the judging tent." She folded her trembling hands in her lap. "The jar is from a big batch I made last fall when blackberries were ripe. Doro and I've eaten it over the last few months. A few others have, too."

Doc Silven gave her a thoughtful expression. "And you're sure the jar you took to the contest and put in your basket is from that batch."

"Absolutely sure," Aggie said.

"She's right about the jar being one of many," Doro agreed. "We've eaten a lot of that jam, and so have some of our fellow Wheaton Hall residents."

"Was the seal on the jar secure when you put it on the table this morning?" Doc inquired.

The questions were obviously putting Aggie on edge, but Doro also felt increasingly wary. Was Doc suggesting the jam might have gone bad due to not being properly stored? Could that lead to dire illness?

"I think it was," Aggie murmured. "I opened it myself, and the paraffin was in place."

Several seconds of silence ensued while Doc leaned back in his chair and folded his arms across his waist as he stared into space. "You've given me plenty to consider."

"In what way?" Mrs. Lammers posed the question in Doro's mind.

"I don't want to jump to conclusions, but Ev and Wade may have been poisoned. I've seen similar symptoms in patients who were. Several cases happened when I was in medical school. Unfortunately, a lot of toxins are easily accessible and folks end up getting accidentally affected by them." The doctor's solemn expression, along with his words, telegraphed genuine concern. "I had one patient succumb after long-term exposure to poison."

Doro swallowed hard over the lump rising in her throat. "Is that worse than sudden poisoning?" She hoped so.

"Not necessarily," he replied. "In this long-term case, the man refused to see me. He was sure he'd be fine. A lingering case of influenza, some food allergy, stress from work. Evidently, those were the excuses he used with his wife. When he finally agreed, it was too late..." His voice trailed off. "I shouldn't say more, because it's a private matter, and the family doesn't need to be buffeted by gossip. They've had a hard enough time."

The sentiment was admirable, because tittle-tattle spread rapidly. Most folks meant no harm by repeating talk, but it often hurt those involved. Even so, Doro could not help but wonder who had died.

Someone in Michaw? Evidently, or Doc would not be concerned about the family. Someone she knew? Most likely, because she was acquainted with everyone in the small town. A glance at Wade's mother revealed the older woman had similar questions. Since it made no difference to the current circumstances, Doro dismissed the past and focused on the present. "You're sure Ev and Wade didn't get lethal doses?" Doro asked.

A hesitation preceded his reply. "Fairly sure, but I can't be positive. As I said, they're otherwise healthy, and that's important. So was getting them here. That's where long-term exposure can be worse. When I don't know someone might've been exposed to poison, I can't provide proper care."

All three women were momentarily mute. Mrs. Lammers found her voice first. "Did you ask what they ate earlier, before the contest and the auction? Wade keeps rat poison in the storage area of the constable's station, along with some foodstuffs. He knows to be careful with toxins, but anyone can make a mistake."

Doro silently blessed the constable's mother for suggesting something other than Aggie's jam might be the culprit, although she doubted Wade would make such an error.

"I asked about what they ate earlier and where," Doc replied. "Wade was able to say neither had breakfast because of judging the cakes. The rest of what they ate, you all know."

"*Able to say*," Aggie echoed as all remaining color drained from her face. "How sick is he?"

The indicators already listed by the physician were alarming, but symptoms could range from mild to severe. Aggie clearly figured the men's ailments were in the former category, while Doro feared the latter better described them.

The doctor's grim expression foreshadowed his words. "Very ill.

Both of them are, although Ev is worse, as I said already. I won't leave them alone for long, not in their current conditions."

With her pulse pounding in her ears, Doro felt dizziness hit hard. While she had been prepared for a tough siege of sickness, Doc's admonition about an uncertain outcome added to her apprehension. "You think they'll recover, but what chance do you give it?" Her voice came out thin and thready.

Doc's countenance did not lighten as he faced her. "Better than fifty-fifty."

"Those aren't good odds," Aggie murmured.

Mrs. Lammers patted Aggie's arm. "As Doc said, Ev and Wade are generally healthy. That's in their favor." Despite her optimistic statements, the older woman looked and sounded tense.

As she fought for control. Doro folded her hands in her lap and clasped them together. Her thoughts were a jumbled mess.

"I've only spoken with Ev in passing before now. Does he have relatives?" The physician addressed Doro.

As the question registered, her fear escalated. "Ev has a younger sister, but I don't know her last name or address. She's married with small children."

"If she's his next-of-kin, the college should have the information," Doc pointed out.

"Of course," Doro murmured. "I can ask Mrs. Jones."

The physician shook his head. "We don't need to alarm his sister, and she can't do anything to help, so let's wait a while."

Ev had left the Prohibition Bureau to ease his sister's mind, so he would not want her contacted prematurely. And, if the worst happened...Doro did not allow the thought to form. "All right," Doro replied. "We can wait."

Doc turned to Aggie. "If Ev continues to do worse, I'll be inclined to think it's because he ate more jam than Wade."

The two young women looked at one another, and Doro noted Aggie's hazel gaze filling with guilt. She wanted to offer reassurance, but she was grappling with the situation herself.

"As we told you, Ev put lots of my jam on Doro's shortbread." Aggie made the confirmation. "Like I said, Doro and I have consumed more than one jar from that batch, so I can't figure out how poison would've gotten into that jar."

"Maybe not accidentally," Doro made the statement and waited for Silven to respond. Would he accuse her of letting her love of whodunits guide her comment? Everyone knew she was a mystery enthusiast.

"I agree that's a possibility," the physician said, "especially if the jar in question was part of a larger batch."

"It was," Aggie confirmed.

"And neither of you consumed any today?" the man asked.

"Both of us had a bite of jam roll, and we're fine," Doro replied.

"No extra jam on the cookies like Ev and Wade?" Doc asked.

The young women shook their heads. "Doro and I had thin pieces of cake. Since we taste-tested the recipe many times over the past couple of weeks, neither of us wanted more. We didn't put extra jam on the cake or the cookies, either," Aggie said, in a troubled tone. "I sealed the jars right after making the jam, which was in September. I used a few of them over the winter and gave some away. Like Doro said, others in Wheaton Hall ate it."

"Are you experienced in canning?" Doc's tone was benign, not accusatory.

Aggie nodded. "I canned various foods at home, and I've made jam many times. The jars got sterilized, and I bought paraffin from the general store right before I got the blackberries. Like always, I stored the jars in a cool, dark place."

"You're sure the jars weren't tampered with?" Doc asked.

His repeated concern bothered Doro. What exactly was he suggesting?

"They looked fine when I opened one yesterday to use jam in the rolls," Aggie replied. "I made a second cake for my auction basket with the same jam."

Doro struggled to picture the jam jar from early that morning, but she had not been concerned about the seal, either. Since she had never canned herself, Doro was not familiar with the process, but she had watched her friend. "I was with Aggie when she made the jam, and no poison was near the workspace. She's too good a cook to make that kind of mistake."

A long moment of silence preceded Doc's response. "Where is the jar now?"

"There was also a full, fresh jar in my picnic basket, so Wade gave the opened one to Ev to put on the leftover shortbread," Aggie replied. "It was nearly full before lunch, and about half-full after."

"I'd like to examine it. I can't test it here, but I'll contact the county sheriff. He'll have someone who can do it for us. Wade wants me to call him anyhow," Silven said.

"Do he and Ev suspect poisoning?" Doro inquired.

Silven shook his head. "Right now, they're too sick to think much about what happened and how it did, but neither of them will be at work for a few days, maybe longer. Wade wants the sheriff to know."

"That's my boy," Mrs. Lammers said. "He takes his responsibilities to heart."

"He does," Aggie seconded the observation. "Maybe Doro and I can fetch the jam jar and get it to you, Doc."

"Of course," Doro agreed. "With Ev so sick, I'll pick up Tee and keep her with me. We can get the jam at the same time."

"Good," he said, "but I feel fairly confident about poison being in it. That's the only idea making sense of the entire situation. If I'm wrong, tests will reveal it."

"But how would poison get in the jam?" Aggie asked again.

Silven's mouth flattened. "You said everyone went to the bandstand for the announcement of winners."

"That's right," Doro said. "Almost everyone in the tent went." Lila Billings and her uncle hadn't, and neither had Betty Stanley. And they had seen Parker and Harland in the area, not to mention the Fultons.

"The baking contest was the last one, but there were two others beforehand. First was fried chicken, since contestants brought hot food straight from home," Aggie added. "The second was bread."

"Neither Wade nor Ev judged any of those foods?" Doc asked.

"No, only the jam roll contest," Mrs. Lammers told him. "Wade has judged the baking competition for years, because he's got a sweet tooth."

Finally, the tension left Aggie, and she smiled. "He does."

Under other circumstances, Doro would have teased her friend about entering the baking contest to please Wade, but she could not shake her uneasiness long enough to engage in kidding. The image of Ev crumpling to the ground remained in the back of her mind, while finding out who was responsible was in the front. "We all left the judging table for the awards ceremony, so anyone could've tampered with the jam jar."

"But why?" Aggie asked.

"That's what I'd like to know," Doro said.

"If it is a toxin, all of us would like to know why and who." Dr. Silven shoved his hands into his jacket pockets.

Mrs. Lammers nodded. "What kind of poison could it be?"

Silven braced his elbows on the edge of his desk and steepled his fingers. "One possibility is arsenic. Folks have easy access," the doctor replied, "and it's colorless and tasteless. I saw several cases when I was in medical school. All but one was accidental. As you noted, Mrs. Lammers, rat poison is in many offices and homes."

A shiver rippled through Aggie. "No one would carry rat poison around without a reason and, since my jam seems to be the only tainted item, the person would've planned to do harm."

Her friend's voice rang with apprehension. Doro wanted to offer reassurance. But how could she? Ev and Wade were ill, probably from poison, and that had not happened by accident. Again, Doro wondered about the people who had been near or in the judging tent. Lila, her uncle, Betty, and the two boys might want to make Aggie suffer. But surely not the Fultons.

"It certainly seems that way," Silven agreed. "Mercury is also colorless and tasteless, but no one has it sitting on a pantry shelf. Although it's in thermometers, handling it is trickier. I'm not sure it wouldn't change the texture of jam. Did it look unusual?"

Doro and Aggie agreed it did not have an odd appearance.

The physician ran his fingers across his forehead. "Some plants cause gastric distress, but getting them into jam would take some doing."

"Perhaps, it was a prank gone wrong," Mrs. Lammers said. "Some years ago, a boy slipped opium into one of the desserts. One made by a girl who turned down his invitation to a party. He didn't want to kill her or no one else. His aim was to embarrass the girl, and he succeeded for a while because the cause of the judges falling ill wasn't immediately obvious. Eventually, his folks noticed a good deal of his grandmother's medication was missing. They confronted him, and he admitted to the prank."

"How awful," Doro said. "I don't recall it, though."

Mrs. Lammers smiled. "You were a babe in arms back then. The family eventually moved away, and the girl did, too, after she married. Her folks are all gone, so there's not been no talk about it in years. It was an ugly event, but opium used to be in many remedies years ago."

"Before the Harrison Narcotics Act banned it," Doc said. "I was just beginning medical school when that happened. It was a wise law, since both opium and cocaine can be dangerous and need regulation. As your story points out."

"Do you think someone was merely making mischief by tainting my jam?" Aggie asked, her face pale and her eyes wide.

Doc's shoulders rose and fell. "Mrs. Lammers' example isn't the only one I've heard about. Usually, kids are involved. Just like the boy using opium, they seldom realize the dangers of certain substances, especially when the toxins are in homes everywhere. Not as many medicines have opium in them nowadays, and it's much more controlled, but rat poison is everywhere." The physician braced his elbows on the desk before focusing on Aggie. "Do you have any disgruntled students? One who has argued over a grade or assignment?"

One hand flew to her mouth. "Yes. One young man is unhappy with his mark on the last essay. If his final paper isn't much better, he'll get a C, which will keep him off the Dean's List."

"And that's important to him?" Silven asked.

"Very much so," Aggie replied. "His family expects him to excel, and he has in other courses. Unfortunately, the young man isn't interested in poetry, and his disinterest shows in my class and in his writing. He only took my class because it fulfills a requirement."

"We saw him and a buddy when we left the tent. They were rude and nasty to Aggie," Doro commented."

"They were," Aggie added.

Silven turned to Doro. "You're familiar with the young man?"

Doro nodded. "He comes to the library for research, although he doesn't do much work. Mostly, he watches the girls and chats with his friends. My boss, Floyd Quartine, has asked Parker to leave several times. It's a tricky situation because his uncle is on the Board of Trustees."

"Which Parker mentions often," Aggie added.

Doc's brow puckered. "Only a couple of trustees live in Michaw."

"Garrett Matthing, Parker's uncle, lives in Toledo," Doro said. "He only comes to town for the board meetings, but he lets his ideas be known then."

Wade's mother posed a question. "What sort of ideas?"

"The college reverting to its original all-male status is his primary interest," Doro replied.

A chuckle left Doc Silven. "He's going against the modern tide with that idea. More women are working and going to college. I don't see it changing."

"He's in the minority," Doro said, "but he's outspoken, and so is Parker."

"Then, he may be the culprit," Mrs. Lammers said.

"Sounds possible, but let's not jump to conclusions," Doc observed. "For now, I want to check the jam, see if it's been poisoned, and, if so, with what."

Should Doro mention Lila and Betty? Maybe not yet. And the Fultons? Revealing their behavior seemed wise. "Mr. and Mrs. Fulton were in the tent when we went back. They hurried off after we tried to chat."

"They did," Aggie said.

"The couple who worked for Veronica Parson?" Mrs. Lammers asked. "They was helpful to you girls back in December."

What the constable's mother said was true. The Fultons had assisted Doro and Aggie, along with another woman, after they escaped from a murderer. "They were," Doro agreed, "but they rarely come into town. From what I hear, they go to Toledo for their supplies." Lingering suspicions about the pair surfaced in the recesses of her mind. Veronica Parson's husband had been suspected of dealing with bootleggers and, after his death, she had most likely carried on the trade. Since the Fultons had come to Michaw with her, they had to know about the rumrunning—and maybe be involved themselves.

"That's true," Doc said. "They even see a doctor in the city. Always did, though. I was surprised they didn't go back to Toledo after Mrs. Frotis' murder and everything that occurred afterward." The widow of the previous town doctor, who had passed a number of years ago, had been killed just before Christmas. She and Mrs. Parson, her next-door neighbor, had been at odds repeatedly before the homicide.

"It's been the topic of town talk off-and-on." Mrs. Lammers folded her hands in her lap and bent her head. "I've asked Wade about them, but he's real close-mouthed."

The observation magnified Doro's hunches. On several occasions, she had broached the topic of bootlegging with Ev, and he had brushed it off. Evidently, Wade did the same. But was it a far-fetched idea to believe the pair would taint the jam to disable the local lawmen? Doro needed to give it more thought before voicing the possibility.

"I'm more concerned about Aggie's student," Doc said, "although it seems strange for him to carry poison with him."

"Maybe he was hoping for an opportunity," Doro suggested, since Parker was a strong suspect. "It wasn't a secret that this year's bake-off was all jelly and jam loaves, so even students could guess extra jars would be available."

Mrs. Lammers nodded. "Many bakers provide more with their

cakes, so the boy coulda guessed. Or maybe he planned to find Aggie's picnic basket and poison that food."

"Maybe," Doro said, "but we kept ours in Wheaton Hall, not at the church."

"If the boys looked, they must've realized that," Aggie observed.

A memory surfaced in Doro's mind. "One day in the library, Parker was telling a buddy about playing a prank on a high school teacher who gave him low marks. Evidently, he flattened two of the man's tires, which broke the axle. They were guffawing about the incident. I had to tell them to be quiet or leave. Parker had the gall to say it'd be too bad if my Essex got scratched or dented. I told him I'd know who to pursue, if it did. Not that I could prove it."

"Doro, you never said anything about that." Aggie turned toward her friend.

"I didn't believe it was important. Now, I can see him plotting some prank," Doro said. "If he thought Aggie was bringing the leftovers home, she would've gotten ill."

Aggie wrapped her arms around her waist. "Parker is smart enough to know arsenic can be lethal. The same with mercury." Her voice trembled, and a shiver went through her.

Doro laid a hand on her friend's arm in a silent act of support and comfort. But she did not know what more to say.

"Is he smart enough to know not to use too much?" Silven inquired.

For several moments, silence echoed in the room. Finally, Aggie replied. "He is. More than once, he's mentioned how much more interesting and useful the sciences are than literature and composition. He's majoring in chemistry."

"I've heard the same from him," Doro added, "so, it's possible he decided some arsenic or mercury in Aggie's fare would either make her sick or affect others and make her look bad."

Doc rolled a pencil between his hands. "If the boy has relatives who are doctors, and he's studying chem, you're probably right about him knowing enough to use a poison that could be easily hidden and feel cocky enough to think he'd be able to put a minimal amount in the jam. Targeting a teacher before now is not a good sign. Neither is threatening to damage your vehicle, Doro."

She nodded. "He's a troublemaker."

A disturbed expression crossed Mrs. Lammers' lined face. "A few folks in town gossip about Wade and Aggie, but would students know?"

"I'm afraid so," Doro replied. "At least Parker and Harland did, because they mentioned it when we crossed paths this morning."

"They did," Aggie added.

Mrs. Lammers patted Aggie's shoulder. "I'm so sorry. Folks oughta keep quiet, especially young'uns."

"I agree, but your observation brings up the fact that others who were around the tent might've been responsible," Doro said.

"You've already mentioned the Fultons," Doc replied, "but it's hard to believe they'd resort to using poison, and what would their motive be?"

Since she was not sure how involvement in bootlegging would lead to poisoning the jam, Doro went on to another suspect. "Betty Stanley was a contestant, and she's been spreading gossip about Aggie and Wade stepping out. She disapproves. What if she wanted to make Aggie look bad?"

Doc's eyes widened. "Mrs. Stanley has had a difficult time since her husband died. Raising their son alone is a tough task. I can't see her as a poisoner or understand why she cares about who Wade sees."

Mrs. Lammers pursed her lips. "She's been after my boy ever since his wife died. Margie was in her grave less than six months when Betty began bringing meals to his house. My sister, my niece, and I pitched in to see he and the children was well-fed and cared for. I told Betty as much, but she insisted he needed someone like her. Such vanity." Disdain laced the woman's voice.

Although Doro had not heard the details before, she was hardly surprised. Mrs. Stanley had set her cap for Wade. That much was clear. But would she poison Aggie? Or attempt to poison her?

Doc cleared his throat. "Mr. Stanley and young Mrs. Lammers died within a few weeks of each other. Sometimes, widows and widowers find solace in sharing their losses." He drummed his fingers on the desk. "I know very little about town talk, so I'm not aware of Mrs. Stanley pursuing Wade. My practice and my family keep me busy."

"I'm sure they do," Aggie observed. She gripped the chair arms. "Mrs. Stanley has been hostile to me and to Doro." She briefly went over the woman's complaints at the cakewalk.

"I see," Doc murmured.

Doro was not sure he did, but she was about to mention Lila Billings when he spoke again.

"My primary concern is getting Ev and Wade back on their feet. Secondarily, I want the jam tested. As for figuring out who tainted it, if it was indeed tampered with, I'll leave that to the lawmen," Silven stated, as he got to his feet. "Please get the jar here as soon as you can."

"Of course," Doro replied.

A tap on the door interrupted the conversation before the doctor's wife stepped into the office. "I wanted to let you know we're back. The children are getting ready for bed. I'll fix them a snack and get them settled, but I can help afterward." Her gaze traveled around the group. "How are Ev and Wade doing?"

Her husband got to his feet. "Not well. While they're apt to recover, they're both in awful shape right now. The cause probably isn't contagious, so we can spread the word and ease people's minds. I'll be happy to have your help, though, because I don't want to leave them alone for long periods yet."

"I'll be back in a few minutes." Magenta looked at the three women again. "We'll take excellent care of those two, so try not to worry." Then, she slipped out of the room.

The door had barely closed behind Mrs. Silven when Wade's mother spoke. "I can spend the evening and help out. I'd like to call my sister and let her know. She's got Wade's children, and they'll enjoy spending the night with her. I should take Aggie and Doro to get the jam first, though. Then, they won't have to walk."

Doc nodded. "All right. A few hours of your presence would ease the burden on Magenta."

"Aggie and I could stay," Doro pointed out.

"Yes, we could," her friend agreed.

"I appreciate that, but Ev doesn't want an audience. As for Wade, he wants you to go home and rest, Aggie." Doc cleared his throat. "Besides, I'm not sure how townsfolk would take it if two unmarried ladies sat at the bedsides of two unmarried gentlemen." Doc looked at Mrs. Lammers.

An inaudible sigh escaped the older woman. "I'm afraid you're right." Her gaze, full of sympathy, went to Aggie and Doro.

Doro noted her friend's blush and, although she wanted to argue about old-fashioned rules, she resisted. Aggie and Wade were already the topic of town gossip, and they didn't need more under the current conditions. As for Doro and Ev...well, there was no Doro and Ev, even if folks speculated about them.

"If you'll show yourselves out..." Doc's voice trailed off.

"Certainly," Aggie agreed.

"I'll be back within a half-hour," Mrs. Lammers said.

The physician acknowledged her statement with a lift of his chin before the women murmured their goodbyes and left.

CHAPTER SIX

"I can take you to Ev's apartment to get the dog and jam, drop you off at Wheaton Hall, and go back to the Silven place," the older woman said after taking the wheel.

"Thank you," Doro agreed.

"Of course," Mrs. Lammers replied. "I can call after I get home. I'm sure it'll be before midnight."

"Yes, please do," Aggie replied.

Mrs. Lammers nodded. "I want to check on Wade's children and make sure they're all right. I may keep them home from school tomorrow, since I don't want them hearing no speculation about their father being poisoned or anything else."

By *anything else*, Doro felt sure she meant the relationship between Aggie and Wade. Although she wanted to discuss the case more fully, Doro did not wish to upset the older lady any more than she already was. At the moment, she looked and acted well, but Mrs. Lammers had been hospitalized with a heart attack last fall. "That would be wise."

After Aggie seconded the agreement, Mrs. Lammers drove to Ev's place. The door to the garage was always open, so Doro climbed the stairs and found the apartment door unlocked, as well. Doro called out to Tee before letting herself inside. The puppy launched herself at Doro, who bent down to fuss over her. "You haven't been alone too long, little girl." Nevertheless, the dog danced and pranced, as if she had endured days of isolation. Tee's excitement brought a smile to Doro's face. "Let me find the jam before I get your lead and head out." The jar sat on a table in the middle of the room, while the dog's gear was in its usual place on a hook near the door, so Doro did not go far to fetch them. Within moments, she and the puppy were in the Lammers' vehicle. Tee yipped excitedly as Mrs. Lammers and Aggie made over her. Then, they were at Wheaton Hall. The entire trip took less than fifteen minutes. After exiting the vehicle, both young women thanked their chauffeur.

"If I'm later than midnight, I'll wait until morning to call," Mrs. Lammers said.

"We'll stay in the reception room until then, so we hear the ring," Aggie replied.

Mrs. Lammers nodded before driving off.

When the vehicle turned the corner, Doro addressed her friend. "Ev walked Tee after the picnic, but I should take her for a quick jaunt before we settle down for a while. Do you want to come along?"

"Yes. Some fresh air would be welcome."

Since darkness had descended, Doro led the way along one of the lighted walkways on campus. The gas post lamps, set twenty to thirty feet apart, provided sufficient illumination. As they ambled along, Tee darted from side to side. Occasionally, she stopped to sniff, do her business, and move on.

"She's such a good little dog," Aggie observed.

"She is," Doro agreed. "Ev is the one who got her walking nicely on the leash. Now, she loves to stroll around campus and town."

A chuckle left Aggie. "She doesn't stroll. She trots along at a good pace."

"She does." Although small, Tee was a ball of energy. An adorable ball of energy. With her black fluffy coat and one ear standing up, as if listening for something important, she had a lock on cuteness.

"She's popular with the students. More than a few times, some of mine have been tardy because, according to them, they were visiting with the campus police pooch."

Doro joined in the laughter. "She's too friendly to be a law dog. She loves being out-and-about, though. I won't be able to take her as much as Ev does, since the end of the semester is busy." Anxiety curled in the pit of her stomach. "I hope she doesn't get upset by not seeing him for a time. Dogs can be very sensitive." Doro did not admit how upset she herself was.

"Doc may let her visit when Ev is better. Until then, I can walk her between my classes and office hours. But tomorrow is Sunday, so we'll both be free to fill her time."

"Thanks, Aggie. I can't take her to the library because my boss is allergic to dogs. She has stayed in my apartment while I work, but only for a few hours. If you walk her, she'll get tired and rest while she's alone." Doro bent to pet the dog's sleek head. "Ev will be able to take care of her again soon." She certainly hoped that would be the case.

After strolling around the campus for fifteen minutes, the little group arrived back at Wheaton Hall. "I'm going to get food and water for Tee. I know Mrs. Lammers won't call for a couple of hours, but why don't you wait down here, just in case?"

"Good idea."

When the dog's needs were met, Doro and Tee went back downstairs and joined Aggie, who was sitting on a love seat in the far corner of the reception area.

"I thought this was a good, out-of-the way spot. Residents don't usually come down on a Saturday night, and almost everyone spent the day at the festival, so they're probably resting."

"It was a full day, even without Ev and Wade getting sick. How about a cup of tea while we wait and talk?" Doro asked.

"Nothing for me right now," Aggie replied.

"I'll wait, too." Doro settled across from Aggie on the matching loveseat, while Tee settled at her feet. The pair of settees flanked the massive stone fireplace, while a sofa faced it. In winter, a blaze was kept going all day and into the evening, but spring led to fresh flowers replacing wood in the grate. Briefly, Doro thought about the May baskets being prepared for the following days. While some had been sold before the cakewalk, many folks would make their own. Although she did not expect one, Aggie surely did. But Wade was in no shape to deliver it. Fresh apprehension filled Doro. What if the men took turns for the worst? What if she and Aggie ended up investigating another homicide case—a double homicide? A shudder rippled through her. Although Doro loved sleuthing, she did not want Ev and Wade to die. Or anyone else, for that matter.

"Are you chilled?" Aggie asked, concern written on her face and roughening her tone.

"Maybe a little," Doro replied, although the chill was inside her. Since Aggie had to be worried about the lawmen, particularly Wade, Doro strove to put on a calm façade. "Do you mind discussing possibilities? It has to be upsetting to think about someone wanting to hurt you, directly or indirectly." Doro yearned to identify the culprit, who needed to be behind bars as soon as possible. Waiting for Ev and Wade to get on their feet did not strike her as wise.

"Talking about it isn't any worse than thinking about it," Aggie observed. "In fact, it'd probably be good to go over everything. Ev and Wade can't, and who knows if the county sheriff will investigate even if poison is found? Doc didn't say how long it'd take to get results back, but I'm guessing a few days."

"Maybe not that long," Doro replied. "I recently read a mystery where arsenic was the poison involved, and the test only took a short time. I asked Gladys Hollingsworth about it, and she told me those tests are fairly fast. It doesn't seem like mercury testing would take much longer."

"Since Gladys teaches chemistry, she should know. It'll be a relief to find out what was used, because I don't like a poisoner being on the loose, especially when we can't be sure of the target."

Doro considered the possibilities. "If the Fultons are still involved with bootlegging, they might want Ev and Wade out of the way for a time."

For a long moment, Aggie studied Doro. "Because a shipment of liquor could come through or near Michaw?"

"Exactly."

Aggie frowned. "We don't know that the Fultons took part in bootlegging. There were never any solid clues."

Doro rolled her eyes. "Maybe not, but there was plenty of circumstantial evidence."

"I can't deny that, but it seems like a stretch for them to taint my jam to hopefully put Ev and Wade out of commission."

Once again, Doro reviewed the events following the bake-off. "The jam jar was there for at least twenty minutes. Most folks left the tent area, but we don't know how long Parker and Harland were around. The Fultons could've been in the tent for a while, and Betty lingered." She paused before making an observation. "Any of them could've tampered with the jam."

"I suppose," Aggie murmured. "Since there was a lot left, I told Mrs. Jones I'd be back to get the jar and put it in my basket for the auction."

"Others were around when you said that," Doro put in. "A dozen or so."

"That's right," Aggie agreed. "But most people moved on quickly, since the basket auction was next on the schedule. It's a popular part of the day, and folks had to walk to the church."

"A handful of women went home to get their food, and others retrieved their baskets from the icehouse, so witnesses are apt to be few, if any," Doro said. "With no one watching, anyone could've slipped a toxin into the jar and stirred it up.

Aggie leaned back and closed her eyes. "I'd like to know how much poison, if any, is in the jam."

"I would, too, because that could reveal the poisoner's intention." Doro stopped before suggesting murder, not assault, might have been the intent. Aggie was not only astute, she was attuned to the undercurrents among a handful of townsfolk like Betty and Lila. Although others disapproved of Wade stepping out with a young professor, who would want to kill one of them? Or even harm them? The Fultons would not go that far, would they? Or could they be partnering with a bootlegger, who wanted to get even with Ev for some past clash? Other Prohibition agents had been targeted by gangsters. Shaking her apprehension proved difficult. What if someone else, someone they had not yet considered, was to blame? But who and why? Because she did not want Aggie more upset, Doro hurried on. "I'm sure it was only to make you or Ev and Wade ill." But she was not sure. Hunches were plentiful. Turning them into clues would take more time and effort. A lot more.

One of Aggie's shoulders rose and fell. "Probably so." Her tentative tone telegraphed doubt, as she cast a troubled glanced at Doro. "You seemed uneasy over Doc Silven's focus on the boys being responsible."

Doro leaned back on the loveseat and drummed her fingers on the arms. "Not entirely. It just doesn't seem like a prank to me, and Doc was dismissive when I mentioned the Fultons."

Aggie rolled her eyes. "He indicated town talk is of no interest to him, which is understandable. His practice and family keep him busy."

"True, but the poisoning is odd."

"I agree, but you and I are avid mystery readers," Aggie replied with a grin, "and you're a top-notch amateur sleuth. You've solved two murders."

"You helped on both," Doro pointed out, "especially, the one in December. And, we solved our first crime when we met." A decade earlier, Doro had been visiting her professor father when she had overheard Aggie, who was a student worker at the time, being reprimanded by another faculty member for losing his final exam. Because he was also threatening to have her scholarship revoked, Aggie had been near tears. Wanting to help, Doro had suggested investigating the lost exam. With assistance from her dad and another student, the two young women had caught the culprits. In the aftermath, a close friendship blossomed and, after a decade, it was in full bloom. Doro counted their happenstance meeting among her luckiest stars.

"I wouldn't be here now, if you hadn't convinced me to crack the case."

"It was good for both of us," Doro commented. "I always loved solving little mysteries but, up until the missing examination, I'd only done minor tasks. Finding lost pets and mislaid belongings. Nothing too challenging."

"You also got me reading whodunits," Aggie observed. "Before the lost exam, I mostly stuck to poetry."

"Which is still your first love."

Color crept into Aggie's face. "Maybe not my first."

Conflicting emotions assailed Doro. "Wade is a good man." The statement, while true, assumed little. Although Aggie was her best friend, Doro did not press for more information. Aggie wanted to consider her feelings before discussing them. Doro respected that, because she had never revealed the extent of her ambivalence over Ev. Strike that. She was not ambivalent. Her mind was set on being a career woman, but heart pangs sometimes threatened her certitude.

"He is," Aggie agreed. "How are we going to find out who's responsible for him and Ev being sick?"

"We can ask around and see if Betty or Lila was in the tent while we were at the bandstand, but something else bothers me about Betty."

A rueful smile tugged at one corner of Aggie's mouth. "Other than her pursuing Wade and disliking me, what?"

"Remember, Doc talking about someone who died from long-term exposure to poison?"

Aggie nodded.

"He didn't want to say who, because of the family, so the man must've lived in Michaw."

"I suppose so, but what are you getting at?"

"Betty's husband died after a lingering illness, from what I know, which isn't much. It was a few years ago, so after influenza swept through the area."

Aggie's jaw dropped. "You think she poisoned him?"

"I don't know, but it's possible. She could've slipped arsenic or some other substance into his food over a period of time."

"That's awful."

"It is, but Betty can be obnoxious."

"That doesn't mean she'd kill her husband," Aggie said.

"It's just a thought," Doro replied, but one that refused to leave her mind. "She can be further down my list."

Aggie's lips twitched. "Why am I not surprised that you have a list?"

"So far, it's in my head," Doro replied with a trace of defensiveness as she pulled a notepad and pencil out of her pocketbook.

"Do you ever go anyplace without writing materials?" her friend asked with a giggle.

"No. Do you?"

A half-shrug moved Aggie's shoulders. "No, because I like to jot down ideas for poems." Her gaze narrowed on Doro. "You haven't mentioned your book in a while. Are you still working on it?"

"Not much, since I've been busy at the library and teaching my classes. The mystery novel course has gotten more and more popular, so I'll have two sections every term. I'll focus on my book over the summer." Doro had been penning a mystery for more than a year. She loved doing it, but finding time was difficult. "As for our suspects, Parker and Harland should be near the top."

"Not at the top? We know Parker has a motive, and the two of them had an opportunity. The means is available to everyone."

Aggie's points were valid, but Doro could not shake her suspicions. "You agree with me that Lila and Betty have a motive, don't you?"

"They do, but would either of them taint my jam? Betty was close enough to hear me when I mentioned coming back and putting it in my auction basket. Everyone knew Wade would bid on it. And others would let him win in the end. Would she want to harm him when she's been in pursuit for a few years? It seems crazy."

"Or vindictive. If she had no hope of them stepping out, she might."

Aggie's jaw dropped. "What a terrible thought."

"It is, and I'm not sure that's what happened," Doro said. "I'm saying it's a possibility, one we can't overlook. The same is true for Lila, although we need to know if she went back to the tent after we left." She jotted down notes while speaking.

"Someone on the May Days committee might have information," Aggie suggested.

"A great point." Doro tapped her pencil on the pad before writing more notes.

Aggie gnawed on her lower lip. "I hate thinking Wade was targeted because of me."

"If either Betty or Lila targeted him, it wasn't because of you. It was because he didn't kowtow to their wishes."

"I suppose," Aggie murmured. "There's another possibility. Maybe some youngster got in trouble, and Wade told the parents. That would upset a boy, don't you think?"

The entreaty in Aggie's voice telegraphed uncertainty. Doro wished she could vanquish it by agreeing, but she couldn't. Not when other options seemed more logical. "Maybe so."

Aggie's brow furrowed. "But you don't believe that's the case."

"I don't, but we won't dismiss it." She rolled the pencil between her hands. "While revenge is an excellent motive for either Betty or Lila, directed toward you or Wade, someone might've wanted both local lawmen out of commission."

"Someone like the Fultons."

For a long moment, Doro studied her friend. "You don't agree they could still be involved in bootlegging?"

"Even if the Fultons are involved, there's been no illegal liquor transported through Michaw," Aggie pointed out.

"That we know about," Doro replied. "Michaw is far enough from the city that Prohibition agents aren't around, and it's situated close to

Chicago Pike. By driving a couple of miles south, rumrunners could hit that road and be on their way. The Fultons are staying on for some reason. Making money through rumrunning seems like a powerful motivation. It's happened in other towns around here, so why not near Michaw?"

"No good reason," Aggie admitted. "And they were in the tent when we got back from the awards presentation."

"Plus, they rushed off," Doro added. "So, you agree about putting them on the list?"

Aggie nodded. "It seems even harder to find out about them and rumrunning, but Ev and Wade could learn more."

The observation reignited another suspicion. "They might already know something. If there's any evidence of the Fultons' involvement in bootlegging, Ev's former boss could've contacted him."

A puzzled expression blanketed Aggie's face. "The Parsons' involvement came up in the Frotis murder case, but I wasn't aware of Ev talking to anyone from the Prohibition Bureau at the time or since."

Doro's lips flattened. "Neither was I, but he can be very close-mouthed, especially about his old job."

"That's sensible, since it's a dangerous one involving sensitive information. I'm sure he doesn't want to inadvertently reveal something important."

A harrumph left Doro. "There's no chance of that. When I've asked if he knows anything about bootlegging going through Sylvania or Michaw, Ev says that's not his job anymore. Of course, he's also admitted the Bureau would most likely contact him if there was rumrunning here. Especially if a raid was eminent. He won't tell me, though, or anyone other than Wade. I don't suppose he's mentioned anything to you."

"Of course not," Aggie replied. "Wade isn't as reticent as Ev, but he wouldn't reveal that kind of information to a civilian, including me."

"And nothing he's said or done makes you suspicious?"

"No. Has Ev given you any clues?"

"Only to insist he knows nothing, and he's very insistent. Almost too strong in his protests." She paused for a long moment. "I don't want to set aside the Fultons sidelining Ev and Wade. Not only was it well-known that Wade would bid on your basket, everyone had to expect me to join you two for lunch, and probably Ev, as well."

"And Ev bid on yours." Aggie's grin returned full-force.

Warmth crept into Doro's face as she avoided her friend's steady gaze. "Ev and I share Tee, and we've gotten friendly. Besides, Ev and Wade are now good friends, and people know you and I have been best friends for years. They might expect the men to both bid on our baskets and then, share them due to that." Because Doro did not wish to delve into her feelings toward Ev, she hurried on. "Getting back to my point, someone might've planned to harm both Ev and Wade, but maybe my imagination is running wild."

A low laugh left Aggie. "Ev would say that."

Under normal circumstances, Doro would have chuckled and agreed. But she was too worried to feel amused. If the Fultons were bootlegging, they had accomplices. What if Ev was the primary target and Wade was secondary? Doro did not voice the idea because Aggie would rightly point out that the poisoner couldn't have known Ev would eat extra jam. With effort, Doro thrust the thought from her head. Her worry about his well-being was intensifying her already vivid imagination. "He would accuse me of being fanciful," she agreed, "but do you?" Anxiety clouded Doro's mind, which made sorting through details difficult. In previous cases, she had not felt as emotional. Logic flew out the window when feelings walked through the door.

Aggie's demeanor again grew solemn. "No, I don't. Even though Ev teases you about reading too many mysteries, I wish we could talk with him and Wade."

"So do I."

Surprise flashed in her friend's hazel eyes. "Usually, you're worried about them taking over."

That had been true at the start of a murder case last fall. As an early suspect, Doro had run afoul of Ev, who was then the new campus security officer. Even after he believed in her innocence, Ev only reluctantly agreed to let Doro take part in the investigation. By the end, mutual respect grew between them, but in the interim, they'd had rough moments. Mostly due to Doro's curiosity about anything mysterious. "True, but in this case, they aren't physically able to take over."

Aggie's lips twisted. "Which is worrisome. Not only did someone taint my jam, Wade is ill. Very ill. Ev is even worse."

The observations wrung Doro's heart. "Doc thinks they'll recover. We must believe that, too." Even as she spoke, Doro felt fresh fear invade every cell of her body. Ev, so strong and healthy, had collapsed like a pierced balloon. Although he had regained consciousness, he was a long way from being well. Doc's reassurances were circumspect, which kept Doro from relaxing. Figuring out who was behind the poisoning would take her mind off Ev's precarious condition. A glance at Aggie revealed she probably needed a distraction, too. "I've jotted down our ideas. We can methodically go over the clues and suspects. Then, when Ev and Wade feel better, we can share what we've learned with them."

Most of the fear left Aggie's expression. "Good idea, but before we do, a cup of tea sounds good. Maybe a sandwich, too, since we haven't eaten for hours."

"We can hear the hallway telephone in the kitchen," Doro said.

After preparing a light meal, and sharing some with Tee, the young women returned to the reception area. Fatigue and anxiety weighed Doro down and, from the look of her friend, the same was true for Aggie. Despite that, Doro broached planning their next moves. "Mrs. Lammers may have good news about Ev and Wade, but neither of them will be up and around soon."

"Not according to Doc Silven, and he should know," Aggie agreed. She slipped off her shoes and tucked her feet up. "What are your plans?"

A chuckle escaped Doro. "Don't you want to talk with Ev and Wade first?"

Aggie rolled her eyes. "You can't fool me, Dorothea Banyon. Your mind has been churning with ideas ever since Doc mentioned poisoning, so don't tell me it hasn't. I know you too well." The assertions were softened by a wink.

Following the release of a pent-up breath, Doro owned up to her mental meanderings. "My first thought was to confront everyone, but that wouldn't be wise or helpful. We mentioned asking if others saw Lila, her uncle, or Betty around the tent while we were at the bandstand."

"That's doable," Aggie agreed.

Doro picked up the notepad, which she had left on the loveseat. After flipping to a blank page, she made notes. "I'll ask Mrs. Jones if any committeewomen stayed near the tent. If someone did, we can talk to her as soon as possible."

The jangling of the hall telephone had both of them jumping to their feet and dashing toward it. Doro let Aggie answer and listened with eager ears. Not that she learned much from her friend's side of the conversation.

As soon as Aggie replaced the earpiece, she turned to Doro. "Mrs. Lammers spoke with Wade, and he's feeling better. Or so he claimed. He insists we shouldn't worry."

Doro's mouth felt like it was filled with cotton, but she choked out a question. "What about Ev?"

Aggie's gaze darted away from Doro. "He woke but was semi-coherent. Doc says it's not a terrible sign."

Not terrible but bad. Were long-term health consequences an issue? Doro didn't know, but the idea was frightening. "Did she say if you and I can visit tomorrow?" Seeing Ev's condition for herself would provide a clearer perspective, although it might not ease her mind.

"Doc wants us to call before going." Aggie sent her friend a reassuring glance. "He wouldn't say they'll recover unless he believed it."

"Of course," Doro murmured. Would Ev's recovery be partial or complete? She moved her anxiety to the back of her mind. "It's been a long day, and we're almost into tomorrow. You'll want to be up early to call Doc, so we should get some rest. We can discuss our plans in the morning." Although she would have liked to get going immediately, Doro knew doing so was not feasible.

"I could drop in my tracks," Aggie replied, "so sleep is a good idea."

Doro nodded, but she was not sure how much slumber she would get. Her mind was filled with worries and wonderings.

CHAPTER SEVEN

As she had feared, Doro found sleep elusive. Tee's small, warm body laying against her back kept Doro from tossing and turning, because she did not want to disturb the little dog. Several glances at her watch found the hours creeping forward until, sometime after four o'clock, Doro dozed off. When sunlight crept into her window, Doro groaned. For several moments, she resisted rising. Then, slowly and surely, the events of the previous day intruded. Her heart raced as she thought of Ev. Was he any better? And what about Wade? To get answers, she and Aggie needed to call the Silven house.

After hurriedly cleaning up and dressing, Doro took Tee out and fed her before heading to Aggie's apartment. A soft knock brought Aggie, fully dressed, to the door. "Good morning," Aggie said as she bent to pet Tee, who did her usual prancing and dancing. "Come in. I made coffee, and I can put toast in the oven."

Doro followed her friend to the small table and sat down. Tee sat on the floor beside her. "Just coffee. Your toasting iron takes too long, not to mention it's a lot of trouble to monitor the bread, so it doesn't burn. You need one of the new pop-up toasters. I love mine. Quick and easy."

Aggie poured two cups of coffee, put them on the table, and joined Doro. "It's not a necessity, though. The toasting iron still works."

"And it always will work, because it does nothing except sit in the oven with bread in it," Doro commented but said no more. Although Aggie had a good job, she still pinched pennies. In some ways, Doro did, too, since a young woman on her own needed to be frugal. Her new toaster had been a gift from her parents, as were many of the niceties in Doro's home. For a moment, she let herself consider the future when her grandmother and parents would be gone, and she would be completely alone. Would she still be living in Wheaton Hall? And what about when she retired?

Aggie's voice broke into her thoughts. "You look far away."

Doro gave a rueful smile. "Not so far. Just thinking." She took a sip of coffee. "It's still early, but I don't think Doc or Magenta would mind if you call."

Aggie's auburn brows rose a fraction. "They wouldn't mind if you called, either."

The comment could open a discussion about Doro's connection to Ev, which was tenuous, at best. Since she did not wish to go over it again, Doro sidestepped that issue. "You and Wade have been stepping out, so it'd be more appropriate for you to telephone."

Something akin to disbelief lit Aggie's eyes. "You aren't usually a stickler for what's appropriate. In fact, you often point out how silly many of society's rules are. That's the main reason you're the faculty advisor to the Young Women Voters for Equality and Justice, isn't it?"

Doro stared into her coffee cup. Her mother had been involved in the suffragette movement and, as a little girl, Doro had attended many events with her. Since Ebediah Banyon supported rights for women, including voting, Doro had grown up somewhat differently than many young ladies. With Michaw being a progressive college, and the town following suit for the most part, her ideas were accepted or ignored. Usually. A handful of folks considered her to be brash, even odd. As she considered her Monday morning talk with Mrs. Jones, Doro wondered if—despite her long-held and well-known intention to be a career woman—her colleagues and neighbors figured she would marry, eventually. Her friendship with Ev might whet their appetites for a full-blown courtship with a wedding to follow. Dismay hurtled through her. Another reason not to contact Doc herself. The call would go through the weekend operator. Sharing the news that Doro telephoned to ask about Ev would delight the woman. "I want to support our female students. Even though we got the vote nearly a decade ago, more progress needs to be made." She drained her cup and looked at her watch. "Maybe we should go downstairs before others get there. I don't know about you, but I'd rather not answer a bunch of questions right now."

Aggie released a long breath. "I'd rather not, either. Let me set the cups and saucers in the sink, and I'll be ready to go. You can leave Tee here. She's stayed before and enjoys snoozing in one of the chairs."

Doro chuckled. "I'm glad her getting on the furniture doesn't bother you. Ev has done a good job of training her, but he sees nothing wrong with giving Tee the run of his place. To be honest, neither do I. Despite her fluffy coat of fur, she sheds very little."

Tee yipped, as if in agreement, and both young women laughed.

Within moments, the pup was snuggled in an easy chair and the friends were headed to the telephone. Again, Doro gained little insight from hearing only Aggie's side.

After replacing the earpiece on the hook, Aggie turned to Doro. "I spoke with Magenta, and we can visit. Both Ev and Wade are awake now."

"Are they better?"

"She wants Doc to tell us the details," Aggie replied.

Doro swallowed hard. "That sounds ominous."

"It makes me uneasy, too, but if they took turns for the worse, I believe she would've issued some sort of warning. She wouldn't want us to be shocked, and she said not to fret. That's a good sign." Despite the assertion, Aggie sounded doubtful.

"Probably so." But Doro was not at all sure. Only a day ago, at this same time, she and Aggie had been preparing to go to the festival. A few hours later, they had been celebrating. Now, both dreaded what they might discover when they saw Ev and Wade. The previous night, going over suspects and clues kept them from falling into despair, although sleep had been elusive. Perhaps her weariness was adding to Doro's anxiety. As she studied Aggie's face, Doro saw dark circles ringing her friend's eyes. "You didn't get much sleep."

Aggie's head briefly fell forward. "Not much. How about you?"

"The same." When she hadn't been fretting about Ev, Doro had been going over and over the suspects and motives. What was the worst option? Bootleggers planning a crime and wanting local lawmen out of the way? A disgruntled student playing a prank? A jealous competitor aiming to harm Aggie? A spurned woman set on getting back at Wade? A gangster seeking revenge against Ev? And would the poisoner strike again? If so, what would be his or her next attempt? Something other than a toxin? But what, and how, and when? Or was the perpetrator lying low? The questions echoed in Doro's mind.

"I had several dreams where someone poisoned everything I cooked," Aggie murmured.

While Doro didn't want her friend to worry, what could she say to ease Aggie's mind? Her friend was already criticized for not being a proper young woman. Fresh annoyance flashed through Doro. *Proper* meaning a female who prepared for marriage and motherhood, not a career gal.

Aggie's voice interrupted Doro's reverie. "I hope Doc has good news."

"They must be better," Doro replied, now in the position of offering reassurance, "or we wouldn't be allowed to visit." Surely that was the case. It couldn't be that the men were failing and wanted to say goodbye. Doro hastily blinked back tears. What foolish, futile thoughts. "Let's not think the worst." The advice was as much for her as it was for her friend.

With her heart in her throat, Doro trudged alongside her friend until they reached the Silvens' front door. After knocking, Doro and Aggie waited only moments before Magenta let them in. A slight smile lit the woman's pretty face. "Come in." Once Doro and Aggie were in the wide foyer, the physician's wife spoke again. "Both Constable Lammers and Officer Mallow are a little better this morning. As you know, they were terribly ill last evening. That continued through the night." She grimaced. "It's awful that poison got into your jam, Aggie, and to think about who put it there."

The woman's observation evoked a question from Doro. "Do Ev and Wade know what happened? What we think happened?"

"My husband told them about a toxin most likely being in the jam. Someone from the sheriff's office will pick the jam up today, so we could have results soon," Mrs. Silven said. "As for what our two patients believe, I don't know that they have coherent thoughts, despite talking to Will for a little while. They're better but weak and exhausted. An hour ago, they were able to keep some broth down, which is positive. We'll try toast soon."

Aggie clasped her hands in front of her and pressed them to her waist. "Do they believe I accidentally got arsenic in the jam?"

Magenta shook her head. "Of course not. Before Will even brought up his supposition, Constable Lammers insisted you'd never be so careless."

Doro saw relief fill her friend's gaze. "We all know that."

"We certainly do." Magenta made the statement with fervor.

"Thank you," Aggie murmured. "Thank you, both."

"Yesterday, we hadn't heard of others getting sick," Doro observed.

"That's still true," Magenta replied. "Will has almost eliminated the idea of something contagious, but a test will confirm that."

"Wade looked terrible yesterday," Aggie said. "I would've thought he was coming down with influenza. At first, I thought both of them were."

"It's fortunate we were at the festivities, so Will could get Officer Mallow here right after he collapsed," Magenta murmured. "Will would like to speak with you two in his office before you visit our patients."

Doro wanted to hear from the physician, so she readily agreed. Aggie did, as well.

Magenta ushered the women into her husband's cramped office. The doctor, his eyes heavily shadowed, rose when they entered. "Sit down, ladies." He looked at his wife. "Thank you for bringing them in. I'll escort them to the patients' room. I won't make it to church with you and the children, but I'll see you all later."

His wife smiled her agreement, went out, and closed the door behind her. After she was gone, the physician gestured for Doro and Aggie to sit down. Once they were seated, he followed suit. "You already know the men most likely ingested poison from something they ate at the festival, probably the jam. I'll be able to say for sure after the tests are done. The county sheriff and his deputies will also cover the area while Ev and Wade are ailing. It's a good idea, even though they expect nothing to happen."

The disclaimer ignited Doro's skepticism. Michaw was a peaceful place. At least it usually was, but two murders had occurred the previous year. Now, poisoning. The crimes were not related, although all were troubling. Did Wade alerting the county lawmen indicate he saw the crime as serious? "Is the sheriff sending someone to be here full-time for a while?"

Doc shook his head. "No, he doesn't have enough men for that. A deputy will drive through every day, and one will pick up the jam sample today. After Wade is better, they can talk about any special issues."

The two friends nodded, and Doro posed one of the issues swirling through her head. "Magenta said no one else has gotten sick."

"That's right," the physician replied. "I spoke with the other three judges, and all feel fine. The one who added a dab of jam is all right, too."

"Good" Doro said. At least no one else was suffering.

He nodded. "Ev and Wade were able to talk a little. I mentioned it being a student playing a prank. They agree that's possible."

The idea did not resonate with Doro, but maybe she had read too many mysteries. If Parker and Harland were the culprits, they weren't on a lark. They wanted to harm Aggie, which was serious.

"Did they offer other ideas?" Aggie asked.

A half-shrug moved one of his shoulders. "No, but I had the feeling both have thoughts on the subject." He glanced from Doro to Aggie. "One of the reasons I wanted to chat was to warn you not to wear them out with a deep discussion of possibilities. They're out of danger, but they could have setbacks. I don't want that."

"Neither do we," Aggie assured him.

"Of course not," Doro added, "but they've speculated, I bet." Although Ev teased her about her armchair sleuthing, he also loved reading whodunits, and their favorite author, Agatha Christie, often used poison as the means in her books. As several stories flashed through her mind, Doro shuddered because the books were murder mysteries. She worked to tamp down the knee-jerk fear. Neither Ev nor Wade would die. Doc had just said as much.

"I walked in on them having a discussion," Silven agreed. "I can't stop that. Neither told me a lot, but they may reveal their ideas to you two. Try to limit the extent of the analysis. They need peace and rest."

"We will," Aggie assured him.

His expression grew somber. "It's lucky neither of you consumed much jam. If you had, I'd have two more patients on my hands." Doc got up again. "I'll let you see the men now. We've kept them in one big room down here."

As she and Aggie followed the physician out of his office and down a narrow hallway, Doro felt a rising tide of dread. When would the pair be well? Would they heal completely?

When they reached the end, Doc opened a door. "Here they are."

Doro stepped inside the room ahead of Aggie. Two beds with a nightstand between them held Ev and Wade, both of whom were propped on piles of pillows. Doro's attention lit on the security officer. With the drapes closed, the light in the room was dim, but she noted his appearance with a sinking feeling. Ev's flushed face, red-rimmed eyes, and drawn features stood out. He looked horrible. Absolutely horrible. She hesitated inside the doorway while Aggie hurried to Wade's bedside.

"Can I bring either of you anything?" Doc Silven asked the men. When the pair demurred, he turned to Doro and Aggie. "Fifteen minutes shouldn't overtire them." Then, he was gone.

"Fifteen minutes," Ev echoed in a voice rough with exhaustion and illness. "We'll barely have time to discuss how poison got into the jam."

His comment did not surprise Doro, but Doc's admonitions rang in her ears. "You two need rest, more than anything." She took the chair nearest his bed as she spoke. "Magenta and Doc told us how sick you've both been, and it doesn't look like you're out of the woods yet." Not succumbing to the poison was good, but lingering illness was not.

"The last sixteen hours are ones I'd like to forget," Wade put in.

"Same here," Ev agreed. After a moment, he turned to Doro. "Tee is at your place, right?"

His concern for the little pup made Doro smile. "You asked me to care for her right before you collapsed, so I picked her up last night after we left here."

Relief slacked his features while color suffused his pale face. "That wasn't my finest moment."

Empathy squeezed Doro's heart. "You were poisoned, but you still thought about Tee."

One corner of his mouth lifted in an attempt at a smile. "I knew you'd make sure she's fine, but I worry about her. She's such a wonderful dog."

Their shared love for Tee had kept their friendship from floundering after Doro informed Ev that her career came first. Ev hadn't argued or belittled, nor had he shunned her when they crossed paths. If he was not as friendly as before her admission, that was to be expected. "She misses you," Doro assured him. "When we walked this morning, she headed toward your apartment."

A wan smile touched his lips. "I miss her."

After resisting the urge to lay a hand on his arm, Doro nodded. "When you're feeling up to it, and Doc gives his approval, I'll bring her to see you."

"Great," Ev replied, but his voice wobbled.

Wade looked at Aggie. "I'd rather my kids didn't see me here, even when I'm a little better. Their mother was bedridden before she died, and I don't want them to get scared."

"I understand," Aggie replied. "Your mother told them you're under the weather, so you're staying here where Doc and Mrs. Silven can care for you. They accepted the story."

Wade nodded. "Good. They're probably still excited about last night's concert and today's parade." His brow furrowed. "Is it over? I've lost track of time."

"That's not surprising," Aggie commented. "It isn't over, but it'll be starting after the potluck, which is in a couple of hours. Your mother will take the children."

Ev pushed to one elbow but quickly fell back against his pillows. "Aren't you two going?" He looked from one young woman to the other.

"We'll see it," Aggie replied, "because I don't want to disappoint the children."

Wade patted her hand. "I appreciate that, since there's no way for me to get there." The constable's disappointment was palpable, and so was his exhaustion.

"They understand, and you'll be there next year. For now, you need to rest," Aggie advised. "Maybe we should go."

When she started to rise, Wade stopped her. "It hasn't been fifteen minutes and, before you leave, we should talk about the poisoning."

His words confirmed Doro's supposition. She looked from the constable to Ev. "Because you two already have."

Ev nodded. "Of course." A note of amusement was in his ragged tone.

"Of course," Doro echoed as she bit back an admonition. Neither man would listen to advice, so letting them voice their ideas was best. As for avoiding an in-depth discussion, as Doc had warned, she was not sure that was possible. The lawmen might be weak, but they were dedicated. "What are your thoughts?"

"Doc is leaning toward one of Aggie's students tampering with the jam when no one was around," Ev replied. "Evidently, you two discussed the possibility with him."

With their fifteen-minute deadline in mind, Doro got to the core issue. She and Aggie would investigate, but professional guidance would be useful. "We did, and Doc settled on that idea for a couple of reasons." She continued by explaining Mrs. Lammers' recollection of the boy who tainted a cake some years back before turning to Aggie. "Does Wade know about Parker?" The question came to Doro for the first time.

A frown furrowed the constable's brow as he focused on Aggie. "No, he doesn't."

Aggie put up both hands, as if to fend off a complaint. "I didn't see a reason to bother you with an unhappy student. I've had more than one, since I began teaching."

Wade's expression softened. "You don't have to share everything with me but, if the kid threatened you, I'd like to know."

She shrugged. "He said I'd be sorry if I didn't raise his grade, which isn't much of a threat."

"Did he say anything else?" Wade asked, his expression solemn.

Aggie summarized the previous morning's exchange.

"Both of them are rude and obnoxious," Ev commented.

"They are," Doro put in.

"With all that in mind," Wade began, "Doc may be right about those two being responsible. I don't know them, do you, Ev?"

"In passing. You're right about their attitudes. They don't respect authority, at all," Ev replied. "I can see them thinking it'd be funny to taint Aggie's jam, but that doesn't mean they did it."

Since Doro felt the same way, she looked at Wade. "What do you think?"

"There's not nearly enough evidence for me to be certain," the constable replied before glancing from Doro to Aggie. "I imagine you two have discussed other ideas."

The observation made Doro look at her friend, who gave a quick nod. "We have." Doro followed with their supposition that the jam was tainted following the contest.

Wade shifted against his pillows. "When Ev and I left the tent, only a handful of folks were still there. Others were outside. As far as I know, the area was empty for at least fifteen minutes, which gave someone a chance to do the deed, just as you two discussed. Maybe someone who wanted to harm Aggie."

Aggie's eyes went wide. "What makes you say that?"

Doro wondered if Wade was skeptical of her friend's feigned surprise. Aggie was well aware she could have been the target.

Wade patted her arm. "For one, you won the bake-off."

When the constable did not continue, Ev spoke. "For another, you've been stepping out with Wade, and a handful of townsfolk have been vocal in their opposition."

Had the men discussed the gossip before now? Evidently so. "Busybodies who ought to mind their own business," Doro muttered.

"True," Ev agreed with a faint smile. "But some of those who've gossiped aren't fond of the college, the employees, or the students. Then, there's the pair of ladies in that group. They both seem sweet on Wade."

Color crept into the constable's face. "I hate to consider either Betty Stanley or Lila Billings trying to harm you, Aggie. Or anyone else, for that matter."

"It's not the only possibility," Ev pointed out.

The remarks from both men meshed with what she and Aggie had discussed, but Doro wondered what else the two had covered. "It seems you've talked a lot about possibilities."

A weak smile touch Ev's mouth. "We have."

Aggie frowned. "Doc doesn't want either of you spending time and energy on ferreting out the culprit."

Low laughter left Wade. "We won't be going anyplace to ferret soon."

"That's for sure," Ev agreed.

With a sigh, Aggie leaned back on the hard chair. "He doesn't want you talking too much, either. A relapse is possible."

Both men groaned. Both women shook their heads.

After a moment, Wade turned to Aggie. "What about your student? Would he really be mad enough to poison you?"

A long moment elapsed before she answered. "He might've wanted to make me sick. He's been pretty upset and, as we've already discussed, insufferable and ill-mannered."

"The kid had motive and opportunity," Ev said.

Wade, his expression troubled, nodded. "And the means is easy to come by. Almost all households and businesses have some sort of poison on hand."

"I'm sure that's the case," Doro agreed, but she was not so certain that Parker was the perpetrator.

"As soon as we're on our feet, Ev and I can talk to the boy," Wade said.

"We sure can," the security officer agreed, but concern wrinkled his forehead. "The problem is, when will we be strong enough to do that? I hate to admit that it won't be as soon as I'd like."

"Or as soon as I would," Wade muttered. "I'm worried about the person trying again. Since we don't know the motive or the target, that could happen."

"It could," Doro agreed. "We heard the country sheriff isn't sending a deputy."

Wade nodded. "He doesn't have the manpower to have someone here all the time. I didn't talk with him myself, since getting out of bed and walking to the telephone isn't doable yet."

"Do you know if Doc told him that Aggie's students might be responsible?" Doro asked.

"He did," Ev replied. "Doc's not as worried as we are. From what we know, the sheriff isn't, either."

"Will Silven isn't one to entertain complicated plots," Wade added. "As for the sheriff, he only knows what Doc told him."

"Dr. Silven also informed us that he doesn't listen to gossip," Doro said.

A grin pulled up one corner of the constable's mouth. "He relies on facts, simple ones. But he's a good doctor. His prank theory has credence, although I'm not convinced it was your student and his pal. I'm leaning toward the culprit having only one target, though."

"Me," Aggie murmured.

With one hand, Wade clasped her arm. "I'm sad to say that seems quite probable."

Her friend's distraught expression tore at Doro's heart. Although she did not want to prolong the conversation, Doro wanted to see how the lawmen would react to another possibility. "What if the two of you were the targets?" As she glanced from Ev to Wade and back, Doro noted surprise and suspicion in the men's expressions. Had they already considered and dismissed the idea?

"What makes you suggest that?" Ev asked in a wary tone.

Answering a question with a question signaled a smokescreen. Doro maintained his steady gaze when she replied. "Because someone might want to incapacitate the town's two lawmen."

Ev's features remained carefully schooled. "For what plausible reason? Hardly any crime happens around here."

"That's right. Last year's murders were oddities. Nothing like that will occur again soon, so there'd be no sense in making us ill. Unless you ladies believe there's a murder plot underway." A note of amusement crept into Wade's voice.

Something akin to a chuckle, a rusty one, left Ev. "You two went over various scenarios and came up with this one?"

For several moments, Doro scrutinized the men's expressions. Both looked amused, but were they? Although she did not think so, Doro wondered if she should explain her ideas about bootlegging as a component. Perhaps, pretending to consider different ideas was wise. Ev would not admit to knowing about rumrunning. Neither would Wade, so she offered a benign comment. "Among others."

"I'm sure," Ev muttered, almost under his breath.

"As am I," Wade chimed in.

The men's cryptic words aggravated Doro and, when she studied her friend, she saw Aggie felt much the same way. Ev and Wade were not being forthright. She sensed it. But why not?

Wade patted Aggie's hand. "You're a far more likely target."

"Maybe," she replied.

The constable's good humor fled as he frowned. "Your student was nearby. You said so yourself. To my mind, that makes him a top suspect. You revealed he may get a low grade in your class, so it stands to reason he wanted to get even by making you sick and miserable. Not everyone knew the jam jar was going into your basket, so he might've figured on you taking it home and consuming it. Maybe someone else is the guilty party, but aiming to poison Ev and me seems highly unlikely."

Doro mulled over the ideas. Many folks had heard Aggie say she'd be back for the jam jar to put it in her raffle basket, a basket that Wade planned to bid on—something that could not have surprised even one town resident and probably few students. "He could've overheard Aggie say she planned to put the leftover jam in her basket, but so could others."

"Maybe, which is why I'm not inclined to jump to any conclusions. I was only mentioning a top suspect." The benign observation was typical of Ev. "By the time the test results come in, Wade and I should be on our feet. Knowing the amount and type of poison in the jam will give us a better idea of the guilty party's intention."

"You mean whether or not the dose was meant to be fatal?" Aggie said.

Once again, Wade patted her arm. "I'd say it wasn't, mostly because Ev consumed a fair amount and, although he's been extremely ill, Doc told us right off that he thought we'd both pull through. The perpetrator probably wanted to cause misery, not commit murder."

Did the men know the physician had put their recovery chances at little better than fifty-fifty? Somehow, Doro doubted it. Silven had wanted to ease the men's minds instead of preparing them for the worst outcome, as he had with the women.

Aggie's expression softened. "I can see Parker doing that to me, but you and Ev are suffering instead."

"I'd rather be ailing than have you endure it," Wade assured her.

Aggie cast a glance at Ev. "I'm sorry you're ill instead of me."

One of his shoulders lifted a fraction before falling back onto the pillow. "I'd hate to have you suffer." His silver gaze moved to Doro. "Or you, and I'll bet you would've eaten some of the tainted jam, too, if Aggie had taken it home."

His obvious concern touched Doro, who decided not to argue over who had been targeted. Or why. She and Aggie could pursue various possibilities. "Probably, since we often have a snack of toast with jam together in the evening. But we wouldn't have eaten so much at once."

"Over time, you'd have gotten sick. Maybe not as dramatically as we did," Wade said in a rueful tone.

"That wouldn't have been fun, either," Aggie commented. "But you two have suffered terribly from what Doc and Magenta told us."

"Let's not discuss details," Ev said with a frown. "I'd rather forget everything that's happened since late yesterday. Doc says it's good that the poison has been purged, so to speak. Luckily, some of it is vague."

"I feel awful about you being struck so hard." As soon as the words were out, Doro hurried to amend the statement. "Both of you."

"We'll be fine." Wade made the additional assurance. "But we won't be able to pinpoint the poisoner soon."

Immediately, Doro's mind churned. But she made an agreeable remark. "No, you won't."

Ev's gaze narrowed on her. "You look a little too happy about that prospect."

"I'm not happy you're incapacitated," Doro shot back. Was he serious or suspicious? Neither prospect pleased her. She understood Ev and Wade were lawmen, so they had both experience and authority, which gave them top status to investigate. Ev was more prone to keep Doro out, but he had failed in two previous cases, and he'd admitted Doro was a skilled investigator. Because he looked grim, she tried for a light note. "You gave me a promotion from armchair detective to amateur sleuth last fall. Am I being demoted?"

A chuckle left Wade, and Aggie followed suit. After a moment, Ev shrugged. "No, but you need to be careful." His gaze went from Doro to her best friend. "Both of you."

Wade's amusement disappeared. "Absolutely."

The warnings indicated neither man doubted the two friends planned to dig into the case. Pretending otherwise would be futile and foolish, so Doro nodded. "We will."

Ev's gray gaze narrowed on her. "You promised to be cautious in December. Then, you ended up being held prisoner by the killer."

"That could've ended in tragedy," Wade said in a tone as rough with emotion as Ev's was.

The men's admonitions revealed genuine concern, but Doro resisted savoring it. Although the ordeal was hardly a fond memory, it had ended well. "We were fine, and you picked up the killer in short order."

"Pure luck on your part," Ev asserted. "I don't want you relying on good fortune again, especially not when the two of us can barely sit up, let alone rescue you ladies."

Doro bit her tongue to keep from saying the men had not saved them, since the friends had escaped their bindings and trapped the murderer themselves. All the lawmen had needed to do was make an arrest. "So, you don't want us to do anything?" She directed the query to Ev.

Once again, he schooled his expression. "What I want and what you'll do despite my advice aren't the same, and we all know it. We've already said the guilty party could strike again. With more than one suspect, it's hard to say when, where, or how."

Wade nodded. "The students, Lila Billings, and Betty Stanley. I hate to think either of the women would want to harm Aggie, but I can't dismiss the idea."

"Good," Doro added, before revealing Lila's snippy comments and reviewing Betty's complaints at the cakewalk. "Betty also got snotty with me because I sat in the section reserved for family at the bake-off. Plus, she looked plenty upset when she didn't even finish second."

"She can be a handful," Wade admitted. "Aggie, I'm sorry you got caught up in this. Whether Lila or Betty poisoned the jam, I know they've been ringleaders of gossip. You don't deserve that, and I should've confronted both of them about their spitefulness."

A soft smile lit Aggie's face. "You're a kind man, so I understand why challenging them would be hard for you."

"But I should have and, even if neither is guilty, I will talk to them," the constable insisted. "If either did it, I'll make sure they're charged. Even if someone only wanted to make you sick, it's a crime," Wade said. "At this point, we need more information and, as much as I hate to say it, you two will have to get it. But carefully. Very carefully."

Doro's spirits soared. "We'll be cautious."

"You know how to gather details without confronting people, and that's what you need to do now. Listen to conversation, but only ask questions of folks who might be witnesses, and then only ask those who won't blab about it. Definitely do not question any suspects." Despite his voice being weak, Ev got his points across.

Wade nodded. "That means no interrogating Lila, Betty, or your students."

"Of course, we won't," Aggie readily agreed.

Doro's concession came more slowly. "We won't."

"If you go to the potluck after church services this morning, you'll hear plenty, I'm sure," Wade said.

"What about the mayor? Did Doc talk to him?" Doro asked.

"He did, and Mayor Brinkley is satisfied that a deputy will drive through town every day," Wade replied. "The mayor won't say anything about the potential cause of our illness, although speculation has started, according to Mrs. Silven."

"The regular town operator doesn't work on Sunday, and her substitute is a prime gossip," Doro observed.

"She is," Wade agreed. "It's too late to stem the tide, but the mayor would like to keep folks from speculating on who might've poisoned the jam, and so would I."

"How?" Aggie asked.

Wade fixed his gaze on her. "We have rat poison in the pantry at the constable's station. We store sugar there, as well. The two substances have gotten confused in other places. Doc shared as much with us a while ago."

The observations had Doro turning to Wade. "You want to leave the impression that you or Ev might've mixed them up?"

"Let's just say, we could let the possibility of us making a mistake surface," Wade replied. "If it turns out to be something else, like mercury, we won't know until after the test. I'll mention the idea to Ma, who will surely share it with others."

Since Mrs. Lammers was a known, albeit harmless, gossip, Doro nodded. "All right, but will people believe either of you would make such an error?"

"No one is perfect," Ev put in, "and we're as apt to err as others. It's just a way to muddy the waters. We don't need the suspects to believe we're on to them."

Doro and Aggie had not mentioned the Fultons. Should Doro do so now? Would either man react in a way that telegraphed their feelings? Uncertainty plagued her, so she tried another tactic. "We haven't talked much about the two of you being the intended targets. You both dismissed the idea, but it is possible." As she watched for reactions, Doro saw the lawmen exchange troubled glances.

"Why would someone want us down and out?" Ev asked. "Like Wade said already, not much happens around here. Surely, you don't expect a bank robbery? Some small towns have been hit in other areas, but not nearby." A slight smile played across his lips, as if this was a ludicrous idea.

His suggestion was far afield from what she was considering, and it made an assumption she had not. During the silence that followed, Doro studied Ev and presented another idea. "Bank robbery isn't a likely motive, but Aggie wondered if some kid who got in trouble wanted to get even with Wade for disciplining him."

Wade's brow furrowed. "I can't think of any time that's happened."

"So, that's out," Ev said.

"What about others who might want to get even with one of you?" Doro asked.

"I can't think of anyone," Wade replied.

"Me, either," Ev put in. "There's been no trouble on campus, other than some hijinks that I needed to rein in. None of the students got upset."

"And no one in your past has a grudge?" Doro suggested. "Gangsters have gone after Prohibition agents in other places."

Ev's jaw tightened. "I'm no longer an agent."

"No, but you probably arrested people who hold a grudge," Doro suggested. "Or maybe you helped shut down their lucrative business."

"Plenty of coppers have done that," he pointed out. "Besides, how would a gangster know I love jam on shortbread? How would anyone know you'd make shortbread?"

"Good questions," Doro conceded. "However, *The Michaw Messenger* ran a front-page article this week about the cooking contests. It clearly stated that jam rolls were the bake sale entries, and it included information about contestants providing extra jam for judges."

"Few gangsters read the local paper," Ev said with a trace of asperity.

His statement did not dissuade Doro. The Fultons might not qualify as hardened criminals, but they might be in cahoots with some. Since she knew, from her earlier conversation with Aggie, that Ev must have contacted his old boss, Doro moved ahead. "There are other possibilities." The suggestion hung heavily in the shadowed room.

CHAPTER EIGHT

Several seconds of silence passed before Ev spoke again. "Are you planning to say what they are?"

Doro glanced from Ev to Wade and back. "Did you contact any other lawmen before this weekend? Someone who might've warned you to be on alert?" When Ev closed his eyes, she had her answer. Nevertheless, she pressed for confirmation. "You did."

Ev put the heel of one hand to his forehead. "You're too astute, and I can't match wits with you in my current state." His voice came out thin and thready.

Part of Doro felt bad about taking advantage of his weakened condition, while another part felt vindicated in her hypothesis. "What did your old boss say?" She felt sure Ev had called the Bureau again recently, but would he reveal the contents of the conversation?

After several moments, his gaze again met hers. Ev ran his fingers through his dark, disordered hair. "The Prohibition Bureau is still under-manned, and he doesn't have time or resources to send anyone out here on a possibility. Not that I figured he would, but I wanted to find out if he knew about current bootlegging activity in the vicinity. The two of us discussed it months ago, because of Mr. Parson's alleged involvement, and his wife possibly continuing on after his death with the help of the Fultons. Even though Mrs. Parson is long gone, the couple is still here, so I talked to my old boss again a week ago."

The statements did not surprise Doro because Ev was too keen a lawman not to have notified his old boss about rumrunners being based near Michaw. "What did you find out?"

A harsh breath left Ev. "The poisoning isn't apt to be related to bootlegging."

"But you contacted the Prohibition Bureau before yesterday," Doro pointed out. "And you'll probably call your former boss as soon as you can get to the telephone."

Ev's dark lashes fluttered shut. "You have me at a disadvantage."

Contrition assailed Doro. "I don't want to badger you." And she didn't. But she wanted more details.

When he looked at her, Ev put both hands up in a gesture of surrender. "If Wade and I weren't down, I wouldn't reveal anything, and what I say cannot leave this room."

"Of course not," Doro readily agreed.

"I won't repeat it, either," Aggie added.

"All right, but I'm only saying this because I'm afraid you'll dig yourselves into a dangerous hole, if I don't," Ev replied in a stoic tone. "It's certain Mr. Parson was involved in rumrunning. As far as anyone at the Bureau knows, he had an interest in a Toledo speakeasy and in a concern bringing booze down from Canada. As for moving the liquor through Michaw, there was absolutely no evidence of it happening in the past."

"What about his wife? Did she continue his business connections?" Doro asked.

Ev nodded. "It looks that way, but the Fultons did all the running to Toledo. Mostly, the man. Since the two of them came to Michaw with Veronica Parson after her marriage, they probably already had connections to bootlegging."

"Are they still involved?" Doro asked.

"My old boss isn't sure. No one has seen Fulton at hotspots in the city recently," Ev replied.

"They keep to themselves at their cottage outside town," Wade said. "Ev and I discussed it, and we have no reason to suspect them of making, storing, or transporting booze from there. Although, like the two of you, we considered the idea."

"You've completely rejected it?" Doro asked as she focused on Ev's face.

He put the heel of one hand to his forehead. "Not completely, but there's no solid evidence. Both Wade and I drive out there a couple times a week. They've seen us, so they know we're watching them."

"All the more reason for them to poison you," Doro said.

"We aren't aware of strangers coming out here," Ev replied, "and the Fultons are hauling stuff away, either."

"I see," Doro murmured. "Aggie and I can still gather evidence." When Ev opened his mouth, she hurriedly cut him off. "Not about the Fultons, but I'd like to ask Mrs. Jones and other committeewomen about who else was around the tent. She went back ahead of the rest of us, so she might've seen something. And a couple of other ladies left after we did."

"It's a small town, and people will find out you're asking questions," Ev pointed out, "and they'll be suspicious."

"True," Wade agreed, "but everyone in town and on campus knows about them investigating the murder in December, and most realize they're mystery lovers. Certainly, their students do. Doro worked with you on the October case, which is also well-known."

Ev's dark lashes fluttered shut. "All true. People, including the poisoner, have to know, which is troubling."

"That doesn't mean we shouldn't do some digging," Doro insisted. "In fact, it's all the more reason to investigate, since the guilty party may already be alerted. Whoever it is will find out Doc suspects poisoning, and that a test is taking place. No matter who's at fault, he or she needs to face justice. The sooner, the better. Besides, we'll tell you both everything we learn."

Wade nodded. "Few folks will think you're doing the official investigation. Doc can let it be known a deputy took a jam sample and allude to the county looking into matters." The constable turned to Aggie. "Be cautious about what you eat and drink and where you go, especially after dark."

Aggie squeezed his hand. "We will."

While silence fell over the room, Doro considered what they already knew. "Did Doc say anything about a local man who died of long-term poisoning some years back?"

"No, and I've never heard about it," Wade replied. "When did that happen?"

"Doc wasn't inclined to provide details, so I'm not sure if it happened here or when he was in medical school, but here, I believe," Doro hesitated briefly before posing a query. "Do you know the cause of Mr. Stanley's death?"

Wade's jaw dropped. "Surely, you're not suggesting he was poisoned."

Doro shrugged, although she felt far from dismissive about the idea. "Who knows? Doc was close-mouthed about that, too."

"That's his way. He doesn't gossip about patients, which I appreciate," Wade said. "So do most other folks."

"True." Doro grudgingly made the admission. At the same time, she resolved to find out about the unknown man. If he had died in Michaw, someone would remember. If not, it wouldn't matter to the case.

"Gossip can be ugly, so I understand Doc's resistance to furthering it," Aggie said. "I hope he's doing the same for me. I don't want people thinking I was negligent and got arsenic or some other toxin in my jam. You know how it is with tittle-tattle. Even though all evidence points to the poison being put in the jar after the contest, some people will say I made a mistake. They probably already are."

"But you and Doro have consumed jam from the same batch, haven't you?" Wade asked.

"We have," Aggie replied, "but folks talk, and I don't want to be labeled careless and unfit." Anxiety knitted her brow.

Her friend did not need to reveal unfit for what. The malicious newsmongers, as few as they were, used the word when they discussed Aggie not being prepared to be a good wife and mother. What they really meant was that, as a college professor, she was not a typical young woman and therefore, not a candidate to wed the town constable. Doro knew, as others did not, that Aggie was uncertain about wedding anyone, mostly because it would end her career. But she cared for Wade, and the feeling was obviously mutual. Once again, Doro wished women had the freedom to work after marriage and motherhood. Perhaps, someday, they would. "All of us know you don't deserve those labels."

"No, you sure don't," Wade said.

Doro slanted a glance at Ev. "What about you?"

"Of course, I don't believe Aggie is careless or unfit," he replied in a tone that clearly indicated she shouldn't have needed to ask.

"Then, you think it's important to catch the culprit," Doro continued.

A frown furrowed his forehead as his eyes closed. Several moments passed before he answered. "I can't argue with you, but don't try to capture anyone."

The wobble in his voice telegraphed his weakness, and contrition hit Doro hard. "I don't want to argue or wear you out, and we won't be physically confronting the culprit."

His dark lashes fluttered open. "I'm already worn to the bone, which is why I'm in no shape to object, and neither is Wade."

"Agreed," the other man said, his voice almost as faint as Ev's was. "You two girls are good detectives. Just be careful. Please."

"Very careful," Ev put in.

The additional warnings gave Doro pause. "The poisoner won't want to be exposed, but he or she isn't apt to harm either of us." Even as she spoke, Doro felt uncertainty rise within her. Did someone hate Aggie enough to want her dead? The idea was an anathema. And what about Ev? Although her idea of a gangster coming to Michaw to issue payback might be far-fetched, Doro could not vanquish it.

"I agree," Aggie agreed with a forced grin.

Wade attempted to smile along with her, but it did not quite reach his eyes. "We can't be sure the perpetrator didn't want to do more than cause illness. Most folks don't know what a lethal dose of arsenic is. Any exposure to mercury is a different story, but Doc thinks it's less likely to be the cause. Anyhow, word will spread that Ev and I are only sick. That will let the person know the dose wasn't fatal."

Aggie's good humor faded. "You've been very sick."

Wade nodded. "True, but what if the person meant for you to get a fatal dose?" His gaze was on Aggie. "He or she might try again and, with the two of us bedridden, up the ante. I don't think it's likely to happen, but it's a worry."

Fresh anxiety roiled inside Doro and, when she turned to her friend, she saw Aggie was as upset. "All the more reason for us to investigate. We don't want a potential killer on the loose."

Every trace of color ebbed from Aggie's face. "What's keeping this person from trying another method?"

Wade laid his free hand over both of hers. "I don't think that's likely. Poisoners generally don't want to use more obvious means. Don't you agree, Ev?"

"What Wade says is true," the security officer replied. "I only ran into one case of poisoning as a cop and none as an agent, but I heard of other incidents, although more people have gotten sick from bathtub booze than have been poisoned."

"Is liquor really made in bathtubs?" Aggie asked, a quizzical expression on her face.

"No," Ev replied with a rough chuckle. "It's called that because the bottles are tall. In most houses, the only faucet high enough to top off the concoction is in the tub."

"How fascinating," Doro said with genuine interest. "Making liquor at home seems risky, so I can understand why homemade brew can be dangerous."

"Very dangerous," Ev agreed. "As far as poisoners, most are women."

"That's true in books, too," Doro added. "I know those are fictional..."

"But they're based on facts," Ev said. "I'm not saying a man didn't do it. We want to stay open to all possibilities at this stage."

"I'm definitely open to looking more at Lila and Betty," Doro said.

"I agree," Ev replied, "but is there anyone else who has an axe to grind with you, Aggie? Another student? A colleague?"

"I try to get along with everyone," Aggie said.

"But even the nicest people have detractors, not that I'm saying you do," Doro said.

Ev focused on Doro. "Do you have someone in mind?"

Doro thought over various discussions on campus. "The female faculty meet every month. At a couple of meetings this year, the topic of women leaving to marry arose."

Ev shifted to sit more upright. "What was said?"

"Concern was expressed because two women left to wed in the past year. Both were replaced by men," Doro replied. "Some are afraid that'll be a trend, which could be bad for the women who remain."

Aggie stiffened. "I wasn't at the last two meetings. The topic was discussed last fall, but did it come up during both recent discussions?"

Doro nodded. "Gladys Hollingsworth is worried. She mentioned Trudy Carstairs not staying at another school because of male dominance. Trudy brushed it off and moved the conversation to another topic, but she looked upset."

"Trudy had to be in her thirties when she came to Michaw," Aggie observed. "Do you remember? She mentioned your dad supporting her tenure."

For a moment, Doro searched her mind. "I don't recall when she came here, but I remember her being the first woman to get tenure, which was a few years ago. I never thought about what she did before. It stands to reason she was at another college."

"I've only seen the two of them long enough to pass the time of day," Wade put in.

"I see them on campus," Ev said. "They're civil, but not overly friendly. Maybe they think the campus security officer is beneath their notice, since I didn't go to college."

His remark gave Doro pause, but she did not voice her thoughts to the men. Trudy and Gladys were academic snobs, so they might not like Aggie stepping out with Wade, who had only completed high school. Or entertaining thoughts of marriage. Trudy had not brought up the topic on Saturday morning, but she and Gladys were both distressed by young female faculty members leaving to become wives and mothers. But how distressed? Not that it had anything to do with the case. Neither professor had been at the baking contest, so they couldn't have slipped into the tent and tainted the jam.

Wade's voice broke into Doro's thoughts. "You're both sure the jam jar was sealed while in the Wheaton Hall kitchen?" he asked.

The question sent uneasiness and curiosity rattling around in Doro's mind. Could the jam have been tainted before, not after, the contest? Doc had brought the idea up, but he had not pursued it.

"Pretty certain," Aggie replied.

When Doro did not speak, Ev addressed her. "You look to be deep in thought. Isn't it possible Professor Carstairs, or Professor Hollingsworth, or some other resident opened the jar, tampered with the jam, and resealed it with paraffin?"

Because she was not sure how to answer, Doro posed a question of her own. "You know how canning is done?"

"Sure, my mother canned fruits and vegetables. She made jam and jelly, too," Ev replied.

Dismay blanketed Aggie's face. "There's been no paraffin left in the kitchen for months. Besides, I can't believe either Trudy or Gladys would taint my jam."

Doro's mind returned to a women's faculty gathering last summer before classes began. "Trudy was distraught at our meeting last August. A man had just been hired in Laura Downes' place. Remember?"

Recollection dawned in Aggie's hazel eyes. "I do."

"Distraught is a strong word," Ev observed.

"It described her reaction," Doro said. "Trudy supported Laura being hired, and she helped her along the way. She seemed to feel betrayed."

"She did," Aggie agreed. "Trudy expressed the hope that no other young women professors would make the same choice as Laura, although one already had."

"Laura was in the science department, so that hit Trudy and Gladys harder," Doro remarked.

"Has either Professor Carstairs or Professor Hollingsworth mentioned Aggie and me stepping out?" Wade asked in a troubled tone.

"Not to me," Doro said, "but she was dismissive about Aggie and me taking part in the May Days events. She thinks we should focus on our careers."

"I see," Wade said. "Has she talked to you?" he asked Aggie.

Aggie shifted restlessly in her chair. "Not exactly," she began. "Gladys hasn't said anything, and I see her almost daily. Trudy and I don't cross paths often, but the last couple of times, she referenced Laura leaving and how that affected other women on campus. She also brought up Wanda Placette, who left last spring."

The revelation surprised Doro. "You didn't tell me about Trudy saying all that."

"It didn't seem important, and it probably isn't," Aggie murmured.

Doro did not concur, but she could voice her concerns later. No need to upset Wade, who already looked anxious.

"Has this woman helped you, Aggie?" the constable asked.

Aggie licked her lips. "She supported me being hired, and she's been kind in advising me about getting tenure. Trudy wants women to have more opportunities."

"She's been helpful to me, too," Doro added. "And to other women on campus. It wasn't easy for her to get her degrees or earn tenure, but I don't know why she left another school."

"It sounds like she didn't want her friend to reveal details," Ev commented.

"No, she didn't," Doro agreed. "Trudy moved the conversation into lighter topics."

"But you'll find out why she left," Ev continued.

His certainty brought a smile to Doro's lips. "I won't ask her."

Relief scored Ev's face. "Good. Be especially careful with her. If this woman is the poisoner, she's closest to the two of you since you all live in Wheaton Hall."

Doro shook her head. "She moved out last summer, and she may not be involved at all."

Ev and Wade exchanged a long glance. After a moment, Ev spoke. "I thought all the unmarried women professors lived in Wheaton Hall."

"Trudy was able to buy a cottage in town," Doro replied. "Besides, living on campus isn't a requirement."

"I see," Ev replied. "Why was she in the kitchen early yesterday morning?"

"She was meeting Gladys," Aggie replied. "They sometimes have breakfast together on Saturday morning."

"Aren't the doors locked?" Wade asked.

"Yes, but Trudy kept her key," Aggie said. "No one had a problem with it, since she also eats with us on Friday evenings and occasionally, she stops by. Like yesterday morning."

Wade frowned. "Keep tabs on her, and don't eat anything that's been left in the shared kitchen for now. She may have nothing to do with it, but you never know who else could harbor a grudge."

"We've promised to be careful, and we will," Doro said.

"I don't think Trudy would poison anyone. She's encouraged all women professors to follow in her footsteps by not marrying, but that's understandable," Aggie said. "The college has a long-standing policy that bars married women from working there, which isn't un-usual. It's the same at most schools."

"Mrs. Jones thinks the college will change its hiring policy," Doro said. "Maybe as soon as this summer. Other schools have. Colorado College has allowed wives to teach for years, according to my dad. Michaw may not be quite as progressive, but it's made strong strides over the years."

"True," Wade murmured. "So, Professor Carstairs may have nothing to worry about."

Doro did not want to agree or disagree, but if Aggie married Wade, she would be both wife and mother. Few schools employed women who held both roles. "I'll talk to Mrs. Jones and see what she knows about Trudy's background. Maybe we can eliminate her."

"I hope so," Aggie said.

Since both Ev and Wade looked increasingly exhausted, Doro went on. "Doc doesn't want us to stay long, so we should wrap up. He gave us fifteen minutes, and we're over that now."

"Will you be back later?" Wade asked.

"We will if Doc allows it," Aggie assured him. "Your mother will stop, too. Right now, you both need rest."

"Yes, because I want to be back on my feet as soon as possible," Wade said. "The spring dance is Saturday night."

A wistful expression crossed Aggie's face. "I was looking forward to going with you."

"We'll get there," he promised.

Disbelief clouded Aggie's hazel eyes. "It's six days away. From what Doc and Mrs. Silven told us, you two will be lucky to be on your feet by then, let alone dancing the night away."

A snort left Wade. "Maybe I won't be able to dance every dance, but I'll be there. With you."

"If you're up to it," Aggie murmured.

"Both of us will be up and about before then," Ev said, although his ragged tone weakened his statement.

Doro got to her feet. "We should go, so we don't tire you two out."

"We aren't children," Ev muttered.

"No, you are sick adults, and we were warned not to let you overdo," Doro reminded him.

"Neither of us have done anything except talk," he replied. "That's hardly exertion."

His increasing pallor belied the assertion, but Doro did not contradict Ev. "All the same, Doc won't let us visit again if we overstay his limits."

As Aggie stood, she glanced from Ev to Wade. "Even talking can be tiring when you're ill." She patted Wade's hands before letting go of them. "Get some rest, and we'll stop again later or tomorrow."

"All right," the constable said. "If you get any good clues, we'd like to hear them right off."

"We can stop every day, while you're here," Doro offered. "But what about the office? If no deputy is coming, is it closed?" For the first time, she wondered about daily doings.

"With both Ev and I out of action, the county sheriff will respond to any major problems, which I doubt will happen," Wade replied. "Colleen can work her usual hours to answer the telephone. If something comes up at night, the operator knows to call the county. Doc saw to that for us."

Colleen O'Shea was the seventeen-year-old clerk who had worked for Wade since January. Formerly a housemaid, the girl was alone in the world. Since the constable's office had needed help, Wade had hired her—partially due to Doro's encouragement. What she lacked in office skills, Colleen made up for in determination. "She's doing all right?"

"She's agreeable, reliable, and eager to learn," Wade replied. "I trust her to watch the office, which says a lot."

"Good," Aggie replied. "All you need to do is relax and get better."

"That's my goal," Wade said. "I've got a date for Saturday night, and I don't want to miss it."

Color bloomed in Aggie's cheeks. "Only if you're well enough."

"We'll be fine by then," Ev agreed. As he struggled to sit up, sweat popped out across his forehead.

Without thinking, Doro put a hand on his shoulder. "Take it easy. There's no need to overexert yourself."

"No, there isn't," Aggie agreed, but she addressed Wade.

"Believe me, I couldn't overdo even if I tried. I feel weak as a newborn kitten," the constable mumbled.

When Ev made no comment, Doro stared straight at him. "What about you?"

A rueful smile touched his mouth. "Sitting up is a challenge. Trying to stand up might lead to me falling flat on my face. Does that answer your question?"

Sympathy filled Doro. "It does."

CHAPTER NINE

After leaving the Silven place on Sunday, Doro and Aggie headed toward town. "Do you really believe Trudy would put poison in my jam?" Aggie asked. "She's prickly at times, but to taint food...I can't imagine her going that far."

"I don't want to believe it, either, but Trudy was upset last summer when Laura left. Even worse than when Wanda did in May."

"She was, and so was Gladys." Aggie shoved her hands into her jacket pockets. "I wonder why Trudy didn't want Gladys saying why she left her last school. Male domination is everywhere."

Both young women chuckled before Doro responded. "I want to find out more about Trudy's other college. Maybe it'll shed light on her attitude. Not that I don't understand her being upset about Laura and Wanda leaving after she did so much for them."

"Trudy has bent over backwards to help every woman professor and many female students."

"Both Laura and Wanda were her students here," Doro said. "As we were."

"Which is part of why she supported all four of us," Aggie observed. "Your dad helped, too. Maybe not vocally like Trudy, but he stood with female students and staff in many ways. I knew that before you and I met."

The observations made Doro miss her father even more, but she had been fortunate to have such modern-thinking parents. "He's always thought women should have the same rights as men. Sometimes, his ideas put him at odds with colleagues. I'd like to know his perspective on Trudy. Writing would take too much time, and a telephone call is cumbersome and costly."

"Not to mention the weekend operator might share every word," Aggie put in.

A frustrated sigh left Doro. "True, but talking to Mrs. Jones might help."

"Agreed."

Doro glanced at her friend. "Being a professor is Trudy's entire life. According to my dad, Trudy fought hard to get more women hired, women who planned to devote themselves to careers, not marriage and family. That's a big reason she supported me."

"And me," Aggie said, "which is why I understand Trudy's concerns. If the college won't keep married women as professors, and more of us wed, her position might become tenuous."

"Mrs. Jones says President Adams is fighting to allow married ladies to continue working on campus. She feels confident about him succeeding," Doro said.

"We'll see," Aggie replied. "Should we go to the church now? The potluck will be well underway. We can use the excuse of you needing to get Tee out to leave early. Unless you want to walk her now."

"She hasn't been alone for long, so we can wait," Doro replied.

"All right." Aggie hesitated for a moment before continuing. "I'm not looking forward to folks staring at me. Few will speculate to my face about being careless and accidentally poisoning the jam, but some are undoubtedly whispering about it."

"Very few," Doro responded, not only to allay her friend's anxiety, but because the vast majority of townspeople were kind and tactful.

"I hope you're right."

"I'm sure I am. Most of the speculation will be about who the culprit is. Since both Lila and Betty have made their interest in Wade more than obvious, they should be scrutinized. And there's their open hostility toward you."

"Other than mingle and listen for gossip, what's the plan?" Aggie asked.

"Mrs. Lammers may have already spread the word that Ev and Wade possibly got rat poison into sugar at the office. I'm not sure how many people will believe the story, but it'll present another possibility."

"Which is Wade's intention, but we can't be sure arsenic was the toxin."

"No, but others won't realize that, so we'll stick to the story."

"How are you going to do interviews?"

"Not formally, since we promised to be cautious."

Aggie snorted with laughter. "When has that stopped you from snooping around?"

"I prefer to call it sleuthing." Doro failed to withhold a chuckle.

"Of course you do," her friend said, still chuckling.

"A few questions can lead to important details. So, can reviewing what we already know."

"Which we've done to some extent."

"We have, but later I'd like to talk about other female faculty members who may have been influenced by Trudy. Gladys comes to mind, but there may be others who interact with her often." A soft sigh escaped Doro. "Tomorrow, I'm scheduled for noon to closing, so my morning is free. With exams this week, people's schedules are different from usual, so we might run into some neighbors in Wheaton Hall."

"Mrs. Farmer will bring over breakfast every morning, so most of us will gather in the reception area. Gladys will be there, I'm sure. I don't have an exam tomorrow, but I'll need to be in my office at some point. I can linger at breakfast."

"Good. As for right now, just mingling and listening is about all we can do. I didn't take notes while we talked with Ev and Wade, and I won't during the potluck. I'll want to get everything we've learned down soon afterward, though."

"Wise idea. I think we'll recall everything of importance."

"I'm sure we will." Doro cleared her throat. "I was surprised when Ev admitted he'd contacted his old boss. He clearly didn't want to tell us, although Wade seemed readier to talk."

A chuckle emanated from Aggie. "Ev's more reserved and regimented than Wade, which probably comes from having been a city policeman and a federal agent."

"I suppose."

"But you'd like him to speak more openly with you," Aggie suggested.

Doro shrugged. "About this case." Chatting too much with the handsome security officer was not wise.

The community church, a small white frame building with a modest bell tower, sat amongst a woods on the northern edge of Michaw. As Doro and Aggie approached, they were greeted by Pastor Winters, a lean man of middling height and middle years. "Good afternoon, young ladies. I'm glad you could join us." His expression grew solemn. "Do you have news about our local lawmen? We said a prayer for them at services. I spoke briefly with Wade's mother, who told me the terrible news."

His wife, a petite brunette, joined them. "Of course, everyone wondered about Officer Mallow's collapse. Some feared another influenza outbreak, but Mrs. Lammers eased minds on that score." One hand flew to her mouth. "Poisoning is dreadful, too. I just meant it wouldn't spread through town like the flu did."

"That's definitely a cause for relief," Aggie said. "Ev and Wade are slightly better, but complete healing will take time. Probably a few days."

"As soon as Doc gives me the go-ahead, I'll visit with them," the minister said.

"I'm sure they'd appreciate that," Doro said.

Mrs. Winters glanced from Doro to Aggie and back. "Help yourselves to the food. As always, there's more than enough to go around."

"Thank you," Aggie replied. "We both planned to bring a dish, but Ev and Wade falling ill took precedence."

"It's probably just as well." As soon as the words were out, the woman clapped a hand over her mouth. "I'm sorry. It's only that..." Her voice trailed off.

Aggie, who had gone beet red, stood speechless. After several uncomfortable moments of silence, Doro stepped into the breach. "I hope a few malicious gossips aren't causing trouble, especially at a church potluck."

The minister's wife blushed as deeply as Aggie. "I've done my best to quell that sort of talk."

"Thank you," Aggie murmured.

Doro did not echo the gratitude because, although Mrs. Winters was kind, she was also quiet and circumspect. While she would not repeat gossip, she wasn't apt to confront it, despite her assertion.

Pastor Winters shifted from one foot to the other. "We need to mingle. Please let Ev and Wade know they're in our prayers." With that, he ushered his wife away.

"Let's get something to eat," Doro suggested. "Then, we'll find a place to sit and observe."

"All right."

The two friends crossed the side yard to where several long tables groaned with an array of dishes. "I know we promised to be careful, but everything looks delicious, and I'm starving," Aggie said.

"I doubt if anyone poisoned food for the potluck. All the same, I'm sticking with dishes I recognize. Mrs. Jones probably made the baked beans and brought ham. Mrs. Winters is famous for her cornbread, and Mrs. Willoughby always brings deviled eggs. Plus, I recognize their plates, so we're safe with those items."

"Good to know," Aggie replied before helping herself. After selecting some items, they headed to where others were eating.

Mrs. Jones was the first to greet them. "Girls, join us over here."

Because the older woman was sitting at a picnic table with two other committeewomen, both of whom were pleasant, Doro accepted the offer. "Thank you."

After Aggie chimed in with her agreement, the two friends sat down.

"Congratulations on your win yesterday," Polly Springs, a slender blonde in her late forties, said. "I didn't have time to speak with you after the awards ceremony. I was busy in the judging tent and then, I had to talk with the school music teacher about last evening's concert."

The observations provided an opening to inquire who else might have been near Aggie's jam jar. While her friend expressed her thanks, Doro formulated her next comment. When an opening came, she took it. "There was a sizeable crowd at the bandstand for the official ceremony, but some folks seemed to stay in the area around the tent," Doro remarked, "even though another event wasn't scheduled in the tent."

"The contestants who didn't win gathered their entries, at least what was left," Mrs. Springs replied, "and a handful of people wondered if samples of the entries were available to taste. A couple were students."

"Male students?" Doro asked.

A smile lit the lady's face. "Yes. They're the ones who are always hungry. The girls usually watch their diets. It was easier when I was young, because skirts were long and full. The straight lines and raised hems of today make it hard to hide extra pounds."

Doro did not comment, but Mrs. Springs had no additional weight to conceal.

"That's for sure," Aggie murmured.

"Dieting too much isn't healthy. I've heard flappers live on cigarettes and celery. At least, that's what my niece in Chicago says," Ella Marker, a plump widow nearing fifty, put in. "Styles come and go, but being well-nourished is always important, which is what I told the girl."

"Very true," Doro put in before the conversation got further off-course. "About the students. Did they take samples?"

"I said they shouldn't because I knew Aggie would be back for her jam jar," Mrs. Springs said.

"So, they took off," Aggie suggested.

Doro hoped the causal comment evoked an additional detail.

Mrs. Springs nodded. "They did. When I left a few minutes later, they were headed toward town with some other boys. So loud that I couldn't help but hear them even when they got a hundred yards away."

Doro could hardly wait to discuss this development with her friend, because it should move the boys off their suspect list. "They are boisterous," Doro agreed. "They didn't come back?"

"No, they disappeared," Mrs. Springs said before turning to Aggie. "We all know about Constable Lammers and Officer Mallow falling ill, but I've heard conflicting rumors. Not that I listen to gossip."

"You don't have to listen to hear it," Mrs. Marker added. "Only a few folks are blathering nonstop, but the ones behind me in church were chattering away. At least they stopped after the sermon started."

While the revelations were not surprising, they were bothersome. "Who was gossiping?" Doro asked.

"Lila Billings and her uncle were telling the folks in their pew that Aggie mixed up some ingredient with rat poison, which is ridiculous," Mrs. Marker replied. "I told the entire row as much when the service ended."

"Thank you," Aggie murmured, as she laid her fork aside and stared at her barely touched plate.

"Of course, it's absurd," Mrs. Jones agreed. "Wade's mother told me that rat poison is stored near the sugar at the constable's office. Each of our lawmen has a sweet tooth, so they put sugar in their coffee. They might've made the mistake themselves."

"I heard that, as well," Mrs. Springs confirmed.

"Rat poison is clearly labeled," Ella Marker said. "I can't believe either man would mistake a box of it for sugar."

The conversation indicated Wade's mother had carried the tale, as planned. While many folks would agree with Mrs. Marker, some would wonder, which had been the constable's intention. Doro was glad Wade wanted to protect her friend.

"Colleen, the new clerk, buys and stores some pantry supplies. Her reading isn't up to par," Mrs. Marker said in a calm, composed voice. "The girl might've made a mistake. I'll ask you all to keep the possibility to yourselves."

"It seems strange, but I won't argue over it. Colleen is a sweet girl, and she wouldn't mean to hurt anyone," Mrs. Springs put in. "Especially not Ev and Wade."

The women's revelations caught Doro off-guard, since Wade had not mentioned Colleen at all, and she felt sure his mother hadn't. "No, she wouldn't," Doro put in. "I agree about not repeating the story, since it may have no credence."

"You're right, Doro," Mrs. Marker said before gathering her plate, cutlery, and purse. "I'd like to get home and freshen up prior to the parade. It's a warm day."

"So, would I," Mrs. Springs added, as she also prepared to leave. "And I certainly won't carry tales about Colleen."

When the other two women were out of earshot, Mrs. Jones turned to Doro and Aggie. "Mrs. Lammers also told me that Wade wanted the story repeated, but no mention was made of Colleen."

"Wade wants to avoid speculation, so he and Ev concocted the story about improperly storing the rat poison near the sugar. The intention was to put blame on them, not Colleen," Doro said.

Aggie frowned. "Colleen's a hard worker and needs the job. I don't think the men figured she would be blamed. I didn't."

"People speculated about various possibilities as soon as Magenta passed on the news that it's not contagious," Mrs. Jones replied. She rubbed her forehead. "I agree about not wanting folks to panic about another influenza epidemic, but I'm not sure blaming arsenic from the constable's pantry will work. With luck, the tests will come back from the county in short order. Mrs. Lammers hoped so, as well."

"A deputy should've picked up the jam by now," Doro put in.

"His arrival may alert folks, too." Aggie pushed her plate away.

Mrs. Jones laid a reassuring hand on Aggie's arm. "Don't worry, my dear. The truth will come out. Ignoring gossips isn't easy, but it will pass. Both you and Colleen will be in the clear. I'm sure of that."

"If Mrs. Lammers and others are promoting the idea that the poison came from Wade's office, I find it even more suspicious that Lila and her uncle are spreading rumors about Aggie's jam. We know it was tainted, but who else, other than the poisoner, knows for sure?"

Aggie's eyes widened and hope flared in them. "That's a good point."

The older woman was less enthusiastic. "It's a valid thought, but anyone could use the fact that arsenic is the likely cause of the lawmen's illness and create doubt about the source. We've all heard of arsenic being confused with sugar or flour. And about it inadvertently getting mixed into those substances. Lila could simply use it to make you look bad, Aggie. After all, it's something she's tried for a while."

All optimism fled Aggie's gaze. "You're right."

"I still think it's a sign of possible guilt," Doro insisted.

"It well could be," Mrs. Jones agreed. "But I doubt if she's your only suspect. Not that I expect you to reveal every clue. Or any, for that matter. But you asked about the students and about Lila."

Doro released a long, low breath. "The boys interested us, but it sounds like they left before the poisoning could've occurred."

"It does," Aggie agreed, "and I'm glad. I hated to think any of my students, even ones like Parker and Harland, would do something so awful."

"We'll move them down the list, since it's not likely they went back," Doro said.

Mrs. Jones nodded. "But what about Betty? She's made no secret of her interest in Wade, and she was upset with the two of you manning the prize table at the cakewalk. Also, she stayed in the tent to gather her entry and supplies after most others went to the bandstand."

Because the older woman was the soul of discretion, Doro did not mind a short discussion of the case. "Aggie and I don't know her well, but she was in your knitting group during the Great War, wasn't she?"

"She was. Her husband was still living back then. He passed a few years ago, about the same time as Wade's wife. Mr. Stanley felt poorly for a while, but he kept active until he suddenly went downhill. On the other hand, Wade's wife was bedridden for nearly a year." The secretary took a drink of lemonade.

"Do you know what caused Mr. Stanley's death?" Doro asked. "I don't recall hearing details."

The secretary's forehead furrowed, as if she was deep in thought. "He died in the summertime, so you must've been in Colorado. You were in graduate school at the time, too."

"Then, I wasn't in Michaw long enough to find out," Doro said.

"I wasn't, either, since I spent the summer with your grandmother and went back to school when you did," Aggie added.

"There wasn't a lot of discussion about his death," Mrs. Jones said. "Doc Silven is close-mouthed about his patients, which is good. Of course, Betty was devastated, so no one asked her questions. All I recall is that Mr. Stanley didn't feel well over a period of weeks. He'd been going back-and-forth to his mother's house in Bowling Green because she was ill. At first, Betty figured he was worn out and, like many men, he refused to go to the doctor. When he was flat in bed, Betty called Doc. Unfortunately, it was too late."

"What about his mother?" Doro asked.

"She passed a month before he did. A bad heart, I believe," the secretary replied. "Margie Lammers died about that same time. It wasn't long after Mr. Stanley's death that Betty began taking meals to Wade's house."

"And Lila did the same," Aggie commented.

"She did," Mrs. Jones agreed. "Lila was sweet on him when they were in school."

"She hasn't made it a secret," Aggie murmured. "But we don't know if she went back to the tent."

Mrs. Jones drummed her fingers on the table. "Unfortunately, no committeewomen were there the entire time. A couple stayed after I left, so they might help with that. If I'd known you need information, I would've asked Polly and Ella how long they were there."

The names were a nice lead, so Doro thanked the secretary. "We'll ask them. Lila and her uncle left quickly, but that doesn't mean they didn't return."

"Lila can be snide, but to poison the jam. I don't know." Mrs. Jones looked and sounded anxious.

"In a way, I feel sorry for her," Aggie said. "I understand her liking Wade and not wanting to be alone."

Although not surprised by her friend's empathy, Doro pointed out an obvious fact. "She has her uncle, who is as prickly as she is."

"But he's up in years," Aggie replied. "He won't always be here, and she has no one else."

Doro shook her head. "You're so soft-hearted."

A slight smile played across Aggie's lips. "You usually are, too. But you're a loyal friend, who always comes to my defense."

"As a true friend should," Mrs. Jones said. "You're right about Doro being kind. She always has been, but she's always been staunchly loyal to friends and relatives, too."

The praise made warmth spread into Doro's cheeks. "Listening to people belittle others is disloyal and wrong. If I hear it, I have to speak up."

"And you do," Aggie said with a chuckle. "Which I appreciate because I'm not as outspoken as you are, although I try to be a faithful friend."

"You are," Doro hastened to assure her before again addressing Mrs. Jones. "At the last meeting of women faculty members, Gladys Hollingsworth mentioned Trudy Carstairs leaving her previous school due to some issue with the men there. Do you know what it is?"

The secretary rubbed her temple as if warding off a headache. "Professor Carstairs met with President Adams alone, but I couldn't help but hear her crying."

Surprise hit Doro. "It's hard to imagine Trudy breaking down."

"It certainly is," Aggie agreed.

A rueful smile touched Mrs. Jones' lips. "She wasn't so outspoken or opinionated when she arrived here." Several moments passed before the older woman continued. "The president confided a few details, mostly because he wanted to ensure Trudy felt welcome. I know neither of you will repeat them."

Aggie and Doro agreed they wouldn't with one caveat: Wade and Ev might need to know.

"Of course," Mrs. Jones said. "I'm not sure it has anything to do with the case, but Trudy was stepping out with another science professor at her previous college. He had tenure. According to her, the man offered assurances that the school would keep women who got married. With that pledge, she accepted his proposal."

Doro's amazement continued to mushroom. "She's never been married, has she?"

Mrs. Jones shook her head. "That's the sad part. Evidently, her sweetheart ran into criticism for supporting her tenure and for keeping married women as professors. Since he hoped to become the department chairman, he hastily ended their betrothal and, when her tenure came up, he didn't support her."

Aggie's hand flew to her mouth. "How mean."

"It is," Doro agreed, "and it explains, in part, why she's opposed to women professors marrying." Perhaps, Trudy saw her younger self in them. Perhaps, she feared they would be hurt like she had been.

"Or even courting," Aggie added.

Her friend's statement reverberated through Doro's mind. Clearly, courtship and marriage were sore points with Trudy. But who could blame her? "Thank you for telling us. We'll keep that in mind."

"As part of your investigation?" the secretary asked.

"Neither of us believes she poisoned Aggie's jam," Doro replied, although it would have been more accurate to say neither of them *wanted* to believe the science professor would do such a thing.

"We don't," Aggie added. "Trudy can be prickly, which can make it hard to be pleasant at all times."

Mrs. Jones nodded. "I understand what you mean."

Doro understood, too, but whether or not the information bore on the case remained to be seen.

After bidding goodbye to Mrs. Jones, the two friends mingled with others. For Doro, the next half-hour proved to be a test of her loyalty and restraint. When the young women crossed paths with many townsfolk, they engaged in casual conversation and fended off questions. Most people wondered how the lawmen fared, while a handful made snide remarks about Aggie's domestic skills, or the lack of them. Doro wanted to defend her friend by supplying their working theory, but she hesitated to open the door to more queries, so she bit her tongue. Once the case was solved, Aggie would be vindicated.

As they left the church grounds, Doro and Aggie crossed paths with Lila, who was toting a large picnic basket. "I'm surprised you two showed your faces. I suppose you're helping spread the lie that Wade inadvertently mixed rat poison into sugar. Anyone who knows him like I do would never believe that. But you have to take the focus off yourself and your lack of household skills. You ought to be ashamed of yourself." Lila stared daggers at Aggie as she spoke.

"You're the one who's acting shamefully," Doro shot back. "As usual, you're spreading nasty rumors that have no basis."

Red flamed in Lila's thin face. "It's certainly true that Wade would never make such a mistake, and I doubt if your security officer would, either."

Although what the spinster said was true, Doro did not comment. Nor did she point the finger at Colleen, although others were. Instead, she aimed for a general observation. "No one knows exactly what happened or how. Doc Silven thinks poison is the cause, but he can't be sure until the jam is tested. Until then, it's wise to avoid speculation."

"People will talk," Lila observed. "You won't be able to stop that." Then, she stomped off.

"Awful woman," Doro muttered. "She's a little too eager to pinpoint the problem as rat poison, which makes her more of a suspect in my mind."

"Maybe so," Aggie commented, "but she'll keep spreading rumors about me, rumors that could hurt Wade and his family. I don't like that. I don't like it at all."

Doro turned to face her friend. "I don't, either, which is all the more reason for us to do some digging. Let's head back to Wheaton Hall for a while. The parade doesn't begin for an hour, and I'd like to jot down notes for our next talk with Ev and Wade, and include what we heard here."

"Which isn't much."

"No, but every morsel is important, because we don't know what bit might bind other pieces of the puzzle together."

CHAPTER TEN

As they approached the main door of their residence, Doro and Aggie stopped. An envelope was stuck in the mail slot.

"That's odd," Doro said, as she pulled it out. "There's no postal delivery on Sunday."

"There isn't, and our mailman always pushes everything through the opening so it lands in the basket. Maybe it's something important."

Doro turned the envelope over. "Our names are on it, but there's no stamp, postmark, or even an address. Only our names."

"Very strange," Aggie murmured.

Doro broke the seal and pulled out the single page. As she skimmed through it, Doro gasped.

"What's wrong?" Aggie asked.

"Take a look." Doro handed the missive to her friend.

Aggie read the words out loud. *"Stop snooping or someone will be sorry."*

"It must be from the poisoner, who dropped it off since it didn't go through the regular mail."

"Anyone could do that," Aggie commented in a tremulous tone. "With it being typed, we don't have handwriting to compare."

"The writer was smart in that regard." Doro studied the note again. "The type isn't unusual, either, so it could've been written on a few typewriters on campus. Even the one in the library."

"The wording is disturbing," Aggie said. "We expected people to figure we're looking into the matter, but who will be sorry and why?"

The possibilities were ominous, and both young women knew it. "We're being careful. As for Ev and Wade, they should be safe at Doc's place."

"I agree."

When Aggie gave the missive back, Doro put it in the envelope and slipped it into her pocketbook. "It's most likely a hollow threat, but let's not tell Ev and Wade. Or anyone else."

Aggie nodded. "It'd only upset them, which they don't need. For now, it'll be our secret."

"It will," Doro agreed, but was it also a good clue? That remained to be seen.

Relief filled Doro when they settled in Aggie's apartment. Tee's joy at seeing them was unrestrained, which lifted Doro's spirits. With hot tea to sustain them, the pair took chairs on either side of the small fireplace in the parlor, while the little dog settled at Doro's feet.

"We learned a few things," Aggie observed, "and we did it cautiously."

"We did, and we haven't tipped our hand to any suspects. The less we discuss the matter, the better. Like Ev and Wade said, the guilty party knows both of us have an interest in mysteries, and we investigated a couple of murders."

"And a lost exam." Aggie's expression lightened.

Doro grinned in response. "We're a good team." A niggling finger of anxiety traced Doro's spine. How long would that continue? If Aggie and Wade wed, they would be a team. Not that Aggie would abandon her friend, but nothing would be the same. Some other emotion pricked at Doro. Jealousy? She hastily dismissed the thought. Just because Doro planned to be a career woman, she didn't expect Aggie to follow suit. Not when she and Wade were more than smitten.

Aggie's reply returned Doro to the present. "We are, and it seems like we'll be a two-woman team for a while." Her good humor dissipated. "Ev and Wade look terrible, but they've got ideas about the poisoning, which surprised me."

"Me, too," Doro agreed. "I thought they'd be sleeping most of the time. Or too sick to talk much."

"That was a relief."

"Because you like Wade."

Aggie took a sip of tea before sinking back in her chair. "Actually, I more than like him. I'm fond of him, and he feels the same way about me. I'm just not sure about moving from stepping out to courtship. I've told Wade about planning to get tenure."

"What did he say?"

"He thinks, like Mrs. Jones, the college will employ married women because times are changing. But Wade has three children. If we wed, I'd be their mother. They're wonderful, and we get along well, but the college keeping a wife and mother? I don't think so. That's why I haven't talked to you about it. You decided to never marry some time ago, because you want to be the head librarian. For a long while, I didn't think I would be a wife. Now, I'm not sure. I miss being part of a family. Spending time with Wade, his little ones, his mother, and the rest of them...well, I enjoy having close connections again." She drummed her fingers on the chair arms. "My ambivalence upset Trudy when we last discussed my tenure."

The wistful longing in her friend's voice wrung Doro's heart. With both parents gone and her brother living in France since the Great War, Aggie was without relations in the area. Although Doro's parents now lived thirteen-hundred miles away, she not only saw them every summer, her maternal grandmother lived in nearby Sylvania. She wasn't all alone, although she might be in the future. "I'll support whatever decision you make."

A smile wreathed Aggie's face. "I know you will. You're a dear friend. Like a sister, and I appreciate your family's kindnesses to me."

"My parents hope you'll visit sometime this summer. We might convince my grandmother to come out with you." For the past few years, Aggie had gone to Sylvania to stay with Grandmother Mc-Claren. The pair hit it off well, which eased Doro's mind while she was away.

"I enjoy my visits with your gramma. If she wants to go to Colorado, I'll travel with her," Aggie replied as she folded her hands in her lap. "She was upset when we told her about Ev and Wade getting sick. Now that we know the cause, we should call her again."

The friends had telephoned the older lady after getting home the previous night. Doro's grandmother had initially planned to attend Michaw's May Days Festival, but a cold had sidelined her. "Let's wait until we know more. At this point, she'll only worry, when she needs to rest."

"You're right." Aggie finished her tea before setting the cup and saucer aside.

Doro pulled out her notepad and pencil. "Let's review our discussion with Ev and Wade. They had some good points."

"They're lawmen," Aggie observed with a grin.

Which was both good and bad in Doro's mind. "Yep, they are. I want to get their ideas down and note where we have agreement. Let's start with their number one suspects, who was also Doc's first choice, but now, we believe Parker and Harland weren't involved."

"I'd take them off the list entirely. So will Ev and Wade when they know," Aggie said.

After putting pencil to paper, Doro nodded. "I'd rank Betty Stanley above Lila Billings until we know about Lila's whereabouts. Betty isn't as volatile, but she's sly. Her criticism of us working at the main table during the cakewalk is an example. She presented her accusations in a mild manner, like she didn't want any shadow over the event. Just over us."

"She probably wasn't the only one thinking we didn't belong there."

"Maybe not, but we certainly couldn't control who was on each number when I stopped the music, or which dessert a person would choose."

"True, but common sense doesn't always enter the picture when someone is jealous. I've heard Mrs. Stanley is critical of women going to college and on to a career. Not that we've been together in many social situations. Nor does she acknowledge me with more than a nod when we cross paths."

Doro nodded. "She's old-fashioned. According to her, well-bred ladies should prepare themselves to be wives and mothers."

"She'd be both if she married Wade, and it's easy to see why she'd set her cap for him." A rueful smile touched Aggie's mouth. "She has to admire his good looks, pleasant manner, and kind heart."

"And you're not biased," Doro observed with a wink.

One of Aggie's shoulders rose and fell. "Perhaps, a little."

Doro rolled her eyes and grinned. "Let's get back to the case. We can discuss all Wade's wonderful qualities after it's solved."

Color climbed into Aggie's cheeks, but she nodded. "Wade seemed open to the possibility of someone wanting to put him and Ev out of action."

"Ev was more reluctant to agree." Doro studied her notes.

"Because his old boss didn't believe there's a bootlegging connection around here," Aggie said, "and Ev would see signs, don't you think? Or have suspicions if locals are involved? Besides, rumrunning goes on all the time in many places. Unless some major shipment was coming through the area, why put the local lawmen out of commission?"

"What if a big shipment is coming?" Doro's mind whirled with possibilities. "Ev admitted the Prohibition Bureau is under-manned, so they won't send agents on a possibility. Most booze comes down from Canada through Detroit. Or across Lake Erie. Some moves through this area. At least it has in the past." She paused for a moment. "Since Ev dismissed the idea, I didn't pursue it. But the Fultons might be involved. Otherwise, why stay in the area? With no visible means of support, they could still be rumrunning."

After a few seconds, Aggie replied. "I thought you eliminated them after what Ev told us."

"I can't get them out of my mind, because we saw them leaving the tent."

"All right," Aggie reluctantly agreed. "I agree about putting the Fultons on the suspect list. What about your gangster seeking revenge on Ev idea? I have to agree with him about it being unlikely."

"Bootleggers have targeted federal agents."

"Yes, but to come here, poison my jam, and hope Ev ate it?"

"It sounds far-fetched," Doro admitted, "so I'll let it go." Even so, she couldn't get Ev being a potential target out of her head. Maybe not in this case. But was someone gunning for him out of revenge? That thought did not die.

"How do you plan to investigate the Fultons?"

"A fine question." Doro took another swallow of tea as she considered ideas. "If they were up and about, Ev and Wade would monitor their activities. Clearly, Ev wonders about them rumrunning or he wouldn't have called his boss."

"A valid assumption," Aggie agreed, "but neither of them would support us digging into the Fultons' comings and goings, especially with them living outside town. It's not like we can walk by their cottage without being noticed."

"And driving past wouldn't tell us much. Wade might've asked the county sheriff to keep tabs on the situation, as much as possible. But he's shorthanded, too." Frustration filled Doro. How would they check into the Fultons? Doro pressed the heel of one hand to her forehead. "We won't know until we learn more. One way to do that is to head over to the constable's office. Wade said Colleen is working every day until he's on his feet again, so she'll be there. She might've noted something of interest, and she knows the Fultons from working with them at the Parson home. We have a little time before the parade starts, so let's get going."

Aggie grinned. "Very astute reasoning."

"Thank you. We can take a few of my cookies along, so she has a treat, too. Being stuck at the station during the festival can't be fun for a young girl." Neither would being accused of mixing up arsenic and sugar.

After putting some cookies in a basket, the two friends walked back to town. Houses of various sizes and types lined the residential streets. Doro loved how people of great means and those of lesser wealth lived side-by-side. She also liked the variety of designs. For a fleeting moment, she thought about her childhood home. How she would enjoy residing in it again, but it was far too large for one person.

When they got to Main Street, Doro noted how quiet it was. In an hour, that would change because the parade, which started at the church and ended in front of the college, would draw a crowd. She and Aggie were a block from the constable's office when they bumped into Mrs. Marker again.

"Another good afternoon to you, girls." Her voice was as soft as her expression. "Are you going back to visit Ev and Wade?"

"Not until later," Doro replied. "Right now, we're stopping at Wade's office with some cookies for Colleen. While he's out, she's working every day."

Mrs. Marker nodded. "It's a fine idea. Michaw is a peaceful place, so it's unlikely anything will happen but having a plan is wise."

"Let's hope nothing else happens." Because she wanted to know if the woman might have seen others around the judging tent, Doro made a general observation before making a query. "Mrs. Springs stayed for a short time after the contest, but you did, too, right?"

The woman nodded. "Someone needed to be there while the losing contestants gathered their entries and such. The Fultons came in. They missed the contest and wondered who won." A smile lit the woman's face. "They were pleased for you, Aggie."

"How kind," Aggie said.

"Yes, it was." Doro wanted to know more, but how should she ask without being obvious? Mrs. Marker's next comments removed the need to come up with a benign question.

"I know the exact cause of the men's illness hasn't been pinpointed, but I feel uneasy because the table was unattended for a while. Both Polly and I had to leave for other duties. I saw no harm in going, but the jam jar was open." The older woman looked from Doro to Aggie. "What's bothering me is that a potential poisoner had plenty of time to tamper with it. That idea is circulating, but so are others."

For several moments, silence ensued. Finally, Doro spoke. "Ev and Wade will figure it out when they're well." But Mrs. Marker had hit on their working theory. If others were also discussing it, how could they find the guilty party?

"Yes, they will." Aggie made her statement in a noncommittal tone.

"I thought you should know the tent wasn't monitored for a time," Mrs. Marker said. "If it turns out someone poisoned the jam, I'll feel terrible."

Since she already seemed upset, Doro hurried to offer consolation. "Even if that's the case, and we don't know that it is, the blame would lay squarely on the poisoner's shoulders."

"It certainly would," Aggie added.

"Thank you." Dismay flashed over Mrs. Marker's face. "Betty Stanley was taking her time to gather her belongings. I thought nothing of it, since she wouldn't want to witness you being awarded the blue ribbon, Aggie. But now...well, I wonder."

"I doubt if she'd taint my jam, but I appreciate your concern." Aggie offered a smile to Mrs. Marker.

If Doro had not known better, she would have sworn her friend believed the assertion. Betty was a suspect, but what about Lila? "Was Betty the only other one in the tent? Other than the Fultons?"

"Those boys, but they took off quickly. No one else was around when I left," the matron replied.

"No one?" Doro wanted confirmation. If Lila had not returned, she couldn't be the culprit.

A puzzled expression covered Mrs. Marker's face. "No one that I saw." Mrs. Marker laid a hand on Aggie's forearm. "If our negligence contributed to your jam being poisoned, I heartily apologize."

Aggie patted the older woman's hand. "There's no need for an apology. Only the poisoner is to blame. No one else."

Mrs. Marker released her hold on Aggie and stepped back. She glanced from one young woman to the other. "If you're looking into the matter, and I'm guessing you are, please be careful. I don't want anyone else to be harmed."

Because the older woman's genuine worry touched Doro, she offered a smile. "Ev and Wade will be up and about in a couple of days. They'll look into the case then."

"Good," Mrs. Marker said. "I'm sure they'll solve it, with you two helping. Now, I'd best be on my way."

After they said their goodbyes, Aggie and Doro continued on. As they did, Aggie shot a glance at her friend. "You made it sound like Ev and Wade will be fine in a couple of days. Doc wasn't that optimistic."

Doro shoved her hands into her skirt pockets. "If I'd revealed that, she'd worry more about us investigating."

"Because she knows you," Aggie said a wry tone. "Everyone does."

"She does, but I don't want her fretting or others gossiping more than they are already."

"Or alerting the mayor, who might convince the county sheriff to put a deputy here full-time until Ev and Wade heal."

A harsh breath escaped Doro. "We don't need a deputy here. You and I are good at ferreting out facts, and we got details without even asking."

"About Lila not going back to the tent," Aggie suggested.

"Exactly," Doro replied.

"Now that we know there's speculation, how are we going to learn more?"

"By investigating, which we will do with all restraint."

"All restraint?" Aggie echoed with a smirk.

Doro grinned. "Perhaps not all, but certainly enough to avoid provoking the poisoner, whoever he or she may be." Even as she spoke, Doro wondered about her assertion. They had suspects—widely disparate ones whose motives were quite different. Getting down to one was key.

CHAPTER ELEVEN

When Doro and Aggie arrived at the constable's office, they found Mayor Ed Brinkley chatting with Colleen. The man, short and slight, turned toward them. "What brings you two here?"

The blunt question, posed without a greeting, momentarily held Doro silent. After a moment, she offered a bland response. "We brought some cookies for Colleen. Since she's working extra hours, she deserves a treat."

Aggie lifted the basket to support Doro's statement.

The young clerk smiled. "Thank you for thinking of me."

Brinkley's scowl put additional lines on his ruddy face. "While Constable Lammers and Officer Mallow are laid up, the county sheriff has jurisdiction."

His words rang like a warning, which was his typical style. Although Doro had known the mayor all of her life, she did not consider him a family friend. While he and her father had gotten along, the two men held radically different ideas about women's roles, which put Brinkley at odds with Doro, too. Since October, when she had solved a murder with Ev, the man had mentioned his objections to her being involved. Luckily, they seldom crossed paths as the mayor rarely set foot on campus, and he holed up in his office often. "So, we heard," she replied.

The mayor rocked back on his heels as he focused on Doro. "Who told you that?"

Because their visit with Ev and Wade wasn't a secret, Doro answered honestly. "We spoke with Constable Lammers and Officer Mallow today."

A harrumph left the mayor as he glanced at Aggie. "Doc Silven says arsenic was probably in the jam. He wouldn't pinpoint the source, but you're not an experienced cook, are you?" The question held a sharp edge.

Aggie's jaw dropped. "I've made blackberry jam many, many times," she said in a firm tone. "And the jam roll is a variation on an old family recipe, so I'm familiar with it, as well."

"I'm sure your mother supervised you as you were growing up. Nowadays, you must be busy with your job." The man put a slight negative note on his final word. "And your social schedule."

Scarlet surged into Aggie's freckled face. "I cook as often as I can, since it's an enjoyable pastime."

A slight smile played across Doro's lips. Her friend's response was perfect—not defensive or argumentative. "She does, and I benefit from it."

"Because you can't cook yourself." The mayor's derogatory tone left no doubt that he considered Doro to be an odd female. Not that he hadn't made that observation more than once in the past. Such small-mindedness was not worthy of a retort, so Doro asked a question herself. "How often will the county sheriff send a deputy out this way? Or will one be assigned to the office until Wade is back?" She knew the answers, but Doro wanted to hear them from Brinkley.

"He doesn't have enough men to put one here. Someone will drive through, when possible, and come, when necessary." The mayor looked at Doro like she was a fool to ask.

"Then, they won't investigate who tainted the jam?" Doro asked.

"No need. Ev and Wade can look into the issue when they're on their feet." The man glared at Doro before turning to Aggie. "You two better not be making a mountain out of a molehill. We all know Dorothea fancies herself as an armchair detective, and I suppose you feel the same way. Keep your noses out of the case. It's straightforward, and I don't want you creating crazy theories. Read your mysteries. Write them. Teach about them. But don't investigate this minor problem. It's likely to be a mistake, nothing more. I don't want townsfolk overwrought, especially with an election coming in the fall."

Not for the first time, Doro wished someone else would run for mayor, but Brinkley had not had an opponent for years. She bit back an objection. Contradicting the mayor would not help, but Ev and Wade being deathly ill was hardly a minor matter.

When none of the women spoke, he pulled out his pocket watch. "I have a meeting before the parade." Brinkley's gaze rested on Colleen, whose heart-shaped face was drawn with worry. "Someone will be along to lock up later. Don't leave before then."

"Yes, sir," the girl replied.

After nodding to Doro and Aggie, the man left without another word.

Doro scowled at his retreating figure while Aggie put the cookies on the counter. After a moment, Doro joined the other two women. "Awful man," she muttered. "If Ev and Wade weren't out of commission, he wouldn't be bullying us."

Aggie shifted from one foot to the other. "Wade mentioned the mayor criticizing him for letting you help Ev last fall."

Her friend had never revealed the information, which gave Doro pause. "Wade's mother was in the hospital, near death. He needed Ev to work the murder case."

"I know," her friend readily agreed.

"When did Wade say this to you?" Doro inquired.

Aggie's immediate response was to open the basket and take out the cookies.

"Aggie?" Her friend's hesitation bothered Doro.

After a moment, Aggie faced Doro. "When we began stepping out."

"In December?"

"Yes. He asked me not to say anything to you. Ev doesn't even know, and Wade would rather that continues," Aggie said.

Briefly, Doro considered the implications. "Does the mayor want to fire Ev?" While Ev Mallow's primary job was as Michaw College's campus security officer, he held special deputy constable status, which meant he could help Wade or act in Wade's absence. Being fired from that position would be embarrassing, and Ev didn't deserve that kind of treatment.

"According to Wade, that won't happen. The town councilmen all support Ev continuing as a deputy." Uneasiness clouded Aggie's gaze. "What worries me is Mayor Brinkley's warning to us. He's gotten pricklier over the past few years, and I don't want to cause trouble for Wade. If we dig around too much, his job might be in jeopardy. The mayor thinks women belong at home, as you well know, and he believes the husband should be in control."

A snort escaped Doro. "Such archaic ideas."

"I agree, but Wade needs this job. He could go back to working as a security guard on the railroad, but his children need him here, and he wants to be with them."

Aggie did not need to say she wanted him nearby, so Doro issued encouragement. "If the councilmen support Ev, they must back Wade. After all, he's been a respected member of the community for years. The Lammers family was in Michaw before the Brinkleys arrived, so I'd say his job is safe. The mayor isn't getting younger, so maybe someone will finally run against him. At nearly seventy, he ought to bow out."

"Maybe he will," Aggie suggested before addressing Colleen. "I suppose you've heard the gossip about me stepping out with Wade."

The suggestion emphasized Aggie's angst about the situation because mentioning such a personal matter was not at all like her friend. When Doro looked at Colleen, she noted the young woman's embarrassment. No wonder Aggie was uneasy. While only a few townsfolk engaged in malicious blather, almost everyone seemed to have heard it. The clerk's response confirmed that idea.

"It's spread through town, but it's not right to talk about you and the constable. What does it matter if he's older or if you're a modern woman? You're both nice, good folks." Colleen's voice rang with certainty.

"Thank you," Aggie murmured.

Colleen nodded. "And most people think it's fine that you two investigated the murder at Christmas. I always say how glad I am you did. I was real worried for a while."

The girl's comment provided an opening for Doro to ask about the Fultons. "You didn't work at your old job very long." Colleen's employment with Veronica Parson had lasted only a few months, but the girl had not been at fault. The December murder had changed her situation. Luckily, Wade had needed a clerk.

"Only a few months, and I was glad to leave," the girl confirmed. "I didn't know much about being a maid, but I tried to do my best. No one helped. They all found fault." Her frown turned to a smile. "I'm not no experienced clerk, neither, but Constable Lammers is patient and kind. He shows me what to do and how to do it. Officer Mallow is nice, too. Both of them is real encouraging." Her gaze filled with some emotion.

"I'm so glad. Not that I expected anything different from either of them," Aggie replied.

"They're both good men." Because she wanted a wider discussion, Doro made a suggestion. "Why don't we sit down and have cookies?"

"I made a pot of coffee when the mayor called to say he was stopping by," Colleen said, "but he didn't want any."

"That sounds good to me," Aggie replied.

After the three young women settled at the table near the back of the office, Doro let Aggie serve cookies and Colleen pour coffee before speaking again. "You mentioned being criticized when you were a maid. Was it only your employer, or did the housekeeper and handyman find fault, too?"

Colleen's pretty features became bleak. "They was as bad. Both of the Fultons told me to stay in my room at night and not be nosey." She took a bite of cookie. "That was after I went to the kitchen one evening for a snack. Got bawled out bad, so I didn't do it again."

Doro exchanged a passing glance with Aggie. "Were the Fultons up when you went downstairs for food?"

Colleen nodded. "He was just coming in. Before they seen me, I overheard her asking if he put the crate away like he was supposed to. He said he'd be a fool not to, but there was a couple of bottles for her and him." The clerk gripped her mug tighter.

Concern assailed Doro. "You know about bootlegging."

"Sure," Colleen replied. "I come here from Toledo. Lots of bootleggers and speakeasies in the city. I didn't know none myself, although a couple of neighbor boys run errands for one of the gangsters who owned a place down the street. My gram told me to stay away from them, so I did."

"Very wise," Aggie observed.

"It certainly was. Bootleggers can be violent, and they don't care who gets in their way." As she spoke, Doro mulled over Colleen's revelations. "Did you ever tell Ev or Wade about what you overheard or that you were told to stay in your room at night?"

"Officer Mallow asked about the Fultons, when I first took the clerk's job, so I told both of them what I heard." Colleen set her mug aside. "They said not to talk about it with no one else cuz there's been suspicions about Mrs. Parson's husband being involved in rumrunning, and her carrying on after he died. Since Officer Mallow was a Prohibition agent, he ought to know, although he didn't give nothing away. I said I wouldn't tell another soul, and I haven't until now. But you asked…" Her voice trailed off as a worried expression blanketed her face.

"Don't worry," Aggie assured her. "Doro and I won't say a word. Ev and Wade only wanted to keep nasty gossip from spreading, since the Fultons are still in the area."

"That's what they said, but neither of them seemed happy about them two staying," Colleen observed. "Constable Lammers drives out their way sometimes. Officer Mallow does, too."

"Did Mrs. Parson have liquor in the house?" Doro asked.

"Yep, but supposedly, it was from before Prohibition started." Colleen took a bite of cookie. "Would anyone keep it around for almost ten years? Besides, Mrs. Parson had a drink most every evening, and the Fultons had a couple or more sometimes. Doesn't seem like the booze would've lasted with three folks at it."

Doro shrugged. "It's not likely that liquor lasted for nearly ten years, if it was being consumed regularly." She glanced at Aggie. "Our suspicions are confirmed."

"They are," her friend agreed.

Colleen clasped her hands together as her glance darted from one friend to the other. "You figured they was all involved with bootlegging?"

Doro met the girl's gaze. "Folks wondered about Mr. Parson from years ago. Talk died down, but many suspected his wife of carrying on the trade, especially when Mr. Fulton took a lot of trips to Toledo." Veronica Parson was not missed, but Doro withheld the observation. They had enough to consider in the present. No point in getting bogged in past investigations when the current case offered a wide range of suspects and motives.

"I hardly ever see Mr. or Mrs. Fulton, and I'm glad. Whenever I do, they look at me funny. Sort of scares me." Colleen stared into her empty mug.

"How do you mean?" Doro asked.

The girl's gaze, clouded with worry, met Doro's. "Like they think I know more than I do, and I told Constable Lammers and Officer Mallow. They said not to fret."

With her pulse pounding in her ears, Doro struggled to maintain her composure. What if Colleen was right? If she was, the Fultons might have poisoned the jam with the confidence that Wade, who was expected to bid on Aggie's basket, would consume enough to get sick. And if Ev hadn't fallen ill, too? Would the pair have incapacitated him in some other manner? The possibility sent fresh alarm hurtling through Doro. How far would they have gone? *Quite far* was the answer that came to mind. Maybe Ev was lucky he was only sick.

"They aren't the friendliest people," Aggie observed, "so I wouldn't worry about them."

Colleen offered a slight smile. "That's what Constable Lammers told me."

"He wouldn't say it if he didn't believe it," Aggie assured her.

For the next few minutes, the young women conversed casually. "When will you close up?" Doro asked as she got to her feet.

"In a couple of hours," Colleen replied. "I'm mostly here in case someone needs help. I'll call the county and the mayor, if that happens."

"It's good of you to work extra time," Aggie said, as she joined Doro.

"I'm glad to have this job, and a nice place to live," Colleen replied. "Mrs. Lammers treats me like a daughter, and my room is lovely. I help with chores on my time off, so she don't charge me as much as her other boarders."

"Wonderful," Doro said, and Aggie echoed the sentiment.

After finishing their refreshments, the two friends bid farewell to the clerk and went outside. Doro turned to her friend. "Did Wade tell you about Colleen overhearing the Fultons and such?"

Aggie frowned. "He didn't." Annoyance crept into her tone.

"Both he and Ev seemed forthcoming earlier. Now, I realize they still withheld some key details." How many remained to be seen.

Aggie laid a hand on Doro's forearm. "Ev sees how intrepid you are, and he doesn't want you getting hurt. That's why he holds information back. Not because he doesn't trust or respect you. Because he clearly does."

Although the observation held validity, Doro felt a growing chasm between herself and Ev—one created by her unwillingness to step out with him. Since Christmas, the handsome security officer had kept her at arm's length, or even more distant. But wasn't that what she wanted?

"Doro?" Aggie's voice interrupted. "You look like you're miles away."

With effort, Doro pushed back personal considerations. Her conflicting emotions were unusual, and she didn't enjoy experiencing them. Doro preferred to feel calm and confident, like she typically did. Everett Mallow evoked new feelings. Shoving them down was her strategy, although that was not working well. Spending the summer in Colorado would surely help. "I was thinking about the Fultons." Not quite true. However, she should think about them. "They have motive, means, and opportunity. Considering Colleen's disclosures, I want to look more closely at them and their activities."

"You're not driving out to their house." Aggie's words were more question than statement.

Several seconds preceded Doro's answer. "The old Farmington place is about a quarter-mile away. It's closer to town, and there's a back way from the main road. Since it's abandoned, we could park there."

"Doro, we cannot stake out the Fultons' residence," Aggie insisted.

"Why not? It'd be perfectly safe," Doro replied. "And we won't stay all night. We'll go around dusk. I can leave my automobile in the Farmingtons' barn, so it won't be seen. And neither will we. If there's a shipment of booze coming through here soon, we could see some pre-planning activity. Other people or Mr. Fulton coming and going would be clues."

"And, if we witness any of that, what would we do?"

The demand went to the heart of the issue. "We'd have to tell Ev and Wade, or alert the county sheriff."

Aggie laid a hand on each hip, as she faced her friend. "Ev has called his old boss, who isn't sending anyone."

"They have trouble keeping up surveillance and raids in cities. They can't send agents into the countryside on a possibility." The policy was understandable, but what would Ev do when he was well? Most likely, he and Wade would investigate, because Doro could not shake the idea that both lawmen were as suspicious as she was. "Doc indicated Ev and Wade will be weak for a while, even after they're out of bed. If we look around the Fulton cottage, we can save them time and energy."

Her friend's gaze narrowed. "Is that your only reason?"

The query emphasized how well Aggie knew her, which made Doro grin. "I'm curious."

A chuckle left Aggie. "Of course, you are."

"You are, too, aren't you?"

"I am, but I'm also hesitant. Ev and Wade won't like it, and the mayor warned us not to dig around," Aggie replied. "I don't want to get into trouble or end up held captive in a cellar again."

Doro ignored the reference to their December detainment. "The mayor isn't a lawman. He's an old fuddy-duddy."

"I don't disagree, but as long as Ev and Wade are out of action, he can call the sheriff. Then, a lawman woud say to back off."

The anxiety roughening Aggie's voice and clouding her gaze reminded Doro of her friend's sensitive nature. While they were alike in most ways, Aggie was reticent, whereas Doro plunged ahead. The balance between their personalities proved useful at times. But not at the moment. "Even if he finds out, which he won't, Mayor Brinkley won't call the sheriff. He'll berate us and tell Wade."

"Who will be upset that we took such a risk," Aggie pointed out.

Frustration assailed Doro. "It's not risky, since we'll be cautious. Very cautious." When Aggie did not comment, Doro continued. "If you don't want to go along, that's fine."

Aggie pursed her lips. "I won't let you go by yourself."

"I'd be fine, but having company would be nice." And reassuring. Doro believed they weren't taking a major chance, but hovering around a vacant home while spying on another place gave her pause. Once Aggie nodded, Doro went on. "The parade will start soon. While we're watching, we may hear something useful. Let's keep our ears open."

"We're more apt to be asked questions," Aggie pointed out.

"We can find Mrs. Lammers and stand with her. She'll field any impertinent queries."

Aggie grinned. "I'm sure she will."

People had already assembled along the curbs as the two friends ambled along. They exchanged greetings with townsfolk but did not stop to chat. They had covered almost a block when Mrs. Lammers called out.

"Aggie and Doro," she said. "Join us over here."

The young women hurried to where Wade's mother and aunt were standing. Their vantage point would let them be among the first to see the parade coming. After an exchange of greetings, the two older women stood on either side of Aggie and Doro, so they were not exposed to passersby.

"I'm glad you made it," Wade's Aunt Nola said. "The children are disappointed by their father not being here, but they so wanted you to see them, Aggie."

"I wouldn't miss it," Aggie replied.

The first strains of music from the high school band, which was moving out of the church parking area to the north of uptown, sounded, and all conversation ended. For the next fifteen minutes, parade participants passed. Boy Scouts and Girl Scouts marched with their troops. Around Doro, applause surged when Wade's middle child, Adora, went by with her sister scouts. The girl beamed at her family. Her big brother, Alan, had already marched by, since he was in the band while her little brother, Davey, came along in a wagon filled with other children, all of whom tossed bouquets of flowers to the crowd.

"It's lucky, the town is filled with lilac bushes and forsythia," Mrs. Lammers observed.

"And that they're blooming now," her sister added. "I recall a few years when a chilly spring led to the children making paper flowers."

"I do, too," Doro put in. "That happened one time when I was in grade school."

"It's a lovely custom to toss bouquets to the crowd," Wade's mother remarked. "Although plenty of people receive May baskets, not all do. For them, this is a treat."

The comment had Doro glancing at Aggie, who had surely expected a basket from Wade, but her friend was smiling. "That's so nice."

"Miss Aggie, Miss Aggie." Davey's voice interrupted.

Doro turned to see him leaning over the edge of the wagon to extend a nosegay to her friend, who stepped forward to accept it. "Thank you, Davey."

The boy blushed but grinned before offering two more bouquets. "For Gramma and Aunt Nola."

After gathering all three bunches of flowers into her arms, Aggie rejoined the group. A brilliant smile lit her expression. She handed bouquets to Mrs. Lammers and her sister. "Davey is a thoughtful little boy."

"Wade was like that," his mother said with a pleased expression.

A twinge of something akin to envy pierced Doro's spirits, but she quickly dashed it. "Look. The dogs are coming along. I should've brought Tee." For several years, people had brought their pups—most sporting bandanas and a few with flowers tucked into their collars—to wrap the parade.

"She's still a puppy and excitable," Aggie observed. "You and Ev can put her in the parade next year."

Doro's discomfort escalated. By next year, Ev was apt to be courting someone else. Another twinge scraped Doro's heart. He might even be married by then. Would he and his wife want Tee? Most likely. A spouse would not like Ev sharing custody of the darling pup with another woman, and Doro couldn't spend as much time with the dog as Ev did. She'd have to do what was best for Tee.

"Doro, I suggested you and Ev put Tee in next year's parade."

Her friend's voice broke into Doro's reverie. "That's a good idea." But she still felt distracted.

Aggie gave her an odd look. "I'm sure Davey didn't mean to slight you."

Realizing her distraction was misunderstood, Doro hurried to correct the impression. "It's not that. I was thinking about Tee being in the parade next year." With Ev and his bride. She shook off the errant idea. "It looks like the end of the parade has passed, so I should get Tee out for another walk."

"I hope you two will join us for supper later," Mrs. Lammers said. "It won't be fancy, but it'll be fun for the children, who will chatter about the concert last evening and the parade today. Before then, I plan to see Wade again. I suppose you'll go back this evening, too." She looked from Doro to Aggie.

Before her friend could reply, Doro spoke. "Doc made it clear we shouldn't wear them out, and you want to see them." Mostly, Doro wanted to observe the Fultons, and she couldn't do that if she and Aggie went back to the Silven place.

"Doro is right," Aggie agreed. "You go today, and we'll stop tomorrow morning. Doro is going to work at noon, and I don't have any exams, so we'll have time."

"All right," the woman agreed. "But come for supper around six o'clock."

"Thank you," Aggie replied. "We'd love to."

After making their farewells, the two friends ambled down the street. When they were out of earshot of others, Doro glanced at Aggie. "We can ask a few subtle questions at supper tonight." Wade's mother had always been in on the town gossip, so she could have helpful information, especially since Mrs. Otten, the Frotis housekeeper, had stayed there for a few days before leaving town. The woman, who had been held captive by her employer's killer, along with Doro and Aggie, had spent time at the boardinghouse until her family came for her. She and Mrs. Lammers, long-acquainted, had enjoyed each other's company. Perhaps, that had led to sharing details. "I didn't want to spoil her enjoyment of the parade by bringing the idea up." Or have others overhear.

Aggie looked skeptical. "What if she later tells Wade we asked about bootlegging?"

For a long moment, Doro considered the possibility. "I doubt she will, since she'll want him to rest and recuperate."

After a few seconds, Aggie nodded. "That's reasonable, but how are you going to ask in front of the children?"

"We can go a little early and help in the kitchen. We can begin with our concerns and then, casually ask if Mrs. Otten is still in touch. That wouldn't reveal our suspicions."

"True," Aggie replied. "If they're corresponding, Mrs. Lammers will share any news. She loves to do that."

"She is a talker, which could be good in our situation," Doro agreed. As they made their way down the block, her mind filled with other ideas, while she and Aggie exchanged greetings with townsfolk and college people. None of them seemed like strong sources of information, so she focused on other matters. "Both the Frotis and Parson houses are still empty."

"I thought they'd be sold by now."

"I did, too, but who knows what's going on legally? As long as no one is in either of them, we could look around. The houses are secluded, with no other neighbors nearby, so we wouldn't be seen if we go after dark."

Aggie stopped and turned toward Doro. "You want to search those places tonight, too? Before or after we stake out the Fultons' house after supper at the Lammers boardinghouse? Honestly, Doro, we're armchair detectives, not policewomen."

"We're amateur sleuths," Doro corrected her friend.

Aggie rolled her eyes. "Ev told you that was a level up from armchair detective to please you, but I see no difference."

"There's an obvious difference. An armchair detective doesn't go out and investigate. He or she stays in a comfy place, reviewing clues. An amateur sleuth is on the move, pursuing justice."

"Is that what Ev said?"

Doro shook her head. "No, but I'm sure it's what he meant."

"Maybe. Maybe not. But if you follow those definitions a step farther, the detective isn't only comfy, she's safe. The same cannot be said for the sleuth, as we learned the hard way in December." Aggie shivered.

The words provoked images that made Doro quake, too. "We weren't searching for clues. We were trying to save Mrs. Otten, and we did."

"With a lot of luck, since we could've all been killed."

"But we weren't, and no one is around those houses now. I only want to see if there's any evidence pointing to ongoing bootlegging."

After falling into step next to Doro, Aggie continued. "Why would the Fultons go back to the Parson place? Even with no neighbors around, that seems risky."

"The houses are on the side of town nearest the Fultons' new home. They could store booze in the Parson's cellar. Maybe that's implausible, but couldn't we check?"

Aggie threw her hands in the air. "Let's go back to your apartment, so you can get Tee out before supper. We can decide about your idea afterward."

Doro and Aggie continued to Wheaton Hall. By the time they got to the edge of town and entered the campus, they passed only a handful of people. Since no one else engaged them in conversation, some of Doro's tension seeped away. It returned when they entered the women's faculty apartment building to find Trudy Carstairs descending the main stairway. She stopped on the bottom step, which put her above the two friends. How the woman loved to be in a superior position. Perhaps, considering her history, that made her feel better.

"Good afternoon, Trudy," Aggie murmured.

"Doro, Aggie." The science professor peered over her spectacles at each of them. "I suppose you've been frolicking about town."

"We went to the potluck and parade," Doro replied. "It's fun to take part."

A frown pulled down the corners of the older woman's mouth. "You're a local, so it's not surprising you enjoy small town entertainment." Trudy cast a look at Aggie. "Is Constable Lammers well enough to participate?"

The question held no note of concern, so why was Trudy asking? Doro listened with interest.

"I'm afraid not," Aggie replied. "He and Officer Mallow were still quite ill this morning. They won't get out of bed today."

Trudy's thin brows shot up. "You surely didn't visit them."

"Yes, we did," Doro said.

The older woman swiveled to focus on Aggie. "Is that wise? You've stepped out with the man, but to see him when he's not properly dressed. That indicates a depth of familiarity that may impede your pursuit of tenure."

"The door was open, and the Silvens were nearby. We did nothing out of order," Doro said.

"Since your father still has many friends here, you'll get tenure, unless you do something unpardonably foolish," Trudy said. "My concern is for Aggie. She needs to be cautious, or maybe she's set her cap for the constable."

"She hasn't set her cap for anyone," Doro replied, angry that Trudy would say such a thing.

"No, I haven't." Aggie enunciated each word. "And Doro is right. We did nothing unseemly."

Trudy's features softened, although her lips did not form a smile. "Of course not, but others may not see it that way." The science professor's tone became conciliatory. "After you won that contest, plenty of people—town and college—started chattering about you and the constable as a couple. Now, they're blathering about you possibly poisoning him, which won't help you win the man over."

"How did you learn all of that?" Doro asked.

Trudy blinked hastily. "Although I don't take part in little town doings, word reaches me. Especially when gossip is rampant. Gladys hears more than I do, since she still lives here. She shares the news." The woman focused on Aggie. "She mentioned two of your students being the guilty ones."

Doro did not comment on the boys. Instead, she wondered why Trudy was back. Was she visiting her friend again? For gossip? Or to cover her tracks? Had Gladys taken part in the poisoning? While not as outspoken as Trudy, the other professor held similar beliefs about women leaving to marry. "What brings you back to Wheaton Hall?"

Trudy virtually ignored Doro and, instead, continued to focus on Aggie. "When Gladys and I were in the kitchen a while ago, we saw some of your jam jars. You need to throw them out before someone else is harmed."

"There's nothing wrong with that jam," Aggie replied in a calm, composed tone. "All the jars are from the same batch, and many of us—Doro and I, most especially—have consumed it over the past few months."

Trudy's nostrils flared with a sharp intake of breath. "You indicated Constable Lammers and Officer Mallow are quite ill."

Doro nodded. "They are, but the cause is in question." That was not precisely true, but Trudy need not know.

"They don't have influenza or some other communicable disease, do they?" Trudy asked.

"As Doro said, Doc isn't sure what's wrong with them," Aggie replied, "but he doesn't believe it's the flu or anything contagious."

A skeptical expression tightened Trudy's features. "I see."

The urge to ask the science professor more pointed questions goaded Doro, but she resisted. Trudy would not reply honestly, and there were other ways to find out if the woman was the poisoner. "If you'll excuse us, I need to get Tee and walk her."

"She shouldn't be here on a permanent basis," the older professor said.

As her annoyance escalated, Doro fought to maintain control. Trudy often made mild comments with an edge. "She won't live here. She's only staying with me until Officer Mallow can go back to his apartment."

"I hope that won't be too long." Trudy descended the last steps and headed toward the kitchen.

"Let's go upstairs," Aggie suggested.

"Good idea." After taking Tee outside, Doro and the little dog went to Aggie's apartment. The two young women settled in the fireside chairs, while the pup stretched out on the floor.

"I want to jot down what we learned at the potluck and parade," Doro said as she once again extracted her pencil and paper.

"All right," Aggie murmured.

Doro studied her friend's face. "You don't sound enthusiastic. Are you tired or worried? Or both?"

With one hand, Aggie smoothed back her hair. "Both, and I'm upset about all the gossip. I know word spreads fast across campus and through town, but Trudy's comments put me on edge." A harsh breath left her. "It's not exactly what she said, but how she said it."

"I understand, and why was she visiting Gladys Hollingsworth again? Are they in cahoots?"

Aggie chewed on her lower lip. "Since they're both in the science department, Gladys probably feels beholden to Trudy, who assigns classes and committee assignments."

"The chairman should do that, but he's close to retirement," Doro said. "He lets Trudy run the department. She'd like to run other things, too."

A faint smile touched Aggie's lips. "You let her know Wade and I stepping out is none of her concern."

"It isn't, and it's none of her business if you court and marry."

Aggie's amusement fled. "We haven't discussed it much, but do you think I might harm women faculty members by seeing Wade?"

Although her friend had not mentioned courtship or marriage, Doro figured both were on her mind and responded accordingly.

"Not really. We're fairly confident that the college will employ married women soon."

Aggie gnawed on her lower lip. "But not mothers."

"Probably not yet, but you wouldn't be the only female professor to leave due to becoming a parent. Ellen Burns did a few years ago. That's how I got my job." Ellen had wed a widower with two children, so her position had been like Aggie's. Or what Aggie's situation might be soon.

"That's a good point. Not that Trudy will stop mentioning it. She's never blatantly critical, but she makes subtle remarks like today."

Doro considered the older woman's demeanor. "Her being in the kitchen before anyone else got there yesterday morning bothers me. She claimed to be meeting Gladys, but don't they usually eat upstairs?"

"If it's just the two of them, they do. But Trudy comes on Fridays for fried chicken. Maybe she hoped some was left, so she could take it home."

"I hadn't considered that. A few pieces were left." Mrs. Farmer, the cook at the girls' residence hall, sent over food three nights a week, and her fried chicken was a favorite among the faculty, including Doro. "That's possible, since it's first-come, first-served on leftovers."

"But that spoils your idea about her poisoning the jam," Aggie observed with a chuckle. "And don't say you weren't considering her as a top suspect, because it's written all over your face."

"You know me too well," Doro admitted in a rueful tone. "Although there are other, maybe better, suspects, I'm putting Trudy with several others at the top of the list. Ev and Wade mentioned Gladys donating a May basket. Ev opened the auditorium around eight o'clock, and the baskets sold out a half-hour later. I suppose Gladys could've hurried off, but I'd like to know more about when she left the auditorium."

"We can ask Ev if he knows. He left and came back, though, and Gladys wasn't there when we arrived."

"You're right, but Trudy goes on the list."

For several moments, Aggie sat in silent consideration. "At the top?"

"I think so. Trudy seems to have a motive," Doro pointed out. "She'd like you to give up on Wade. Or vice-versa. No matter which one of you got sick from the tainted jam, you'd look negligent in maybe confusing arsenic with sugar."

"You mean when I originally made it? Would it remain potent for months? I hadn't thought about it until right now."

"Me, either. We can ask Doc Silven. For now, Trudy is someone to consider because, as a science professor, she has more knowledge about poisons than most people. But it's not plausible that you got poison in it last fall. We've eaten plenty and stayed well." Doro scanned the other information. After petting Tee, who stirred before settling again, Doro continued. "We got some good tips in regard to the others, too."

"We learned about the extent of the gossip," Aggie put in. "I hope we find answers soon, so that will end."

"Which is why I didn't want to wait for Ev and Wade to feel better."

"A good point," Aggie admitted. "I hate being fodder for blather, and Wade would, too. Luckily, he doesn't know."

"Ev wouldn't like the chitter-chatter, either, but we should have a good handle on the guilty party by the time they find out what's being said." She paused briefly. "What did you think about Mrs. Marker's observations?"

"She mentioned a few people being in the tent after we all left. Most of them are solid suspects." Aggie scratched her head. "But how can we learn more without talking to them?"

"That's where it gets sticky," Doro replied.

"Maybe we should wait until after tomorrow to head out to the Fultons' cottage. We may learn enough to eliminate them. After all, we have plenty of other suspects."

For several moments, Doro considered the suggestion. "We have several," she admitted. "Trudy, Betty, and the Fultons remain. Lila, too, until we know for sure she didn't go back to the tent."

Hope leaped into Aggie's hazel eyes. "Then, you agree about waiting."

While she could not shake the idea that the Fultons were involved in bootlegging, Doro realized that did not mean they had tried to waylay the local lawmen with poison. "I do."

Relief slackened Aggie's features. "Good. Your theory about them is possible, of course, but I think the poisoning is more directed at me. The guilty party couldn't know for sure that Ev and Wade would consume a lot of jam, while we didn't, so using the jam to put them out of commission seems like a futile effort. Some other means would work better."

The observations were sensible. "I've already admitted I can let my imagination run away with me. Maybe I am in this case, but I still wonder about Mr. and Mrs. Fulton and rumrunning."

"I do, too. Even if they aren't involved in this case, the two of them could work with bootleggers."

Doro nodded. "And, as much as I'd like to see if they are, we need to focus on finding the poisoner."

"That's important, especially considering the note. The person may be watching us, so driving out to the country doesn't seem wise at this point."

After considering the missive again, Doro relented. "You're right. We could be followed, although I still believe the warning isn't serious."

"Maybe not, but I'd rather do what we promised Ev and Wade, and be cautious."

"We'll wait."

"Good." Aggie studied her wristwatch. "Right now, we should get ready to leave. If we go early, we can speak with Wade's mother in the kitchen. I'd like to know if she's heard more about how he and Ev are faring."

"So, would I," Doro added because, despite her interest in solving the case soon, Ev was never far from her thoughts.

CHAPTER TWELVE

Since Tee had been invited, she joined the two friends on their walk to the Lammers boardinghouse. When they arrived, young Davey, greeted them at the door.

"Hullo," he said before dropping to pet Tee. She danced around and around, while the little boy lavished attention on her.

"Tee is happy to see you," Doro said.

Davey glanced up, his dark eyes sparkling. "I'm happy to see her, too. It's neat how Tee's one ear is always up, and the other is down."

"I think so, too," Doro agreed.

A voice broke into the conversation. "Come in, come in," Mrs. Lammers said.

After she and Aggie stepped into the foyer, Doro unclipped Tee's leash. "You can play with her, Davey, if it's all right with your grandmother."

"Can I, Gran, can I?" Davey asked in a sing-song voice.

"Sure, but stay in the fenced area out back. We don't want to lose Tee," Mrs. Lammers replied.

"We'll stay in the yard," Davey assured her before turning to the puppy. "Come on, Tee." Then, the two were off.

"He'd like to have a dog," Mrs. Lammers told the young women, "but Wade's got his hands full with work and family. The children come here after school, so I suppose a dog could spend the day with me." Her gaze lingered on Aggie as she spoke.

"Kids love dogs and vice versa," Aggie said. "My brother and I adored both of ours."

"We always had a dog, too," Doro added. "I sure miss Baxter, but I'll see him this summer."

"I remember him," Mrs. Lammers commented. "Glad he's still well, and I hope your parents are, too."

"They are. The dry air in Colorado is good for my mother," Doro replied.

"They won't be coming back," the older woman observed.

Doro shook her head. "No. I'll keep going out there. I leave in less than two weeks."

Mrs. Lammers looked at Aggie. "But you plan to stay here, don't you?"

"Since Wheaton Hall closes for the summer, I'll be with Doro's grandmother in Sylvania again," Aggie responded.

"I know she enjoys having you, but you're always welcome here. My boarders leave when school is out, so it's quiet. Except for the children being with me during the day, and Colleen has her room, but she's a help, not a bother." Mrs. Lammers smiled. "I have a lovely, large suite facing the backyard, where you'd be comfortable."

"Thank you. I appreciate the offer." Aggie did not take it, though.

Since Doro knew her friend's feelings were conflicted in regard to marrying Wade, she turned the conversation in another direction. "We came early to help with dinner."

"How kind," the older woman exclaimed. "Come along. There's not much left to do, but I'd enjoy the conversation." The three women went to the back of the house and settled at the round table. "I'm always glad to have some female company. I love my boarders, but it's all boy talk at the table."

"I can imagine," Aggie observed with a smile. "Have you heard any more about Ev and Wade? Did you have time to visit?"

With one hand, Mrs. Lammers patted Aggie's arm. "Of course, you're fretting over Wade. I should've telephoned you as soon as I got back. They're able to keep broth and toast down, so that's a step forward."

Color crept into Aggie's cheeks as she darted a glance at Doro. "I still feel bad about it being my jam that made them both sick."

"Nonsense," the older woman said. "It isn't your fault someone poisoned it, and all three of us know that had to be what happened. What galls me is the possibility that someone coulda been killed."

The observation reignited Doro's fears. Had murder been the goal? She didn't think so, but it remained a possibility. "Ev and Wade will look into the case when they get on their feet. They'll need to investigate before making any arrests."

Mrs. Lammers turned to Doro. "You're not looking?"

Out of the corner of her eye, Doro saw Aggie bite back a grin. "We'll ask around to save Ev and Wade time."

The older woman's lips twitched. "Doro Banyon, I've known you since you were a babe in arms. You was always curious. Always loved mystery books, too. I remember when the two of you found the culprits who stole that exam." Her attention fixed on Aggie. "You coulda lost your scholarship and had to leave Michaw, since you was being blamed."

Aggie nodded. "I'm lucky Doro came along and convinced me to catch the guilty party."

"We're all lucky," Wade's mother assured her. "Especially my son."

After clearing her throat, Aggie addressed their hostess. "Wade is a good man."

"He is," the constable's mother agreed, "and you're a good woman. Not only that, you make a fine couple. I won't put no pressure on you and ask if I might have a new daughter-in-law, but I'd be proud and pleased, if that happens. I know about your career and all, so that's a lot to consider. Take your time and, if you decide your job comes first, I'd like for us to be friends."

Aggie blinked hastily, as if to hold back tears. "Thank you. I'd like that, too."

As Doro listened to the exchange, she felt a surge of bittersweet longing—for exactly what, she did not identify. Instead, she returned to the matters at hand. "You're right about my inquisitiveness, Mrs. Lammers. We wondered if you've heard any gossip from your boarders."

"A little. When we got back from the parade, several of the boys came into the kitchen for a snack. They all say a student wanted to get even with Aggie." A worried frown creased her forehead. "When I went to see Ev and Wade, I heard them talking as I approached the room. I wasn't eavesdropping, but I couldn't help but hear some of the conversation, and it bothered me."

"How so?" Aggie asked, concern roughening her voice.

Since Doro wondered the same thing, she listened carefully.

"They was talking about Lila and Betty," Mrs. Lammers replied. "Wade is sorry about being so nice to them."

Aggie offered a tentative smile. "Not wanting to wound people is a good quality."

The older woman nodded. "He's put some distance between himself and them, and he told Ev as much when I was there. Wade don't believe Betty was as likely to use poison as Lila," Mrs. Lammers replied. "That's all I heard because Magenta Silven came along and wondered if I was having trouble finding the room again. I had no business listening, so I went in. Not sure if the boys realized I heard anything, but I kept the conversation on how they was doing and off the poisoning."

"Very wise," Aggie murmured.

"Yes, it was," Doro agreed. "How do you feel? Do you believe Lila might be responsible?"

For a long moment, Mrs. Lammers studied her empty cup. Finally, she looked from Doro to Aggie. "I could see her doing it, especially with the support of her uncle. You both know how they tried to cheat during the baking contest a few years back."

The young women nodded. "They were at the contest as observers," Doro added.

"Mrs. Stanley was there, too, but she took part," Aggie said.

"I saw all of them." Mrs. Lammers paused a moment before going on. "But I left right off to see you get your ribbon."

"Thank you," Aggie replied.

"We're not sure about Lila and her uncle, since they weren't seen in the tent after the contest, but Betty Stanley was." Doro wanted to ask about Mrs. Otten and what she might know regarding the Fultons. But how to do it without increasing Mrs. Lammers' trepidation? The older woman didn't need additional worry, not when her son was ill and his three young children were already without a mother. Not when she had battled a heart attack last fall. Finally, Doro made a statement. "The Fultons stopped to find out who won, since they missed the bake-off."

A pause preceded Mrs. Lammers' response. "You know Mrs. Otten stayed here a few days before she moved to be with her brother."

Something between anticipation and apprehension knotted Doro's stomach. A glance at Aggie revealed her friend was riveted. While she had agreed to put the Fultons at the bottom of their suspect list, Doro was more than willing to move them back to the top. "Of course. You were kind to offer a room to her."

Mrs. Lammers bit her lower lip. "The poor woman was more than ready to leave the Frotis house, and get away from the Parson place, since it was next door. It's not a secret that townsfolk suspected Mr. Parson of bootlegging. Not actually doing it himself, but paying others to haul the booze and such."

"I remember hearing gossip going back to the start of Prohibition," Doro commented. "Mr. Parson went to Toledo often enough to give it credence."

"That's for sure," the older woman agreed, "and he started right after Ohio went dry in May 1919, well ahead of the Volstead Act going into effect."

The federal law had made the sale, distribution, and manufacture of alcohol illegal in all forty-eight states. It had also amped up illegal operations, which meant big money for those taking the risk of bootlegging. Mr. Parson seemed to be one of them. When Mrs. Lammers said no more, Doro asked a question. "Did Mrs. Otten see any odd goings on at the Parson house? Living next door, she might've had a chance to observe things."

After peeking into the oven, the older woman faced Doro. "She didn't want to make accusations, and I don't, neither. At the time, I mentioned some of her chatter to Wade, who told me not to worry since Mrs. Parson is good and gone."

"She most certainly is," Doro agreed, "but the Fultons aren't." The observation should elicit more information.

A smile creased Mrs. Lammers' plump face. "I knew you wouldn't miss that point."

"Doro doesn't miss much," Aggie said with a smile.

"Bootlegging is lucrative, and I doubt if the Fultons got rich working as a house couple, yet they have no jobs now," Doro pointed out.

"And they're renting a nice place." Mrs. Lammers sat down and clasped her hands on the table. "Ev and Wade must be monitoring them. Wade kept an eye out for rumrunning in the area as soon as he got hired as the constable. Nothing turned up, but most of the doings are in Toledo. At least, that's what he told me after Mrs. Otten stayed here. Maybe that was true then, or maybe he didn't want me to do no fretting. In any case, I can't shake the feeling something is going on now, and both local lawmen are out of commission."

The observation proved Mrs. Lammers was as suspicious as Doro and Aggie. The woman was sharp. Even so, Doro hesitated to state her own ideas. A quick sidelong glance at Aggie revealed she looked pensive. Would Aggie change her mind about snooping around the Fultons' cottage? Should they? Doro remained uncertain. "Most liquor comes across Lake Erie or down from Detroit to Toledo. At least, it did," Doro said. "Now, with the Fultons living outside town, I wonder if a load is coming through there."

"Maybe," Mrs. Lammers said. "Mrs. Otten was wary of the Fultons, and I am, too. Even though they helped you girls in December, it's odd they're staying on when they're city folks."

"It is," Doro agreed.

"You two have your hands full," the older woman observed.

When Aggie frowned, Doro sensed her friend's ambivalence and anxiety. To allay both, she said, "If we discover something important, we'll tell Ev and Wade. They can contact the sheriff and Ev's old boss in Toledo." As she spoke, Doro again wondered how much the two lawmen suspected and had already passed on. More than they had shared.

"Of course, we will," Aggie agreed. "But the poisoning and boot-legging may not be connected."

What her friend said was true, so Doro nodded. Wade's mother was also right: the two young women had much to unravel. When Davey and Tee entered through the back door, Doro wrapped up with a gentle comment. "Thank you for talking with us, but we should get supper on the table."

"We should," the older woman agreed before directing an order to Davey. "You clean up and let the others knows food will be ready in ten minutes."

"Yes, ma'am," he said before rushing out of the kitchen. Tee, her nose twitching, stayed behind.

As all three women rose from the table, Mrs. Lammers spoke again. "I've had misgivings for months. Wade listens but mostly pacifies me by saying Ev knows about bootlegging, so he'd contact the Prohibition agents in Toledo, if there was good reason. Maybe he already has. I doubt if Wade would admit that."

Since Wade clearly did not want to alarm his mother, Doro did not reveal Ev had been in touch with the Bureau, but to little avail. Instead, she also allayed the woman's worries. "Wade is right, so there's no reason to be concerned about the Fultons poisoning the jam."

Relief filled Mrs. Lammers' eyes. "I'm glad to hear you say that. Now, let's get supper on the table. A hoard of hungry boys will be down shortly."

After a hearty meal and casual conversation, Doro and Aggie left the Lammers boardinghouse and headed for Wheaton Hall. Tee again frolicked along ahead of them.

"Mrs. Lammers doesn't have as vivid an imagination as you, but she seems as suspicious of the Fultons," Aggie observed.

"Talking with Mrs. Otten influenced her, but I didn't realize how much."

"Neither did I," Aggie agreed. "Wade never mentioned his mother's doubts, but he's evidently been set on easing her mind and not alerting me."

Doro glanced at her friend. "Are you upset with him for not mentioning his mother's concerns?"

A shrug moved Aggie's shoulders. "I shouldn't be, although he might've brought it up when we all discussed the possibilities earlier today."

"It was this morning, wasn't it? Somehow, it seems much longer ago than that."

Laughter left Aggie. "I agree. It's been a long, long day." A soft sigh left her. "But I believe what I said back at my apartment. The poisoning may have nothing to do with rumrunning and the Fultons. Plenty of people were at the festival because it's a big event in town. I hope you haven't changed your mind about driving out to their cottage."

For several moments, Doro ambled along and let her mind roam over the potentialities. "You're right about waiting, because going there probably won't help us figure things out. Besides, we're both exhausted." She cast another sidelong look at her friend. "Do you have a gut feeling?"

Several seconds of silence ticked away before Aggie responded. "Right off, I felt like it was to get even with me. I leaned toward personal jealousy. I suppose I still am. Maybe it's because I'm overly sensitive, as you sometimes point out, but Lila and Mrs. Stanley have been my main detractors. Now, we have no reason to suspect Lila."

"Not when she left the tent before we did and didn't go back, as far as we can tell," Doro agreed. "As far as being sensitive, it isn't an undesirable trait unless you're wounded by gossip. I don't want you getting hurt."

"I know, and I take mean words too much to heart," Aggie admitted. "Plus, I can't shake my guilty feelings about poison in my jam. But I'm trying." Her last words held a light note.

"Good, because it's not your fault." Before Doro could say more, they rounded the corner and crossed paths with Lila Billings, who was leaving her home with a basket, which she gripped with both hands. "Good evening." Doro tried to sound pleasant, but she was not sure she succeeded.

"What are you two doing?" the spinster asked in a tone as sharp as her features. Lila focused on Aggie. "Shouldn't you be grading papers or doing some other schoolwork?" She made the word *schoolwork* sound nasty.

Aggie's chin lifted as she met the other woman's gaze. "It's Sunday."

While the statement did not answer the question, Doro was proud of her friend for not getting rattled. Too often, Aggie mumbled various excuses when confronted.

Lila blinked. "It is."

The answer indicated the other woman was caught off-guard, so Doro pressed the advantage. "What are you doing? Delivering a May basket?" Lila taking a gift to someone other than Wade seemed unlikely, but would she be so bold as to do that?

"That's none of your business," Lila snapped.

"And what we're doing is none of yours," Aggie replied.

A smile rose unbidden to Doro's lips. They might learn nothing from Lila, but Aggie was showing spunk. "We didn't see you after the baking contest. At least not until the potluck," Doro said.

"Unlike some, I made a hot meal to auction off. That took time. Not that the men in this town appreciate such effort," Lila replied. "I need to be on my way," the older woman said before pivoting on her heel and stalking off.

"Maybe I should've been less strident," Aggie said when Lila was out of earshot. "We might've gotten a little information from her."

"I doubt it. Besides, I'm proud of you for showing pluck."

Aggie chuckled. "Being best friends for a decade has finally rubbed off on me."

"I'm flattered," Doro said with an answering laugh before she became serious again. "I'd like to know what she's up to."

"Who knows?" Aggie said. "But her taking a fresh from-the-oven meal to the auction adds to no one seeing her back in the tent. As far as I'm concerned, Lila isn't a strong suspect."

Reluctantly, Doro nodded. "I'd like confirmation from someone else, but right now, I wonder where she's headed. She carried the basket like it was heavy."

"Observant, as always. But what does it mean? May baskets have flowers and sometimes candy, not that she'd take one to anyone other than Wade."

"Exactly."

Aggie's forehead furrowed. "What are you thinking?"

"Lila might take a food basket to Wade. Maybe a far-fetched idea." When Doro spoke it out loud, the possibility seemed silly. "Would Doc let her in?"

Aggie chewed on her lower lip. "Ev and Wade are better, but they weren't eating much. What would she take?"

"Who knows? Anything to curry favor with Wade, although he's more apt to be annoyed since he's been fending the woman off for years."

"His mother is right about him being too nice to Lila. If he'd been more abrupt years ago, she wouldn't still be bothering him."

"Have you told him that?"

Aggie shook her head. "No, but he is doing a better job at dismissing her now, so he wouldn't welcome a visit. Lila might not care, though."

"Probably not," Doro agreed. "Let's head toward the Silven place and see."

"Have you given up on snooping at the Frotis and Parson houses?"

Doro did not miss the optimistic note in her friend's voice. "After talking with Mrs. Lammers, yes. It sounds like any current rumrunning operation wouldn't come through town in the next couple of days. Maybe in the future." After sliding her arm through her friend's elbow, Doro gave Aggie a slight tug. "Come on."

A few minutes later, the pair was back on the street where the Silvens lived. "There she is," Doro said as she came to a stop. With one hand, she pointed toward Lila, who was mounting the porch steps. "Let's wait here." Doro gestured to a hedge. She breathed a sigh of relief when Tee occupied herself with sniffing.

Aggie nodded, and the two women stepped behind the bushes. "I can barely see over these."

"You're a little shorter than I am," Doro commented, "but the main thing is, we can't be seen easily."

After rising to her tiptoes, Aggie agreed. "True."

Doro kept her attention fixed on the Silvens' front door, which opened to reveal the doctor's wife. Too far away to see the expression on Magenta's face, Doro waited for some other sign of what Lila was saying. Several moments passed before Magenta stepped aside, and Lila entered the house. "I can't believe that woman got inside. Surely, she won't get to visit Ev and Wade."

"Mrs. Silven is gracious to everyone, so keeping anyone on the porch would be unlike her. Besides, we don't know what Lila told her. Maybe she mentioned feeling ill herself."

"I wouldn't put it past her, but how did she explain her basket?" Doro asked.

"Who knows?" Aggie asked before shifting from one foot to the other. "We can't hide behind these bushes for long. Someone will notice and wonder what we're doing."

Although the point was well taken, Doro was not ready to leave. "Let's wait a couple of minutes. Maybe Magenta will send Lila packing."

"We can hope. Neither Wade nor Ev needs to be bothered by too many visitors."

"Magenta knows that, and she knows Lila." Doro's statements proved prophetic because, less than two minutes later, Lila exited the Silven home. With the basket now swinging over one arm, she stomped off. "I'd like to know what Lila said. I don't think it'd look odd for us to stop back and ask how the men are. You're naturally concerned about Wade."

When Aggie faced Doro, she grinned. "Don't pretend you aren't worried about Ev."

While she couldn't deny the assertion, Doro shrugged. "Let's go."

A knock on the Silvens' door brought Magenta to answer in short order. "I didn't think you two would be back today." Her questioning glance went from Doro to Aggie to Tee. "I see you have an additional friend." With a smile, she bent to pet the puppy, who rolled over to show her belly. Magenta chuckled before giving it a quick rub.

"We're sorry to bother you, but we wondered how the men are doing," Doro said. "Aggie is especially concerned about Wade."

"As is Doro about Ev," her friend put in.

Magenta grinned as she stood and glanced from one young woman to the other. "Of course, you are. It's hard when our menfolk are hurt or ill."

Doro wanted to quell the idea that Ev would ever be *hers*, but ignoring the comment might be best. "We don't want to bother you, but Aggie is fretting."

A slight smile played across Magenta's lips. "They're both resting comfortably. Mrs. Lammers spent some time with them." Her good humor disappeared. "Lila Billings just brought custard, bread, chicken soup, and cookies. Constable Lammers and Officer Mallow aren't up to that much food, which I explained to her. But she insisted on leaving it."

"She didn't want to see them?" Doro asked.

"She did, but I put my foot down. She's not a relative or a friend, and my husband clarified visitors must be limited." Magenta sighed. "He's on house calls, but he'll check on the men when he's back. Of course, I peek in on them periodically."

"Thank you," Aggie murmured.

"Certainly," the older woman replied. "They're sleeping now, but I can call you first thing in the morning with an update. Or you're welcome to come back then."

"We know you're busy," Doro said. "We'll stop back tomorrow morning before work, if that's all right."

"Please do," Magenta agreed, "and I'll tell them you were here."

"Wonderful," Aggie replied.

Doro could not bring herself to chime in, so she merely nodded. On the way back to the main sidewalk, she remained silent. However, Aggie did not follow suit.

"Magenta seems to think you're sweet on Ev, and vice versa."

"You promoted that idea," Doro shot back, "and I have no idea

why, except you're starry-eyed over Wade. Just like he is over you."
Why she was so annoyed, Doro could not pinpoint. Or maybe she
preferred not to delve into her feelings, which often confounded her.
When would she go back to being her calm, composed self? Perhaps,
over the summer. She hoped so.

One of Aggie's shoulders lifted and fell. "We're fond of each other.
Quite fond. Maybe you and Ev aren't there yet, but—judging by how
you two acted at the town Christmas celebration—you could be soon.
If you allowed it."

The repeated reference to the kiss under the mistletoe stirred up
ambivalent emotions in Doro. She could not deny, at least to herself,
enjoying the embrace. "I hope we weren't seen by many people, but
you're the only one who's brought it up. From what Magenta just said,
she might've noticed. But she's not a gossip." Realizing she sounded
defensive, Doro stopped.

"I shouldn't tease you," her friend said. "I didn't see you two outside, although I noted you danced near the doors before disappearing.
Magenta might have, too."

Surprise rippled through Doro. "So, you don't know if we went
outside?" Or, more to the point, what they had done.

"I do, but only because Wade saw you two come back in. The next
day, he teased Ev, who got red in the face and stammered something
about you wanting to see the arbors with mistletoe, since that was one
of your decorating suggestions." Humor riddled Aggie's voice.

Heat scorched Doro's face. "That's not exactly right." Or was it?
Although she remembered the kiss well, Doro wasn't sure who suggested stepping outside. In her mind, it just happened without forethought.

"Ev was flustered, even after Wade said no one else seemed to notice."

The reassurance did little to ease Doro's mind. "When did Wade tell you?"

"Recently," Aggie replied. "He wondered why you and Ev aren't stepping out, so I explained about you wanting to keep working."

"Did he understand?" So many folks didn't. Would most people eventually accept married women pursuing careers? Doro wondered.

"He did, and we talked about what the college's current policy means for you and for me." Aggie's expression grew somber. "Time will tell, I suppose."

"Yes, I suppose it will." With determination, Doro vanquished all thought of courting and career. "We need to get some rest."

"Good idea," Aggie agreed before the pair, now quiet, returned to their apartments.

CHAPTER THIRTEEN

Although Doro slept better than she had the previous night, morning came far too soon. Even Tee, who was cuddled against her, seemed to agree because she burrowed under the pillow when Doro arose.

After getting ready for the day, Doro took the puppy out. Since the campus was stirring, she exchanged greetings with a handful of folks. Most smiled and greeted Tee with a pat on the head, but, as Doro and the dog passed College Hall, they encountered Trudy Carstairs, who offered a faint, fake smile.

"You're spending a lot of time with that dog. When will Officer Mallow take it back?" the other woman asked in a voice filled with contempt.

"As soon as he's well enough." Surely, the woman did not think Ev had recovered already.

Trudy pursed her thin lips. "A little arsenic shouldn't put a healthy, young person out of commission for long."

The comment put Doro on alert. "How do you know it was arsenic? And just a little? Not even Doc Silven is sure. He mentioned mercury as a possibility."

Color surged into the professor's angular face. "I've heard folks talking about it, and that's what they're saying, and it's far more likely than mercury."

"Why?"

Trudy cleared her throat. "If you had paid more attention in your science courses, you'd know."

Doro opened her mouth to say the town physician didn't know, so how would she? Then, she thought better of it. Instead, she repeated an observation. "It's not like you to accept and spread rumors."

A harrumph left Trudy. "You were raised around this campus, so you ought to realize a lot of information is first passed as gossip."

Since Doro could not deny that fact, she shrugged. "Maybe so, but I hope you won't repeat talk that may not be factual. Ev and Wade will investigate as soon as they can. Then, the truth will come out, and the guilty party will be held to account."

"Held to account? I'm surprised you want your friend's mistake to lead to culpability. Aggie would be wise to stop pursuing the constable and concentrate on her career."

The older professor's demeanor disturbed Doro. If she asked what the campus gossip mill was churning out, she would be as bad as those she had just criticized. If she didn't ask, she wouldn't find out much. In the end, Doro defended her friend. "Aggie didn't make a mistake. I'm sure of that."

"Even if you thought she had, you wouldn't admit it." Trudy switched her briefcase so that it was in front of her. "I need to get to my laboratory, but I suppose the two of you will snoop around most of the day. You care more about playing amateur sleuth than you do about being head librarian. That could come up when your tenure does."

The thinly veiled threat had Doro grinding her teeth to keep from snapping back at the woman, who turned on her heel and strode off. For several moments, Doro fought to regain her composure. When Tee whined, she bent to pet the dog's ears. "I know. I'm not sure what to think, but I need to talk with Mrs. Jones about her." Doro headed toward Wheaton Hall. The telephone was ringing as she entered, so Doro rushed to answer. Surprise and relief collided when Doc Silven's voice came across the line. After a brief conversation, she returned the earpiece to the cradle and addressed Tee. "Ev and Wade can leave Doc's place today." A sharp yip left the puppy, who seemed as happy as Doro.

When Doro went to her friend's apartment, Aggie was equally pleased to hear the good news. "Are they going to the Lammers' boardinghouse?"

"No, Doc doesn't think that'd be a restful place, and I agree. With students in and out and two of Wade's children needing to stay for a while, there's a lot of commotion. Mrs. Lammers and Mrs. Islington will look in on the men at Wade's house. Mostly, they need more rest, but they can be up and around a little. They both had toast and a little oatmeal this morning, and they're sitting in chairs. Big improvements." Doro was not sure if that was good or not. If they were a lot better, both would get involved in the case, and as lawmen, they had every right. "After lunch, Doc is going to drop them off on his way to make house calls. He'll check back later, but he wondered if you and I could stop this afternoon. Adora is staying with Mrs. Islington, but Mrs. Lammers has the boys and her boarders to take care of. She's dropping off bread and soup for Ev and Wade."

"You told him we'd go over, right?"

"Sure," Doro replied. "The library isn't open yet, but I'm going to ask Floyd if I can take off early and work on Saturday instead. You don't have an examination to give until tomorrow, right?"

"No, but I planned to be in my office for a couple of hours between ten o'clock and noon. We have to do a lot already."

"We sure do," Doro agreed. After a glance at her watch, she sighed. "I could smell the aroma of breakfast downstairs, so we better go before people start leaving. I'm hoping we get some additional details."

"I do, too."

When Tee yipped, Doro ruffled her floppy ears. "Sorry, sweetie. We can't take you down to breakfast, but I'll bring a treat, if I can."

Aggie chuckled. "She'll be spoiled by the time Ev gets her back."

"When he cooks eggs, he makes enough for Tee, and he shares his toast," Doro replied with a grin.

"Then, we must try to get both for her," Aggie said, her laughter increasing.

As the two friends descended the staircase, they heard a plethora of voices. "It sounds like we're among the last to get here."

The statement proved accurate, since the large dining room across the main hall from the reception area, was filled. A chorus of greetings rang out as Doro and Aggie entered.

"Help yourselves," Mrs. Farmer, who stood beside the massive buffet, said. "There's plenty."

"As always," Gladys Hollingsworth, a laden plate in hand, put in.

Since she wanted to talk with Gladys, Doro rushed to get food and hurried to grab the seat next to the other woman. The offerings from Mrs. Farmer were safe, and Doro was glad because hunger pangs gripped her. "I hope you aren't saving this chair for someone." Trudy was not present, but she could be coming.

A slight smile moved Gladys' full lips. "No, I'm not."

After seating herself, Doro aimed for a casual tone. "Trudy isn't coming."

"No, she's busy with end of the semester tasks. She performs most of the department chairman's duties," Gladys replied.

"I've heard that," Doro said. Out of the corner of her eye, she saw Aggie settle at the other end of the table, which was a sound strategy. With luck, they would double their cache of information. Since pelting Gladys with direct questions would be a foolish ploy, Doro tried for a casual note. "Trudy mentioned having a garden at her cottage. Is she growing flowers?"

"No, but there are forsythia bushes around the house." Gladys took a bite of eggs.

Asking outright when the woman had taken her May basket to the auditorium could trigger suspicion, so Doro was cautious. "I love forsythia. It looks pretty with other spring flowers."

"It does," Gladys agreed.

When the science professor did not continue, Doro focused on Trudy's garden. More information about when Gladys dropped off her basket, and how long she had stayed in the auditorium, would have to come from someone else. "Trudy sounded happy about having a garden."

"It's an advantage that we don't have here," Gladys said, "and it will be helpful for someone to grow plants we can use in our teaching."

"It would make botany more interesting. What kinds of plants is she growing?" Doc Silven had mentioned toxic plants, but he'd indicated getting them into jam would be challenging. Trudy, being a science professor, might have the knowledge to hide flora in food. If she did, Doro wanted to know the possibilities.

"Various types." Gladys stopped to study Doro.

"I see," Doro murmured, but she did not see much because the other woman was sharing little. After a big bite of eggs, Doro tried another foray. "Trudy has a lot of responsibilities. When I was a student, the chairman unlocked the supply cabinet before our laboratory sessions. I suppose she does it now."

Gladys did not stop buttering her toast, but she nodded. "She does, and she has to go back at the end of every laboratory class to ensure the room is locked again. Some instructors aren't responsible enough to do it themselves, and it wouldn't do to have dangerous chemicals stolen."

"Of course not," Doro said. "But that makes me wonder."

Gladys' beady black eyes narrowed on Doro. "About what?"

"Doc Silven thought Constable Lammers and Officer Mallow might've been exposed to mercury. Maybe a student took some from the lab closet," Doro said.

With a piece of toast halfway to her mouth, Gladys paused. "Unlikely, but mercury is in thermometers, so anyone could break one and get the substance out. They'd have to be cautious, though. Touching mercury is dangerous. Besides, it wouldn't dissolve into jam like powder would."

Since Trudy had said much the same thing, Doro made another suggestion. "Powder like arsenic."

"Yes. I thought arsenic was the cause. That's what I've heard," the older woman said as she went back to eating.

"Perhaps," Doro replied, not willing to give a lot away, either. "I don't recall it being used in science classes when I was a student."

Gladys sent Doro a look of disbelief. "It isn't, but it's available in many places, as I'm sure you know."

"True, which will make it difficult for the lawmen to find the culprit."

"You don't believe your friend made a mistake? I like Aggie, but she's not an experienced homemaker."

The assertion galled Doro, who fought back a harsh retort. "I'm sure she didn't make an error."

"Friendship can blind one to faults." With that, the woman shifted to talk with the person on her other side, leaving Doro to chat with two other Wheaton Hall residents, neither of whom had useful knowledge, only gossip. When Aggie rose thirty minutes later, Doro excused herself and met her friend in the main hall.

"Let's chat outside," Aggie said.

After they had walked twenty yards, Doro could no longer withhold her question. "Did you learn something?"

"Not a lot, but Trudy was upset when she first got here, just as Mrs. Jones said."

"Due to what happened at her old school?"

"Yep," Aggie replied. "She talked a lot about not trusting men, and how marriage is a trap for women."

"That meshes with what Mrs. Jones told us, but we can't discount Betty."

"No, we can't. I noticed you sat by Gladys. Was she any help?"

"Not really, although she said much the same as Trudy about mercury. She also said Trudy was busy with end-of-year work, which is why she didn't come to breakfast."

"She always has, even when she's busy."

Doro shrugged. "Maybe she didn't want to talk to me again. I couldn't get Gladys to admit she made a May basket, although we know she did. Finding out how long she was gone from Wheaton Hall on Saturday morning was impossible, because there was no opening. She said there's forsythia at Trudy's house." Doro summarized the rest of her conversation with Gladys and finished with a conclusion. "The other part that seems important is arsenic not being used in the labs. Trudy might've put the items in a department purchase order. If not, we can check with local merchants. Trudy rarely leaves town during the school year. Only in the summer and then, not for long. She had to get the items locally or place an order."

"If she's the culprit."

"She's slipped with some of her comments." Doro searched her mind for ideas on how to catch Trudy, if she was guilty. "She's not only focusing on you not having good domestic skills, she mentioned campus gossip about Parker and Harland. Maybe to keep attention off herself, especially after I called her on identifying the amount and type of poison."

A worried expression crossed Aggie's face. "You didn't say the boys are in the clear?"

Doro shook her head. "I didn't want to alert her. It's better if she thinks we have several other suspects."

"Good, because she might try to harm you, if she believes you're on to her."

"That's possible but not probable. Since she mentioned a little poison not having long-term effects, Trudy might've only wanted to cause trouble for you. Doing something to me is more apt to create a problem for her. A big one."

"In any case, we need to be extra vigilant. We've already decided not to eat anything stored in the kitchen downstairs," Aggie warned. "I'm going to dump my other jam jars, in case she tinkered with them."

"Let's keep them in your place. When the test comes back, Ev and Wade may want all of them tested."

"I hadn't considered that," Aggie murmured.

"You had the one in your basket, which indicated you were taking back. But she couldn't know for sure you wouldn't switch it out. Remember her advising you to dump all the jars?"

Aggie's face went pale, leaving her freckles standing out in stark contrast. "There are only four left. Let's get them now."

After putting the remaining jars in Aggie's apartment, the friends went to Mrs. Jones' office, only to find the woman had driven into Toledo to pick up items for the dance on Saturday night. As they stepped back into the main corridor, Aggie looked at her watch.

"I should go to my office for a couple of hours."

"And I want to report to the library early, so I can leave before three o'clock and get to Wade's house about the time he and Ev do."

"I'll come by shortly after two-thirty."

Doro rushed to get to work on time. Because her desk was piled high with paperwork, she sat down and sorted through it. Concentrating proved difficult, as her mind kept straying to the case.

Floyd Quartine agreed to Doro taking a few hours off, so, when Aggie came to the library at quarter before three, the two young women made their way to Wade's house. They barely got off campus when her friend addressed Doro. "You don't think it's inappropriate for us to be in the house with two unmarried men, do you?" The question was barely out, when she chuckled. "Of course, you don't."

"I'm not completely lost to propriety, you know," Doro said with a trace of asperity. "Wade's mother wants us to help, and Doc seemed all right with us checking on them. We won't stay long, if that eases your mind."

"I suppose it's fine," Aggie said.

"Before we get there, did you hear anything else worthwhile?" Doro asked.

"Not really. Just speculation."

"Since Mrs. Jones is working late, due to being away for a while, we can stop at her office later. I'd like to see the purchase orders from the science department. Doc mentioned plants being toxic, and Trudy's growing some for the botany classes. Maybe she made the leaves, or berries, or stems, or whatever into a paste or liquid. She is a science professor."

A chuckle emanated from Aggie. "It's clear you aren't. I'm not, either, but I feel pretty sure *whatever* isn't toxic."

Doro rolled her eyes. "You know what I mean."

"I know." Aggie's expression grew somber. "If Trudy ordered toxic plants, she might've been planning ahead, which is awful."

"Or she had them for classes and got the idea when she discovered you were in the baking contest. That seems more likely." Doro chewed on her lower lip. "Contestants were announced almost a month ago. If she ordered arsenic and paraffin about that time, we'd have some powerful evidence."

"We would, along with other bits and pieces," Aggie agreed.

Within a few minutes, the two friends were on the front porch of Wade's white frame two-story cottage. A knock at the door brought him within moments.

"Ma said you two would check on us," the constable said as he let them in. Stubble lined his face, but he was dressed in pants, a shirt, and shoes. "Come on. Ev and I are sitting in the parlor."

Ev heaved himself to his feet as soon as the women entered the room, but he wobbled enough that he braced one hand on the chair arm.

"Sit down," Doro said without forethought. "Both of you." Although dressed similarly to Wade, Ev looked worse. Not only did multiple days' growth of beard obscure his square jaw, his eyes remained heavily shadowed and red-rimmed. Why had Doc released this pair? Due to their insistence? Doro would not be surprised.

"Ma left some food for us, but she said you two would be over and heat it up," Wade said. "It's just soup and bread she made."

"I can do that," Aggie said. "Why don't you sit at the table while I fix a light meal?"

"Sounds fine," Wade agreed.

After Wade followed Aggie into his kitchen, Doro sat across from Ev, who finally collapsed into his chair. Anxiety constricted her insides as she studied his countenance. "Maybe you should've stayed at Doc's place another day or two." Or more.

His dark lashes fluttered down before opening again. Ev shook his head, as if trying to fend off fatigue or clear his mind. "If you'll give me a ride after supper, I'll be fine at my apartment."

The urge to chastise him for being foolish hit Doro hard, and she took a deep breath to rein it in. "I doubt if you can climb a flight of stairs when you can barely stand up." Getting to his garage attic apartment would be a sore trial.

Color seeped into his face as his gaze skittered to a point past her. "I can manage."

The protest came from bravado, not honesty, but Doro's intention was not to shame him. She wanted Ev hale and hardy as soon as possible. Seeing him laid low had evoked deep-seated anxiety and something more, something she did not stop to examine. "You don't need to manage on your own. Wade invited you to stay here, and Doc released you based on that."

Ev's head fell back against the chair, and his eyes again closed. Every line of his body radiated frustration and fatigue in equal measure. "We need to find out who tainted the jam. I don't like Aggie being under suspicion, and neither does Wade. Or Colleen being scrutinized."

His vexation, a palpable force, resonated inside Doro. "You'll be back to normal soon. If you follow Doc's orders. If not, you may prolong the problem. You don't want that."

He shook his head. "No, I don't. I hate being incapacitated."

Doro thought back to the previous October when Ev, still working his old job as a Prohibition agent, had been shot in the thigh. Despite the wound, he had insisted on investigating a campus murder, even though he had not officially started as the Michaw College security officer. "I know. You revealed that when you were limping around last fall instead of resting your leg."

His lips flattened. "The former president put pressure on me, and I wanted to get off to a good start here."

"You hadn't officially left the Prohibition Bureau," she pointed out.

"No, but it all turned out fine. We caught the killer, and I kept my new job."

"Two new jobs," she added.

One of his shoulders rose and fell. "Being a deputy constable doesn't add much work, and Wade needs help at times. Like now. Unfortunately, neither of us is able to do a lot, and it annoys me not to be out investigating."

Since his frustration was back full-force, Doro pointed out a fact. "Your ideas have helped us put the situation into perspective. That's really important."

For a long moment, he studied her face. "Wade believes the two of you aren't digging deeply into the case. He thinks you're just discussing ideas and doing a cursory investigation."

The statements hung heavily in the air between them for several seconds. His insights were not surprising, but they were alarming. Doro refused to reveal all her suspicions until Ev was stronger. Poisoning was serious. Although he was no longer at death's doorstep, he was far from well. "I suppose the two of you kept discussing the case when you should've been resting." The comment did not answer his implicit query, but she had no intention of doing that. Even the tiniest tidbit would evoke more questions.

A scowl formed on his handsome face. "Of course, we did. We're lawmen, and it's our responsibility to solve the crime. Something we haven't even started. Now that we're on our feet, we have to investigate."

She did not point out that he could barely stay on his feet. As Doro studied Ev, she searched her mind for something to say that would help. When he did not speak or move, Doro tried again. "It's a temporary situation. In a few more days, you'll be back to normal and on your own. For now, both you and Wade require rest and help. The two of you are no longer bed-ridden, but you're not ready to go out and investigate. That's why you need to stay here, not in your own place. How would you manage?" Doro hoped Ev would respond to the immediate issue of the two lawmen still being out of commission instead of prying into exactly what she and Aggie planned to do.

After a long moment, Ev met her gaze. Although exasperation still shone in his silver eyes, resignation joined it. "You're right. Doc lectured us about not doing too much, too soon." A rueful grin tugged at one corner of his mouth. "He doesn't want to see us back in his patient rooms because we didn't listen to him. His words."

Relief filled Doro, and she smiled in return. "I'm sure he doesn't. Neither do Aggie and I." She bit her lower lip. "It has to be hard for both of you to be laid low."

"It's tough. I've hardly done a thing for myself since the baking contest. I can't even shave." A harsh exhalation left him as Ev ran one hand over his stubbled jaw. "I'm afraid to look in a mirror."

Doro had to hold her tongue not to say he was still too attractive for her peace of mind. She and Ev were friends, good friends, but they would be nothing more. How could they when marrying would end her dreams of being head librarian? "Shaving isn't important. Regaining your health is. A few more days of rest won't make a big difference in pursuing justice, because it's unlikely the perpetrator will go after anyone else or try to commit murder."

His gaze narrowed on her. "What have you uncovered?"

While Doro inwardly chastised herself for the slip of the tongue, she weighed how to proceed. Luckily, Aggie's appearance offered a delay.

"Supper is ready, and we're going to eat in the kitchen," her friend said.

"Great." Doro jumped to her feet and headed to the other room because she wanted to avoid more queries from Ev. Not that he wouldn't pose them at the table, but she needed time—and Aggie's support—to consider her responses.

Wade, already seated, gestured to the chair next to him. "Sit down, Ev."

After waiting for Doro to take a chair, Ev did, too.

"Your mother said Doc Silven advised bland foods for a while longer," Aggie, an expression of concern on her face, observed.

A smile tugged at one corner of Wade's ample mouth as he stood and held a chair for Aggie. "Truth be told, I couldn't face anything too heavy or spicy yet."

Doro could not help noticing Ev failed to admit such weakness, which was typical. Once again, she was reminded of how solitary his life was. What if he had succumbed to the arsenic? Would she have been the one to contact his sister? A shiver rippled through her at the idea.

"Doro, are you cold?" Aggie asked.

Immediately, Doro strove for a casual expression. "Not really, but a hot meal will taste good."

"It sure will. Chicken noodle soup is heartier than bowls of broth and cups of tea," Wade said as he smiled at Aggie, who placed a bowl in front of him.

"Start with that," she said with a smile. "If you're still hungry, there's plenty more."

After a quick nod, Wade picked up his spoon. Meanwhile, Ev reached for the plate of bread, which Aggie had sliced. She hesitated for a heartbeat before passing it to him. Doro noted her friend hung on to one end of the plate. "Just take however many pieces you want," Aggie suggested with a benign smile.

Relief filled Doro, who feared Ev remained too weak to hold the platter.

"Thanks," Ev said before taking one slice.

Doro followed suit, and Aggie served herself. Once they all had food, the group ate. Within moments, Doro felt some of the tension seep away. Perhaps, they could bypass a further discussion of the case until another day.

All too soon, Wade laid his spoon aside. "It's a wonderful meal, but my appetite isn't as good as I thought." He glanced at Aggie. "You knew I couldn't eat much."

One of her shoulders lifted and fell. "Doc warned about the two of you needing to build up slowly to a regular diet and normal portions."

Although Ev had not consumed as much as Wade, he also laid his utensils down. "I hate to admit he's right."

For a moment, Doro studied his expression. "So, you'll stay here for a few days and take it easy, like Doc ordered." She put a slight emphasis on the last word.

"Both of you," Aggie added, her attention on Wade.

The constable grinned. "Yep. Doc and Mrs. Silven took great care of us, but I don't want to go back anytime soon."

"Or ever," Ev muttered. After a moment, he glanced around the table. "He didn't say we couldn't discuss the case more. I don't have to remind you about Wade and me being lawmen." But he was reminding them. All four of them, and most especially Doro, since his attention riveted on her.

When a potent silence filled the room, Doro glanced at Aggie, who looked as guilty as she felt. They had extended their investigation beyond the parameters set by the men, but they had not gone too far afield. At least not in her opinion.

"We can't chase down leads or suspects," Wade said in a benign tone. "We just want to know what you two know. Maybe a discussion among the four of us will move the investigation forward."

Again, a period of quiet ensued before Aggie, concern shadowing her face, focused on Wade. "We told you about the various suspects. Since we last spoke, we got additional information." After sharing the news about Parker and Harland leaving the tent well before the jam might have been poisoned, she said, "That clears them."

"It does," Wade agreed. "Any other progress?"

Doro took up the response by reporting on Lila before making a final observation. "The timeframe is too narrow for her to get back to the tent and taint the jam before people started returning from the park. In addition, she took a hot meal for the auction, which meant she had to be home cooking for a time."

Ev focused on Doro. "Let's get corroboration, but Miss Billings is way down my list now. That means we've got Betty Stanley and Professor Carstairs."

"And you're sure the Fultons should be off the list, too?" Doro asked.

Wariness put gray clouds in Ev's eyes. "Why is this coming up again? Have you been asking about them? Or talking to them?"

"No," Doro replied.

His gaze narrowed. "Why do I not believe you?"

The skepticism annoyed Doro, who laid down her fork. "We didn't go around inquiring about the Fultons, and we definitely didn't confront them. Why is that so hard to believe?"

A snort of laughter escaped Ev. "Because I've gotten to know you over the past eight months, and you love to pursue your hunches."

"You can't deny that," Wade added with a chuckle.

"No, you can't," Aggie said."

A look of triumph crossed Ev's face. "See. We all agree you're inquisitive, sometimes too much for your own good."

Doro shot her friend a quelling glare. "I didn't ask until someone shared information with us," she said in a stiff, stilted tone.

"That's true," Aggie agreed.

"Who told you about them, and what was said?" Ev asked.

After glancing at Aggie, who gave a slight nod, Doro responded. "Wade's mother mentioned having concerns."

Wade sat up straighter. "What did she say?"

Aggie shifted to face him. "That she'd told you about Mrs. Otten's worries concerning the Fultons, but you said to forget about them."

Silence echoed in the room. Doro looked from Wade to Ev. "Neither of you has anything to say about that? I assume you discussed what Mrs. Lammers and Mrs. Otten talked about." The men failed to meet her gaze.

"The four of us discussed them as possible poisoners," Aggie said. "You two let Doro and me believe there wasn't sound evidence of their involvement in rumrunning."

Wade slumped back in his chair. "Gossip about the Fultons died down over the past few months, and I wanted to keep it that way."

"Your mother and Mrs. Otten talked at Christmastime," Aggie pointed out. "You must've been told soon after."

The constable ran one hand over his face. "I was."

When Wade did not continue, Ev jumped in. "When he told me, I said we should keep it to ourselves. And I didn't say there was no evidence at all."

Doro ignored his last comment and focused on the first. "Because you didn't want me finding out."

Ev picked up his spoon but didn't continue eating. "You're an intelligent person, so you know bootleggers can be dangerous."

"I do," Doro agreed, "so I wouldn't take chances."

A look of incredulity shadowed Ev's features. "You wouldn't have poked around to learn more about the Fultons?"

"I would've observed but not inquired," Doro replied, although she might have asked a few questions around town. Ev need not hear such an admission.

He shook his head. "In any case, I'm to blame for Wade not saying anything about his mother's concerns. We haven't dismissed them, but if I thought there was a bootlegging run coming near here soon, I'd say so." Ev inhaled and exhaled sharply. "My old boss would alert me if there was a possibility. No one wants innocent folks to run afoul of rumrunners, so Wade and I need to know what might happen."

For a long moment, Doro studied him. "You're confident that nothing is." It was a question and a statement.

"I'm confident nothing is going on in the immediate future," Ev replied. "I can't say it never will."

The response made Doro sit up straighter. "So, you think the Fultons are involved in the illicit liquor trade?"

With one hand, Ev rubbed his forehead. "That's quite likely," he admitted before hesitating for a moment. "There will be signs if a run is coming near here, and they're involved."

"What kind of signs?" Doro asked.

Ev shook his head as a rueful smile formed on his face. "If I tell you, you'll be on the lookout, which could get you into trouble. Suffice it to say, I'm on alert for them."

Disappointment hurtled through Doro, but she let the subject drop. Their present concern was identifying the poisoner. Later, she could learn more about the Fultons. "So, we'll take them off the list," she said.

After the group agreed, Aggie turned to Wade. "We haven't learned much about what caused Mr. Stanley's death. I wasn't here when it happened."

"My first wife was ill at the time and passed only weeks later, so I had my hands full," the constable said.

Doro noted he used the term *first wife*, which indicated he was considering a second. Had Aggie noticed? If so, her friend made no sign. "Betty isn't originally from Michaw," Doro said.

"She came here shortly after her marriage," Wade said. "I didn't know her well, but Betty brought meals to us often, following Margie's passing. Her son Mathias and my Davey are the same age," Wade replied.

"She looks to be close to forty," Doro said.

"About that," Wade agreed.

"So, she was older than her husband," Ev observed.

"I hadn't thought about it, but probably so. He met her during his law school days," Wade said.

"Was she married before?" Aggie made the query.

"No," Wade replied. "Betty taught school in the city. She thought about going back to it after Mr. Stanley passed. She spoke with the principal recently, because money is a concern for her."

The information prodded Doro to put forth another question. "What did she teach?"

"I don't know." Wade paused a moment. "Why so many questions about Betty?"

"Just wondering, since she's still a suspect," Doro replied.

"What about that woman professor?" Ev asked. "Any more from or about her?"

After exchanging a long look with Aggie, Doro revealed what she saw as Trudy's slip-ups and ended by saying, "It bothers me."

"She's a concern to me, too," Wade agreed. "For one, I don't like her attitude."

Aggie patted his hand. "She's outspoken with everyone, but it's hard to believe she'd taint my jam. Maybe I don't want to believe it."

"I don't, either," Doro put in, "but the circumstantial evidence gives me pause."

"Me, too," Ev said. "As a science teacher, she'd know how much arsenic would sicken but not kill. The fact that she could also reseal the jam jar with paraffin is another clue against her. Is paraffin used in the science lab?"

"It wasn't when we were students," Doro replied. Then, she revealed Trudy's ability to order and store supplies, as well as her tending plants for classes.

"Interesting," Wade said.

"It sure is," Ev added. "Can you find out what she's ordered recently?"

"Department chairmen approve supply orders, but the records go to the president's office before payments are made," Doro replied. "I'm not sure if we could get the paperwork or not." She didn't say she planned to try, because Ev might object to her methods. Better to present information after the fact than to reveal her strategy now.

Wade ran one hand over his face. "Unless we have more evidence against her, we can't get the information. President Adams is a good man, far better than his short-term predecessor, but he won't like us implicating a professor without sound reasons."

Ev shifted to face Doro. "Do the two of them get along?"

"Pretty well," Doro said. "President Adams fought for Trudy to be hired and to get tenure."

A harsh sigh escaped Ev. "Then, let's not approach him until we know more."

Not wanting to alert the men to her plan to ask Mrs. Jones, Doro presented a suggestion. "Arsenic is being discussed as the cause of your illness. From what Professor Hollingsworth told me, mercury wouldn't be easy to hide in jam."

"I wonder about toxic plants," Ev said. "I'm sure there are many."

"Unfortunately, that seems to be true," Doro agreed. "When I spoke with Professor Hollingsworth, she gave little information, so I don't know what Trudy is growing. At this time of year, the plants would have to be inside." She paused for a moment before mentioning Gladys and the flowers. "Ev, you saw Professor Hollingsworth bring a basket. How long did she stay?"

Ev's gaze skittered away. "I saw her leaving when we came in for the cakewalk."

"Around nine-fifteen?" Doro asked.

He nodded. "She stayed almost an hour. Why?"

"Gladys wouldn't have stayed away so long if she knew Trudy was coming to Wheaton Hall," Doro replied.

"No, she would've been there," Aggie agreed, "although she's known for being tardy."

"So, that's not the final clue," Ev said.

"No, but it's another one to add," Doro replied. "The test results will be, too. When does Doc expect results?" Doro asked.

Ev's gaze narrowed on her. "You're giving up on seeing the invoices right away?"

Drat the man. He was far too perceptive. With effort, Doro maintained a calm demeanor. "Wade wants to wait," she replied before going back to her query. "I hope we won't have to wait on the test, though." She turned to the constable and repeated her query. "Do you know?"

"The deputy told us they'd have the jam tested today," Wade replied. "We could hear any time."

Doro sat up straighter. "Will the sheriff's office call you?"

Wade nodded. "That's the plan."

Although she wanted to find out more about Trudy's involvement, Doro also yearned to get details about the test. A quick glance at her watch showed the time to be quarter to five. Mrs. Jones might be back. Would the secretary let Doro look at invoices? "Aggie and I can wash the dishes while you two rest," Doro suggested.

Wade immediately agreed while Ev, who looked skeptical, followed suit after a moment.

When the two young women were alone in the kitchen, Aggie turned to Doro. "You want to hear about the test, and I do, too. Are you planning to call Mrs. Jones again?"

"You're reading my mind."

The ringing of the telephone interrupted. Since it was in an alcove off the front hall, Doro and Aggie hurried to the parlor. Wade's side of the conversation revealed little, except the caller's identity. The county sheriff was on the other end of the line. After returning the earpiece to the cradle, the constable shared the news.

"As Doc figured, the substance in the jam is arsenic, maybe in the form of rat poison. In terms of the amount, there wasn't enough to be fatal." Wade joined Aggie on the sofa, while Doro took the chair across from Ev.

"Not even if it was ingested over time?" Aggie asked.

"Especially not then," Wade replied. "We would've gotten sick, but not deathly ill."

Ev braced his elbows on his knees and clasped his hands in front of him. "So, either Betty or Trudy could've done the deed."

"That's right," Wade said. "We need to interview them as soon as we're able and get those invoices. I called the college, and Adams is in Sylvania this afternoon. I'll try his house tonight. Ev and I might go over to talk with him."

Doro felt a stab of alarm and when she studied Aggie's expression, she knew her friend had the same reaction. The men could hardly stand up. How would they question people and gather evidence? But they would not need to exert themselves if Doro and Aggie gathered the right evidence in short order.

"For now, you need to rest," Aggie said, in a soft tone exuding concern.

As she got to her feet, Doro nodded. "Yes, you do."

Ev shifted in his chair. "You've done a lot of work on the case. Wade and I will be able to take over soon, so you don't need to do anything now. Except be careful. Narrowing the suspects down to two is important, but we don't know which of them is guilty. Since we aren't sure about the motive, either, caution is best."

"Absolutely," Wade agreed. "We're both getting stronger quickly. By tomorrow, we can get back to work. Even later tonight, we might."

"Let's hope so," Doro replied, but she did not comment on the case or that she and Aggie would keep investigating. Instead, she bid the men goodbye before the speculation darkening Ev's gaze led to him asking more questions or issuing additional warnings.

CHAPTER FOURTEEN

After leaving the Lammers' home, the two friends walked about a half-block before Aggie glanced at Doro. "Ev and Wade seem sure they can investigate tomorrow."

Doubt was in Aggie's voice, doubt that echoed inside Doro. "They're too optimistic, in my view and going to President Adams' house tonight is foolish."

"I feel the same way, but we were being warned off."

Doro chuckled. "It was a casual warning from Wade. Ev was more forceful."

"Which is why you wanted to rush off," Aggie observed.

"It seemed wise," Doro replied. "Since we didn't actually agree, we can pursue a few details. For one, I'd sure like to know what Betty Stanley taught before her marriage."

Several moments of silence elapsed before Aggie responded. "Because, if she was a science teacher, she'd also know about poisons."

"Probably so," Doro agreed.

"You're not going to ask her, are you? She won't say, and she'll get even snippier."

Doro shook her head. "No, but the high school principal should know. He and his wife usually eat at the diner on Monday evenings. We could stop there for a piece of pie and coffee."

"We just had a meal, and I ate two slices of bread."

"You don't have to have the entire piece, but we need a reason to go in," Doro pointed out. "I can go by myself."

"Oh, no. I'm going along."

"Because you're curious, too," Doro said with a grin.

Aggie's lips twitched. "I am."

Since the diner was on the next cross street, Doro and Aggie turned toward the restaurant. As usual, the place was busy during the dinner hour. A quick glance revealed that the principal and his wife, Nick and Fern Willoughby, were seated in a booth toward the back. Luckily, a table near them was available. The couple looked up as the young women sat down.

"Dorothea, Agatha, how nice to see you both," Mrs. Willoughby said with a smile. A petite woman in her mid-forties, she exuded warmth and welcome.

Her husband, only slightly older but taller and leaner, had a sterner countenance. Doro attributed to his years at the helm of the high school. Most students were well-behaved, but a few boys caused trouble from time-to-time, and the principal dealt with them. "Good evening," Doro replied.

Aggie added her response.

Mr. Willoughby did the same before asking, "How are Wade and Officer Mallow?" Although only a few years older than the town constable, the principal had been a teacher when Wade was in school.

"We've been wondering about them," his wife added. "Such a terrible thing for them to fall ill like they did. There's a lot of gossip going around town, but I don't like to listen."

Doro fought back a smile. Fern Willoughby was not known as a town tattler, but she usually lent an ear. At least that had been the assessment from Doro's mother. "I love Michaw, but a small-town is a gossip mill, and so is a college campus." The statement gave nothing away. Should Doro say more? But what? Her primary interest was learning about Betty Stanley. Principal Willoughby surely knew what the woman taught, and his wife could have details, since she served on the town events committee. "We missed seeing you at the baking contest on Saturday morning." The casual observation might be useful. Doro hoped so.

Mrs. Willoughby shrugged. "I missed both the cakewalk and the competition because I was helping with picnic baskets at the church. Keeping them cool and organized is important. I was in charge, so I stayed there until the auction began."

"That had to be a big job," Aggie commented. "We kept ours in the Wheaton Hall refrigerator, but didn't most ladies store them in the icehouse?"

"They did. The majority came early, although there were a couple of stragglers who arrived shortly before the sale began. Betty Stanley was one, because she had a hot meal. So did Lila Billings. She insisted on putting her basket front and center." Mrs. Willoughby sent a sympathetic glance Aggie's way. "She was mighty upset when Wade bid so high on your basket. Betty wasn't happy, either. Maybe I shouldn't say anything, but she's been the source of malicious gossip about you. Although I understand her situation, it's not right to blame you for how Wade feels. Same with Lila."

Her husband cleared his throat. "Mrs. Stanley and Miss Billings don't want to be the topic of tittle-tattle, either."

A flush rose in Fern Willoughby's cheeks, but she held the principal's gaze. "Then, they shouldn't spread mean, baseless accusations about Aggie." When she spoke again, her voice lowered several notes. "Betty's husband didn't leave her well-situated. I believe that's the main reason she set her cap at Wade."

Wade had said as much. Now, Betty's interested in returning to teaching, which makes sense. "She told Wade about seeking a job at the high school," Doro said.

Principal Willoughby released a harsh breath. "Our math teacher, Miss Lowell, is leaving at the end of the year. Mrs. Stanley is interested in the position."

Disappointment filled Doro. Her supposition was wrong.

Aggie frowned. "She taught math before her marriage."

"No, she taught chemistry, which is why I had to say she wasn't a strong candidate," the principal replied in a regretful tone.

"I see," Aggie murmured, but an edge of excitement was in her voice.

Doro felt a similar anticipation. A chemistry instructor would know enough about toxins to choose one that would not be immediately detected. And she should realize what amount would cause illness, not death.

Mrs. Willoughby laid her napkin aside. "Betty feels desperate at this point, and that's making her angry. When Mr. Stanley first passed, we all figured he left her well off. In fact, right after the funeral, Betty seemed calm about her situation. She mentioned being set for life."

"I only have a vague memory of Mr. Stanley dying," Doro said.

"You were away," the principal said.

"He was fairly young. What caused his death?" Doro asked.

The principal's wife shook her head. "He felt ill for a few weeks. Stomach trouble, headaches, fatigue. Betty said he refused to see Doc. Evidently, he blamed it on exhaustion, since he'd been running to his mother's place in Bowling Green every weekend and sometimes going mid-week. He insisted he'd be fine. But he wasn't. A few weeks after he started ailing, he died. Betty had called Doc to the house by then, but it was too late. Such a sad time for her and her boy."

As she listened, Doro felt her heart race. "Did Doc Silven know what was wrong?" she asked in the hope the Willoughbys might know more than others.

"No. If Mr. Stanley had agreed to see him sooner, Doc might've figured it out. As it was, all he had to go on was Betty's observations. Poor thing. She was distraught," Mrs. Willoughby said. "Her only relief was having enough money for the future. Then, when the estate was settled, she got the bad news." The principal looked from Aggie to Doro. "I'm saying all this in the strictest confidence, because you two are discreet and trustworthy."

The young women readily agreed to keep the information to themselves.

"I'm sure it came as a terrible shock," Doro observed, but her supposition about Betty Stanley seemed more valid. The woman could have slowly fed arsenic or some other toxin to her husband.

"It did," Mrs. Willoughby replied, "and it's made her bitter. I'm sure that's the main reason Betty is spiteful. Aggie, I hope you know few folks listen to her gossip."

A soft smile lit Aggie's face. "Thank you. I do."

Mr. Carter, the proprietor, brought more coffee to the Willoughbys before addressing Doro and Aggie. "I'll send a waitress over. You already know the menu, but we have a special on meatloaf today."

"We're having pie and coffee," Doro said, although she would have liked to dash out and find Betty Stanley. Could the woman harbor enough anger to go after Wade again? Or maybe target Aggie with more than tart tittle-tattle? Doro did not want either of them to suffer.

Or anyone else, for that matter.

Regret darkened the owner's face. "Sorry, we just sold the last piece."

"That's all right," Aggie said. "We've had enough sweets for a while, so just coffee."

Doro felt a surge of relief. A little coffee, and they could be on their way. But to where and to do what? She had to organize her thoughts quickly.

After the principal and his wife finished their meals and excused themselves, Mr. Ford brought coffee for Doro and Aggie. When he was out of earshot, Doro laid her cup aside. "Mrs. Willoughby has always been knowledgeable about local goings-on, so we should've sought her out sooner."

Aggie rolled her eyes. "That would've been viewed as odd. What could we have asked casually before now?"

"That's a valid point."

"Besides, it's only been two days since Ev collapsed. We're making good progress." Aggie ran a forefinger around the edge of her cup. "Lila arriving early for the auction confirms her alibi."

"It does, so we were right to move her down the list," Doro replied, but she couldn't shake her uneasiness. Because she didn't want to talk more in the busy diner, Doro finished her coffee quickly. When Aggie did the same, they laid coins on the table and went outside. "Mr. Stanley dying from suspicious causes makes me wonder why Doc Silven didn't suspect her."

"Mrs. Willoughby said Mr. Stanley didn't see Doc until very late in his illness. If Betty acted upset over her husband's death, Doc might not have wanted to bother her more, especially when it's such a horrible idea. A woman killing her husband by slowly poisoning him? I don't know. Betty has been nasty to us, but would she do something so awful?"

"She might for money. From what we've heard, she expected to be well-off after her husband died. Maybe she wanted to be a widow instead of a wife."

"But she's worse off," Aggie replied.

"Which gives her a powerful reason to pursue Wade." Doro slid her arm through Aggie's elbow. "Mrs. Jones is supposed to work late, so I want to stop by her office."

"To look at the invoices."

Doro grinned. "If she'll let me. What I find, or don't find, might eliminate Trudy. Or highlight her."

"Mrs. Jones will bend the rules for you, I'm sure," Aggie said. "Are you calling first?"

"I should, just to make sure she's there. Let's head home."

When they arrived at Wheaton Hall, Doro telephoned the president's office. After speaking with Mrs. Jones, she turned to Aggie. "She'll let us look, and we can take Tee."

After fetching the little dog, the trio hurried along the walkway to College Hall. Doro's mind churned with bits and pieces of information. Usually, Doro got a gut feeling that led to the perpetrator. And she'd had one about Trudy, but she also wondered about Betty.

After entering the school's main building, the friends headed to the president's office. Their footfalls echoed loudly on the hard floors, which seemed to put the little dog on alert. Both ears were up, and a low growl left her.

"You're fine," Doro assured Tee. "You're just not used to being in here at night when no one else is around, since Ev only brings you

during the day." Even as she spoke, Doro wondered if that was right.
"We're all fine." Despite the statement, Doro picked up her pace.

Aggie followed suit. "It's creepy in here after hours."

When they got to the president's suite, Doro tapped on the door
before calling out, "It's Doro, Aggie, and Tee." When no answer came,
she tried again. "Mrs. Jones, it's Doro." Anxiety filled her, and Tee
began to whimper and whine. After inwardly chastising herself for
getting nervous and letting her feelings affect the puppy, Doro bent
to pet the silky head. "It's all right. Mrs. Jones is probably in the
president's office getting something, so we'll wait for her in her area."
After a single step inside the outer office, Doro stopped dead in her
tracks. Mrs. Jones' usually pristine desk was strewn with papers, and
more were on the floor. When Tee darted forward, Doro stopped her.
Something was wrong, but what? Had the secretary stepped out? Had
someone come while she was gone? Or had something bad happened
to her?

"What a mess," Aggie murmured.

When the sounds of a scuffle emanated from the president's private
office, Doro rushed inside without forethought. Tee strained at the
end of her leash, and Aggie was on their heels. Both young women
stopped abruptly at the scene before them. A masked figure was
wrestling with Mrs. Jones.

"Stop," Doro called out as Tee barked wildly and yanked on the
lead. The intruder kicked out, but Doro kept a firm grip on the leash
handle, which kept the little dog from being hurt. "Who are you, and
what are you doing?"

The person did not reply. Instead, he or she shoved Violet Jones
aside and turned toward the wall of bookcases behind the president's
massive desk. In moments, one panel swung out, and the figure disappeared. Doro wanted to give chase, but she first checked on the

secretary. "Are you all right?"

"Yes." The single word was a hushed murmur. "Fine, just rattled."

"We saw papers strewn across your desk and on the floor. What happened?" Doro asked. Getting basic information before pursuing the intruder seemed wise.

Mrs. Jones put one hand to her head and took a deep breath. "After you called, I got the paperwork from the science department out. I hadn't sorted through it, so I put it on the edge of my desk while I finished some typing for President Adams. When I got done, I brought the report in here for him to go over in the morning. As I returned to my desk, I saw someone going through everything, and I called out for the person to stop, but whoever it was grabbed a folder and ran in here. I followed to get the papers back."

Apprehension built inside Doro like the steam inside a kettle. "I couldn't tell who it was. Could you?"

A crestfallen look blanketed the woman's face. "No. The hood had narrow eye and mouth slits. I don't even know if it was a man or a woman."

Doro glanced at Aggie. "We can't let whoever it is get away. Stay with Mrs. Jones and Tee. I'm going after the person."

"It has to be Trudy," Aggie said. "Betty Stanley surely doesn't know about the hidden door or secret passage to the tunnel. She may not even know there's a tunnel."

"I agree," Doro replied. "Trudy has to be the thief and poisoner."

Mrs. Jones went paler. "I'd feel better if you called Officer Mallow or Constable Lammers. I heard they left Doc's house."

"I'll make the calls," Aggie assured Doro.

"Don't. They aren't in any shape to be running around. Call President Adams. I won't try to capture Trudy, just get the file."

"All right," Aggie reluctantly agreed. "We can have Colleen call the county sheriff. I'm sure he'll send deputies to nab Trudy. She may run, but she won't get far in the that jalopy of hers."

Because she was eager to catch the culprit, Doro handed the leash grip to Aggie. As she turned toward the president's office, the secretary spoke again.

"If you're going through the tunnel, take a flashlight. President Adams keeps one handy." Mrs. Jones reached into her desk and gave the item to Doro. "Be careful. Very careful. I don't want to telephone your parents with the news that you were hurt, or worse, while sleuthing."

Doro nodded. "I promise to be cautious."

"Good, but I'm going to call President Adams right now," Mrs. Jones said.

"Go ahead, but be cautious," Aggie urged her friend.

"I will." Doro rushed into the secret passage, eager to confront Trudy and end the investigation.

CHAPTER FIFTEEN

As soon as she stepped inside the hidden door, Doro turned the flashlight on. The narrow passageway was as dark and dirty as she remembered from her one foray into it, back when she and Ev had been investigating the murder of a professor in October. Then, he had been with her, and they had come the opposite way. This time, she had to descend the open, tight spiral staircase instead of going up it. Luckily, she had on sensible, low heel shoes.

Even so, Doro carefully went down to the cellar. Her nose wrinkled at the musty odor, but she pushed on. She focused the beam ahead and tried not to think about what creepy, crawly critters could be in her path. As she reached the main tunnel, Doro heard footsteps echoing ahead of her. While there was a dirt floor in most places, concrete had been poured in other locations. Not wanting to be heard, she quickly shed her shoes and hurried on. When the passage split into two branches after forty feet, Doro hesitated. One led to the male faculty residence hall, while the other went to the library. Trudy was not apt to escape through the apartment building, so Doro turned the opposite way.

Although the library was still open, no one would be in the store-room, which was where her current route ended. Since she still noticed the sound of shoes striking the hard patches, Doro tried to be quiet herself. As she scurried along, Doro considered how and where to confront Trudy. Definitely not on the rickety staircase leading to the library. She would have to let the science professor stay far enough ahead to avoid a dangerous confrontation. But not too far, because the storage area had a back door. Getting the file from Trudy before she took off was essential.

As she reached the steep steps, Doro heard the door above click shut. After a deep breath, she sprinted up the flight and waited. With her breathing coming hard and fast, hearing was not easy. Finally, the sound of footsteps again reached her. After a long inhalation, she eased the door on the landing open. The dark figure, now devoid of the hooded mask, came into view. Blonde hair, cut in a blunt bob, shone in the faint light provided by a single ceiling bulb.

Certainty filled Doro. Trudy Carstairs had taken the papers and, undoubtedly, poisoned Aggie's jam. For a fleeting moment, the woman faced Doro. Then, she spun on her heel and headed to the exit.

Doro shot forward to grab Trudy's arm. "Stop right here."

Trudy, her eyes flashing with rage, turned. "What do you want?"

The disingenuous question annoyed Doro. "The file you stole from Mrs. Jones' desk."

"File? I don't know what you're talking about," Trudy shot back. "I haven't been in the secretary's office for days."

Doro's gaze narrowed on the other woman. Since the papers were not visible, they must be tucked under her cloak. "Yes, you have. I just saw you there. You used the secret passage from the president's office to the tunnel as an escape route."

A cackle left the science professor. "You have a vivid imagination, Dorothea. You always did. But your fanciful nature won't help you gain tenure. Nor will falsely accusing a senior faculty member of theft." All civility was gone from the woman. Only anger and arrogance remained.

Trudy's brazenness only increased Doro's determination. "Do you deny you were in the tunnel just now?"

The professor lifted her chin. "Of course not, but there's access to it from the cellar of College Hall, as well from the men's faculty building."

While both statements were true, they did not mesh with what had happened. "You expect me to believe you went through College Hall and down to the cellar to come over here? Why? The weather is pleasant, so that's not a reason."

A smirk curved Trudy's lips. "What makes you think I wasn't in Maple Hall?"

The query seemed like a diversionary tactic, since women were only allowed in the reception area of the men's apartment building. To access the tunnel, Trudy would need to go into the residence hall proper to get to the cellar, which would be an odd action. "That makes little sense."

"Not to someone like you, who has been sheltered all her life." After a heartbeat, Trudy continued. "You've never had a beau, have you?"

"What does that have to do with you stealing the science department invoices?" Doro asked in a clipped tone.

"Nothing at all," Trudy replied, her own voice cool and dismissive. "Evidently, I need to spell it out for you. Marriage and career don't mix, as you know, but that doesn't mean a woman doesn't like the company of a man."

The assertion was another attempt to camouflage Trudy's guilt, so

Doro called her out. "Whoever you visited could help you establish an alibi, so what's his name?"

Even in the dim light, Trudy's angry expression was obvious. "I don't need an alibi, because I have no reason to steal invoices, but you must stop harassing me, or you will regret it. Rest assured of that."

The older woman's threats would have rattled Doro if she did not feel certain about both her intuition and the evidence. "You have an excellent reason. Those invoices show you purchased arsenic for the lab, a substance that's never been stocked, and that's not there right now. The same with paraffin." While she could not be sure what the paperwork indicated, Doro knew Trudy was lying.

"How ridiculous," Trudy said. "We've always kept arsenic in the lab, which means nothing, since the substance is widely available. The same with paraffin. It can be useful for a few applications."

"Like what?"

Trudy's nostrils flared with a sharp intake of breath. "I do not have to explain my purchases to you."

While the assertion was valid, Doro kept pressing. "There was no arsenic when Aggie and I were students, and Mrs. Jones said she'd never seen an invoice for it. Or for paraffin, and Gladys told me arsenic isn't used in the department." Doro studied Trudy's cloak. Could there be an inside pocket? Were the files in it? Somehow, she needed to get those papers.

"You and your friend weren't interested in science, as I recall. As for the secretary, she only got the job because her husband and your father were close friends. She isn't qualified and never has been."

"What about Gladys? She knows what materials are standard in science classes."

A brief pause preceded Trudy's response. "She doesn't know every-thing I've ordered recently."

Recent invoices would be more powerful proof, if Doro could get her hands on them. "I see," she murmured. "But you'll need to explain the sudden need for arsenic and paraffin. Invoices from the last decade are stored in file cabinets, so we can prove the science department didn't order arsenic or paraffin over the years." At least she hoped they could. Doro was going out on a limb with her assertions.

A humorless guffaw echoed in the small room. "Your ideas are more fantastic than ever, but it's little wonder since you spend so much time reading those foolish whodunits. President Adams approving your course about the mystery novel was asinine. When he leaves, I'll see that ends. You're apt to be gone, too, unless your father's friends rally to save you, but will they also rescue Aggie? Probably not." Trudy turned toward the exterior door. "Now, I'm leaving."

Since Doro knew the woman would destroy the invoices as soon as possible, she could not let her escape. Without forethought, she yanked on Trudy's cloak. A file folder and a mask tumbled out. Trudy bent to retrieve them, but Doro snatched both up and stepped back. "Running off won't help. The papers will prove what you did, and Mrs. Jones, Aggie, and I saw you in this mask." Doro waved the dark cloth in the air.

When Trudy lunged forward, Doro threw her shoes toward the woman, but they hit the door as it closed behind the professor. After donning her footwear, Doro rushed to the door leading into the library. She needed to summon help. Relief hit her when she heard voices near the circulation desk. If the science professor escaped, she could not go far. Nor could she deny her crimes. Not when Doro had solid proof in her hands.

"Doro, what in the world is wrong?" her boss asked as she stopped at the counter.

Nearly breathless, Doro sucked in air before offering a brief explanation. She wrapped up by saying, "President Adams should be coming. I'm sure Aggie and Mrs. Jones let him know I followed Professor Carstairs into the tunnel."

"I was on the telephone with Mrs. Jones when you ran in. She wondered if you were here. She's worried." Floyd Quartine searched Doro's face. "Are you all right?"

"Fine," Doro replied, but her heart was still racing while her breath continued to come in gasps.

"Mrs. Jones and Aggie will be over, along with President Adams, but why don't you sit down and catch your breath?" the head librarian asked, his lined face shadowed with concern.

Because she felt both shaky and winded, Doro agreed. She and Quartine were only in his office for long moments before the president and his secretary arrived. Aggie and Tee were close behind them.

"Are you all right?" Aggie asked.

Mrs. Jones echoed the question.

After she offered reassurances about her well-being, Doro revealed the file of invoices, along with the hooded mask. At the same time, she scooped Tee up. The little dog settled happily in her arms. "I haven't sorted through the papers."

President Adams, clad in a sweater and trousers instead of his usual suit, opened the folder and sifted through the invoices. "Mrs. Jones and Professor Darwine filled me in. This is sufficient evidence to my way of thinking. The science department never ordered either arsenic or paraffin in the past, and the dates are relatively recent," Adams said.

"Within the past month?" Doro asked.

He nodded. "April tenth."

"That's a few days after the baking competition contestants were announced," Doro said.

"Which means Trudy decided to poison my entry then," Aggie

observed.

"It seems that way," Mrs. Jones added.

Adams nodded. "Ev and Wade will have to examine the evidence. Mrs. Jones explained why you didn't want to call them, but they need to know now."

Anxiety squeezed Doro's insides. "They'll try to chase Trudy down, and I doubt if either of them is able."

A reassuring smile lit the president's face. "They're grown men, so they can decide for themselves. If they're not ready, Wade will call the country sheriff."

The remarks did not lessen Doro's concern. A deputy would not arrive soon, which meant Ev and Wade might push themselves to pursue Trudy. Even so, the president's statements were valid, so Doro agreed. "I'll call Wade's house."

After a brief conversation with the constable, Doro hung up and faced the trio in Floyd's office. "Wade insists he can track Trudy down. Ev was in the background saying the same thing, so they're heading to the constable's office," Doro said. "I'd like to meet them there."

"Me, too," Aggie agreed.

"I'll walk the two of you over," Quartine said.

"Good, and I'll see that Mrs. Jones gets home," Adams added.

"Thank you," the secretary replied.

The men's concern seemed oppressive, but Doro conceded. Although Trudy was highly unlikely to lie in wait for any of them, she had few options. The evidence weighed heavily against her. Even if Ev and Wade did not catch the science professor tonight, they would make an arrest soon.

Floyd left Doro, Aggie, and Tee at the constable's office, where the windows were alight. "Ev and Wade must be here already," Doro observed.

"They didn't waste any time," Aggie said.

When the friends stepped inside, they found Wade on the telephone and Ev pacing the length of the room. They did not look any better than earlier, except for the grim determination lining their faces. After Aggie went to stand near Wade, Ev stopped next to Doro.

"Confronting Professor Carstairs could've been dangerous," Ev muttered. "Why didn't you call us?"

The urge to chastise him was a palpable force, but Doro resisted it. "I didn't go to the president's office intending to confront anyone. It just happened that a masked figure was there when we arrived."

A sigh of resignation left him. "But you couldn't know what the professor might do when you followed her. You're lucky the woman didn't attack you."

Again, Doro could not reject a valid point. "I didn't confront her until she was in the library storage room, with other people nearby. We needed to know for sure who it was, and I had to keep her from destroying the invoices. If she'd done that, would you and Wade be able to arrest her?"

His head fell forward, and he rubbed his neck with one hand. "Probably not, unless her department chairman testified to her ordering arsenic and paraffin."

"As the assistant chairwoman, Trudy is the one who handles the orders and invoices. The chairman wouldn't know, and Mrs. Jones hadn't looked at them until this evening after I called, but that would only be one witness." Doro shoved her hands into her pockets.

Ev ran one hand over his face. "True, but I still don't like you taking such risks."

The sincerity in his tone and expression reached past Doro's barriers. "I don't like you getting out of your sickbed to chase her down."

For long moments, they gazed at one another. Then, Wade's voice intruded.

"The mayor and his wife are in Toledo this evening, but I spoke with a couple of councilmen. I let them know we're going to the professor's home. If we don't find her, I'll get some help."

"You have help. At least, you will if you let us drive you over there," Doro said.

"Yes, do," Aggie added. "It will save a little strain."

After the lawmen exchanged a long look, Wade nodded. "All right."

"You two need to stay in the vehicle," Ev said. Although he addressed both women, his attention riveted on Doro.

"Of course," Aggie readily agreed.

Doro's concession came a bit more slowly. "Sure, but let me drive."

Ev looked skeptical, but he nodded. After Wade did the same, the group was on its way to Trudy's cottage, which was near the campus. Silence filled the automobile as Doro drove the short distance and stopped at the curb. No lights were visible from the street.

"The place looks empty," Doro said.

"Maybe she left already," Aggie said.

"Her vehicle is at the far end of the driveway," Doro pointed out.

"Oh, you're right," her friend replied. "Do you think she's inside her house or in the automobile?"

"Hard to say," Ev replied. "Getting away from here is her best bet, although it's got poor odds."

"Where would she go?" Wade asked. "She doesn't have family, does she?"

"An aunt in Indiana, although I don't know exactly where," Doro said.

"Not much future in being on the lam," Ev observed. "It might take time to catch her, but she'd be arrested sooner or later. Running will only give her some extra days of freedom."

"Sooner would be better," Doro put in.

"I agree." As Wade spoke, he opened his door. "Wait here. One of us will cover the back door while the other goes to the front one. She could have a light on that we can't see yet."

As Ev slipped out of the vehicle, Doro felt her anxiety escalate. "Be careful."

"We will," he replied. Then, both men stepped away from the vehicle.

"I hope Trudy doesn't have a weapon," Aggie murmured.

Since that worry hovered in the back of her mind, Doro expressed the same wish. As she stared into the darkness, Doro saw Ev stop at the front porch while Wade disappeared around the side of the house. After a few moments, Ev went to the door. Her heart caught in her throat as the seconds dragged like hours. Did Trudy have an accomplice? If so, she might already be gone. Two main roads led out of Michaw, but how would they figure which one to take or which direction to go? To her aunt in Indiana? Or someplace farther away? Frustration bloomed inside Doro as she stared into the darkness.

Abruptly, shouts pierced the night. Doro, fear weighing like a leaden blanket on her heart, twisted in her seat. Ev rushed down the front steps and to the driveway. Almost simultaneously, Trudy's old Hudson roadster backed out. Wade scurried from behind the house, but neither he nor Ev could catch the car on foot. While her own vehicle was more powerful than the Hudson and could catch it on the road, Doro knew stopping Trudy now was best. Since she had not killed the engine, she pulled to the end of the drive just as the roadster reached that point. The impact sent Doro's larger vehicle into a half-spin, but it stopped Trudy in her tracks.

Seconds passed before Doro, her heart pounding in her ears, turned to Aggie. "Are you all right?"

"Yes, and you?"

"A little shaken." When she got out, Doro realized she was a lot shaken. For several moments, she leaned against the chassis. Otherwise, she might have tumbled to the ground. On the edges of her mind, Doro registered Ev and Wade extracting Trudy from the roadster and, in short order, the lawmen were leading the professor—who was struggling mightily despite having her hands cuffed behind her—to the curb.

"Thanks for hemming her in, Doro," Wade said with a grin.

"It seemed better than chasing after her," Doro replied.

"Better?" Ev echoed. "You may not think so when you see the dent on the side of your precious automobile."

A pang of dismay enveloped Doro. "Oh, no." She loved the Essex.

"It's not so bad," Wade assured her. "Right now, I want to get the professor to the station. Ev and I will put her between us in the back seat."

"Do you think my car is still drivable?" Doro inquired.

"Absolutely," Wade assured.

Doro wanted to rush around and study the damage but that could wait, so she climbed back behind the steering wheel and, when the men and their prisoner were settled, turned toward Main Street.

After Ev and Wade led Trudy into the office, Doro hurried to see the dent. A crease marred the front end of her beautiful roadster, but the constable was right. It could be fixed.

"I'm sorry she got damaged, but you did the right thing," Aggie murmured.

Another pang hit Doro, who always referred to the Essex as *she*. "It's just an automobile." But it wasn't. The roadster had been a college graduation gift from her parents, and Doro treasured the vehicle. People often laughed at her affection for the car, but she was like an old friend. An injured friend now. Doro patted the dent. "We'll get you back to normal as soon as possible." The sound that came out of Aggie sounded like a muffled laugh. Doro stood to face her friend. "I sound ridiculous."

Aggie shrugged, but her hazel eyes twinkled. "Let's go in and hear what Trudy has to say."

Since Doro was as curious as Aggie, she led the way. Loud voices, mostly Trudy's, reached them as soon as they opened the door.

"Stay still and stop shouting," Wade advised Trudy. "You're only making it worse for yourself."

"You are a besotted fool, Constable Lammers," the professor said in a snide tone. "You don't want to believe your precious sweetheart is only skilled in poetry, a useless subject. She was in two of my science courses, and we were lucky she didn't cause an explosion. With that in mind, it's easy to understand how she got poison in her cooking."

"Professor Carstairs, we know you put arsenic in the jam. We've got proof of you ordering the stuff for the science department." Wade lifted the sheaf of papers—which Doro had handed to him earlier—as he spoke. "I've already confirmed that no previous orders were ever made. Add to that, the purchase of paraffin, your presence in the Wheaton Hall kitchen the morning of the baking competition, and the timing of your orders. You had plenty of time to taint the jam and reseal the jar on Saturday. You claimed to be meeting a friend who lives in the residence."

"I met Gladys Hollingsworth," Trudy insisted.

"That's interesting," Ev put in. "Professor Banyon and Professor Darwine saw you in Wheaton Hall around eight-thirty, right?"

"About then," the professor replied.

"At that time, I was letting your friend into the auditorium, since she donated a May basket. She chatted with some of the committeewomen for a while and seemed in no hurry to leave," Ev said.

Trudy's jaw tightened, but she ignored Ev's assertion. "You haven't said what my motive would be."

"You don't like fellow female professors marrying and leaving," Ev said. "That's not in dispute, since you indicated as much to Aggie, Doro, and others more than once. I'm sure we can find people to corroborate that. You've dug a deep hole for yourself by not only using poison, but by also stealing documents from the president's office. If I were you, I'd own up and hope to get a more lenient sentence by being honest."

"I'm sure Gladys will corroborate my alibi. Ask her," Trudy said.

"Maybe she'll lie for you, but Officer Mallow saw her when she was supposed to be meeting you," Doro put in before making another observation. "You said Gladys doesn't know what's ordered, so did she lie to me about arsenic not being used in science courses?"

Rage flashed in Trudy's eyes. "You're disrespectful to senior faculty, Dorothea, and that is foolish."

Out of the corner of her eye, Doro saw Ev shake his head. Trudy was painting herself into a smaller and smaller corner, and they all knew it.

"Maybe Professor Hollingsworth will lie, but she'll get found out," Wade said. "Or maybe she helped you."

"We'll be looking into that," Ev agreed.

For several seconds, Trudy studied the lawmen. "Your tactics won't work on me. I went to Gladys' apartment on Saturday morning. These two," she jerked her thumb at Doro and Aggie, "saw me go up, and I met two other professors on their way downstairs, too."

"But you didn't go to Wheaton Hall to see Professor Hollingsworth," Ev insisted, "because she wasn't there. I'll testify to her presence at the auditorium, and so will others, I'm sure."

Trudy remained stoic.

"Professor Carstairs, Officer Mallow has already pointed out that you were caught stealing papers from the president's office, papers that show you purchased arsenic and paraffin on April tenth. On top of your non-existent alibi, you'd be wise to admit the truth."

"That's all circumstantial," Trudy insisted, but her tone was not as formidable.

"Why take the papers if you didn't want to hide your purchases?" Doro asked.

Although her expression did not soften, Trudy bent her head. For long moments, silence filled the office.

"Trudy, you told me that a little arsenic wouldn't kill a person," Doro put in. "As a science professor, you would know. But most others wouldn't realize how much could cause sickness, not death. Did you want to make Aggie ill? Or both of us? Or harm all the judges and embarrass Aggie? What was your goal?"

Trudy lifted her chin a fraction, but the glare had left her face. "Being taken seriously as a professor is difficult for any woman, and you both know it. I've fought for myself and every women professor at Michaw College. Those who marry and leave make it even harder for the rest of us, because a man is apt to be hired next. It's happened twice in the past year, and it'll happen again when Aggie leaves."

"I've never said I'm leaving," Aggie pointed out.

Trudy's attention strayed to Wade before returning to Aggie. "But you will." Defeat was in her voice and expression.

"What about your job, Professor?" Ev asked. "Your actions will lead to you being fired. Do you think a man will be hired in your place?"

The color ebbed from Trudy's face. "I have tenure."

"That won't do you much good if you're found guilty of attempted murder," Ev said.

"Murder," Trudy echoed. "I didn't plan to kill anyone."

Doro seized on the response. "Then, you wanted to make someone sick."

Trudy put both shackled hands to her face, but she said nothing.

"Professor Carstairs, Officer Mallow already gave you good advice about coming clean," Wade told her. "You'd be wise to do that now. An assault charge would be better than attempted murder."

The professor's shoulders slumped and her head fell forward. "I wanted to make Aggie look bad, and I figured all the judges would add a dab of jam to her cake—only enough to cause minimal symptoms of arsenic poisoning. Since I used a small amount of rat poison, I didn't figure on anyone getting deathly ill. That was never my intention. Please believe me." Her tone grew plaintive. "I've heard talk in town about Aggie not being suitable marriage material, due to her career. I thought if folks believed she accidentally got arsenic in the jam, that would make matters worse and maybe end her stepping out with the constable." Her gaze went to Wade.

The constable scowled. "I'd never believe she'd make such a mistake," Wade said, his voice stern, "so it wouldn't have made a difference to me."

As Trudy turned her attention to Aggie, sadness shone in her gaze. "I tried to persuade you to not give up your career for marriage and motherhood, because you are a fine professor. And you're a wonderful example to our female students. I helped you get hired. I've been a friend and a mentor." A harsh breath left her. "Besides, you love poetry and your students. Being a housekeeper to a passel of children won't be as easy or as satisfying."

"Aggie already said she hasn't decided about her future," Wade put in. "I'm not pushing her to go courting, although she knows I'd like that. Having her be happy is more important than anything. If you were concerned about her welfare, that's what you'd want, too."

One look at Aggie's face had Doro's heart turning over. Wade truly loved her friend. He had not spoken the words, but it was clear in his concern. And everyone in the room knew it.

"You don't know how hard it is for a woman in academia," Trudy murmured, but her tone lacked conviction.

"Maybe not, but you haven't made it easier," Wade replied.

An interlude of silence was followed by Ev speaking. "We need a formal statement." He glanced at Wade. "I'll call the sheriff's department, since we don't have proper facilities to hold her."

Wade nodded. "Sounds fine. I'll take the statement. Maybe Aggie or Doro will jot down the notes."

"Doro is good at that," her friend said.

"I am sorry, Aggie," Trudy said. "For making you look bad and for leaving the note. I wouldn't have done anything else."

Anxiety hit Doro as soon as the words were out of the professor's mouth, but she had no chance to speak because Ev and Wade both expressed shock and displeasure.

"What note?" Wade looked from Trudy to Aggie.

Ev focused on Doro. "I'd like to see this note, if you haven't destroyed it."

Heat flooded Doro's face, but she reached into her pocketbook and extracted the missive before handing it to Ev.

After scanning it, Ev handed the paper to Wade. "You've been carrying it with you but didn't show it to Wade and me."

Wade looked as disapproving. "This is evidence."

"Yes, but it isn't signed and it's typed," Aggie pointed out.

Wade's features softened. "True."

Ev shook his head. "I guess."

After a long breath, Doro smiled. "We planned to show you when you were better. And, well, things started happening fast. But it's all ended well."

"Your famous last words," Ev said, but a smile played across his lips.

Within the next hour, Trudy Carstairs had admitted to being the poisoner, solidified her motive, and offered another apology to Aggie. Doro did not find it sincere, but her friend graciously accepted. Soon afterward, two deputies arrived to take the science professor to Toledo.

When the office was again quiet, Doro studied Ev and Wade, who both looked on the verge of exhaustion. "You two need to get some rest."

"I won't argue," the constable replied with a faint smile.

"Let me drive you home in your vehicle," Aggie said. "Ev can ride with Doro, and then, we'll head back to Wheaton Hall, so you two can sleep."

When neither man resisted the suggestion, Doro realized they were dead on their feet. She was even more certain after Ev climbed into the passenger seat and let his head fall back. "You need to rest tomorrow. So does Wade."

Seconds of silence passed before he spoke. "I agree."

His quick conciliation and ragged voice stoked the embers of anxiety deep within Doro. "Do you need to see Doc?"

Out of the corner of her eye, Doro saw Ev turn toward her. "I'm exhausted, not sick. In a few days, I'll be as good as new."

"Until then, you'll stay at Wade's house."

"I will. Not sure I can do much else."

The admission telegraphed how poorly he must feel, so Doro let the conversation dwindle away. From time-to-time, she glanced at Ev, who had fallen asleep. Her heart turned over. He was such a good man.

The urge to say they could step out rose within her. On its heels came her determination to be the head librarian. Even if getting married did not lead to dismissal, it would be an impediment to any promotion. And what about having children?

As she drove through the night, Doro made a decision. She needed to leave for Colorado as soon as possible, because being around Ev too much, especially in his present condition, was wearing on her restraint.

CHAPTER SIXTEEN

For the rest of the week, Aggie and Doro were busy with end of the term matters. When Aggie brought home a lovely May basket on Wednesday, Doro felt a twinge of envy. Wade had purchased it before the cakewalk and, although some of the flowers were slightly wilted, the thought was beautiful. Aggie's pleasure over the gift reinforced Doro's belief that her friend and the constable would soon go courting.

While Aggie visited Wade's house every day, Doro did not. Instead, she asked about both lawmen and felt happy they were improving, but her decision to leave for Colorado sooner than planned made her hesitate to face Ev. Maybe Doro should have told him herself, but she left the task to her best friend, who had not been pleased to shoulder the responsibility.

On Thursday evening before leaving for dinner with Wade, Aggie said, "You've decided not to step out with Ev, which is your choice, but you aren't so busy you couldn't have let him know you're leaving this weekend. At some point, you'll have to talk because of Tee. I'm not doing it for you."

Embarrassment sent heat into Doro's cheeks. "I don't expect you to."

"Good." Her expression softened. "He's a good man, and he deserves better treatment. If you don't want more than friendship, that's your decision. But avoiding him isn't friendly." After a moment, Aggie gathered her things and left.

Doro shut the door and scooped up Tee. After the pair settled in the window seat, Doro stroked the puppy's head. As usual, one ear bobbed up. "The truth is, the more I see Ev, the more I think about staying here all summer. Or at least not spending all of it in Colorado." A soft whine was Tee's response. Doro smiled. "You'd like that, I suppose, but I've wanted to be the head librarian since I was a little girl. The policy of not employing married women may change soon, but it may not. I don't want to step out with Ev, end up liking him even more, and..." Tee yelped. "All right. End up falling in love with him, and then, find out I'll lose my job if we wed." A self-deprecating chuckle left her. "I'm getting way ahead of myself, because he'd have to fall in love with me, too." Her heart raced at the thought, and at the memory of standing with him under the mistletoe during the town Christmas dance. And not just standing. For a moment, Doro thought about the spring dance on Saturday. Thought about it and dismissed it. By the time the first strains of music played, she would be hours away.

When a call came from Ev on Friday, Doro reluctantly packed Tee's gear and put it in a bag. The little dog danced around, ready for an adventure.

"We're going to Ev's place, since he's home." Doro went to the umbrella stand and hall tree by her front door. Before getting Tee's leash, she looked into the mirror. As she fingered her brown hair, Doro wondered about her appearance. Was she overdressed to drop off the puppy? Her rose silk drop-waist dress was stylish, and Doro topped it off with a matching cloche that sported a pink ribbon and flower. Since extra ribbon had come with the hat, Doro tied a piece on Tee's collar. "We look bright and cheerful, not overdone," she said to the puppy before leaving the apartment.

Within moments, Doro and Tee ascended the stairs to Ev's apartment. To calm her nerves, she touched the gold locket at her neck. The glittering pendant had been given to her mother from her father, and passed on to Doro when Julia Banyon left for Colorado. The feel of it gave Doro strength and confidence.

Doro's knock was quickly answered. When Ev opened the door, the puppy yipped and darted forward. With reluctance, Doro released the leash.

Ev sank to his knees and petted Tee, who licked his face with wild abandon. "I'm glad to see you, too, and I love the ribbon."

When Ev did not comment on her outfit, Doro hurried on. "How are you feeling? Aggie said you and Wade have been improving every day."

As he rose to his feet, his gaze met hers. "We have." The two words sounded clipped and chilly. "That's why I came home today."

Facing him was every bit as difficult as Doro had figured. Maybe more difficult. Part of her wanted to admit the extent of her fear and worry about him. Despite Aggie's reassurances, Doro had fretted about a setback. "No lingering effects from the poison?"

He shook his head. "Not really."

Once again, his response did not exude warmth. Was he upset that she had not visited all week? Doro cleared her throat. "I worked several evenings, so I couldn't make it for dinner. I hope Aggie explained." The truth was, Doro had volunteered to work late because she feared letting her guard down with Ev. When they weren't together, remembering her dream of being the head librarian remained foremost in her thoughts. But when she saw him, Doro felt a connection that could not be denied.

"She did, but I didn't expect you to come. After all, the case was over. Or about over. Aggie will probably tell you later tonight, but Wade spoke with Doc Silven earlier today. He was never concerned about Betty because Mr. Stanley was exposed to arsenic at his mother's home. You might remember green arsenic being used in wallpaper years back."

"I've read about it," Doro said. "That's why his poisoning took place over a long period?"

Ev nodded. "The paper with arsenic was under newer wallpaper, so it wasn't noticed until the house was sold, long after Mr. Stanley got ill, and it was only in an upstairs bedroom. He slept there, but his mother hadn't gone up there in years."

"What a shame," Doro observed with genuine sympathy.

"It is," Ev agreed. "Wade spoke with Mrs. Stanley after talking to Doc and made it clear, as he also did with Lila, that she needs to stop circulating false statements and mean criticisms about Aggie."

"What did Betty say?"

"She's sorry and won't interfere. Miss Billings denied gossiping, but Wade was straightforward with both of them. I don't think they'll bother Aggie again. Wade's days of having women pursue him are over."

The same would not be true for Everett Mallow. Although his face still showed traces of the ordeal, his silver eyes shone as brightly as newly minted coins and, while his dark hair was not as neatly combed as usual, the tousled look did not detract from his appeal. Nor did the stubble lining his jaw. He was handsome, intelligent, articulate, and personable. Plenty of local ladies would set their caps for him, if they had not already. When his gaze collided with hers, Doro felt heat flood her cheeks. A slight smile played across his lips. Hastily, she stared at her notes. How embarrassing to be caught ogling the man. "Did Trudy ever say if she tainted other jars?"

"She said no," Ev replied, "but we sent all of them to the county. No poison was found, but the jam got dumped, which is a shame. I love jam."

Doro smiled. "Strawberry season is coming soon, and Aggie will pick some and make more jam."

"Are you going to bake more shortbread then?" Ev asked.

Although his grin made him even more appealing, the question evoked bittersweet longing, which Doro hastily dismissed. "I'm afraid not, since I'll be in Colorado by the time local strawberries are ready."

As his attention moved from Doro to Tee, Ev's smile flattened. "When do you leave? Aggie said you were going earlier than planned, but not exactly when."

Her friend had not shared that tidbit, but Doro could not be mad. Providing details of her change in plans was her responsibility. Doro swallowed hard over the sudden lump in her throat. "Tomorrow morning."

Shock widened his silver gaze, and he hastily focused on the dog. "Tee will miss you."

"The months go fast," Doro said, although the time loomed longer than it had in the past. Her gaze went to Ev, who was staring down at Tee.

"Yeah, I'm sure it does when you get to see your folks."

An uneasy silence developed before Doro returned to the case. "Will the other suspects be named in the report?"

"No, it's not necessary," Ev replied, "and there's no need to embarrass local folks for no good reason. As far as Professor Hollingsworth, she had nothing to do with the poisoning. She seemed upset and readily agreed she hadn't planned to meet Carstairs on Saturday morning."

"What about the Fultons? Are you planning to monitor them?"

When he looked at her, the corner of his mouth lifted. "You know I am."

"Do you expect them to bring booze through or near Michaw?"

One of his shoulders lifted and fell. "It's not an expectation. It's more of a possibility I can't ignore."

Doro could not help but wonder if he expected something big to occur. When? While she was away? Possibly missing out on investigating bootleggers sent Doro's spirits plummeting even further. With grim determination, she masked her disappointment. As she searched his face, Doro saw mixed emotions there. "You believe they are involved?"

He shoved his hands into his pockets. "I do, although I can't prove it. Wade and I have discussed the situation, and he feels the same way. Even my old boss thinks it's possible. You'll be leaving soon, so you probably won't see either of them. If you do, try not to show any doubt or interest. They know you're an amateur sleuth, and they may suspect you suspect them."

Doro smiled at his turn of phrase before examining the statements. "You don't think they'd try to harm me?"

"Not as long as you don't bother them. Or talk about them with anyone other than Aggie."

"I won't." Making the promise was easy because she'd be gone in twenty hours.

"Good."

"Is that all?"

Again, he did not reply immediately. When Ev did, his voice lowered. "I may be away for part of the summer myself. If I'm not back when you get here, don't ask a lot of questions, all right?"

Apprehension curled in the pit of her stomach. "Are you going back to the Prohibition Bureau on a temporary basis?" Or a permanent one? Had her rejection of his suggestion to step out led to this?

"Of course not. I told you about my promise to my sister. She doesn't want me in such a dangerous job, which is why I'm here."

He had told her about the pledge to his sibling the prior fall, but Doro still felt uneasy about him going away. Where? Why? For how long? Since he was unlikely to provide specifics, she posed a more benign question. "Will you be back when classes start?"

"Long before then," he assured her, "and I've already asked if Wade will take Tee. He will, which his kids will love."

Doro petted the puppy's head. "Good." She yearned to know more but had no right to ask, so Doro voiced some friendly concern. "Whatever you do, be careful."

"I won't be in any danger," he replied in a clipped tone, but his gaze dropped to Tee.

Why wasn't Ev looking her in the eye? Because he wasn't telling the truth? Because he might be harmed? Doro needed to get some distance. "I'll put Tee's gear on your kitchen counter." She rushed to the small alcove off the parlor and stopped in her tracks. On the table was a beautiful basket filled with forsythia and tulips—the one Gladys had donated, the one Ev had fancied. And the one he had clearly purchased. For her? Doro didn't know and couldn't ask, so she hastily deposited the bag with Tee's things and went back to the other room, where Ev was now in an easy chair with Tee in his lap. "You two look comfortable."

"Tee is good company." For a moment, he studied Doro. "Don't worry about her being with Wade's family. It'll be a short time, and she'll be fine."

Doro choked out, "That's a relief." But Doro felt no relief, not about Ev going somewhere for some unknown reason. Quite the contrary. She felt edgy and scared and torn. "I better go, so you can rest."

"Enjoy your summer."

A smile wavered on her lips. "You, too." When Ev stood up, Doro crossed the few feet between them and petted Tee. "Be a good girl. I'll miss you terribly." But her words were not only for the puppy, they were for the man holding the little dog.

WHAT'S NEXT FOR DORO?

Doro's sleuthing adventures do not end with <u>The Jammed Judges!</u> Look for details on Book 4 on my website, in my newsletter, and on my Facebook page! Book 5 will follow at the end of the year.

THANK YOU!

Thank you for reading <u>The Jammed Judges!</u> I hope you enjoyed it. If you have time, please rate or review it. Comments from readers are helpful and appreciated. I am on Goodreads and BookBub. Most retailers also accept reviews.

https://www.goodreads.com/author/show/21325652.D_S_Lang

https://partners.bookbub.com/authors/6026727/edit

For more information, please go to my website. If you sign up for my newsletter, you will get access to free stories! https://www.dslangbooks.com

You can sign up for my newsletter on my website. I share other authors' work, news about my books, a peek into the writing life, historical tidbits, and more. Your email will never be shared, and you can unsubscribe at any time!

About the Author

D.S. Lang started making up stories to entertain herself as an only child, and she is still making them up. Now, she puts them in writing. Her mysteries are set in small town America during the 1920s. The amateur sleuths are young women dedicated to cracking cases with a colorful team of characters.

After earning Bachelor's and Master's degrees in education, D.S. worked as a golf shop manager, teacher (junior high, high school, and college), program manager, tutor, and mentor. She has a lifelong love of history and often gets sidetracked on research when she should be writing.

Acknowledgements

In <u>The Jammed Judges,</u> Doro makes shortbread, which Ev loves. They are my favorite cookie, too. When I talked about adding a recipe to this book, one of my friends said she had a wonderful one for shortbread.

This recipe has a long history, since it was passed down to my friend Terri Kovach through her husband's co-worker and friend, Mike Balow. Mike's grandmother, Paulina Pavlovich Mijatovich (1924-2014) got this gem from a neighbor. Details and Mrs. Mijatocih's signature are on the recipe that follows.

Thanks to Terri, her husband Gary Benore, Mike, Mrs. Mijotocih, and her neighbor Mrs. Henderson, too.

If you make the cookies, I hope you love them as much as everyone else has over the decades!

Mike Babus
Grandmothers
Recipe

June 8, 2008

One of my contemporary dear friends (84) passed on this original
shortbread cookie recipe which she acquired from an elderly
Scottish neighbor in Sudbury, Ontario way back when..... We are
firm believers in passing on rather than hoarding so there are
many enjoying Mrs. Henderson's original. Here goes....

S H O R T B R E A D

1/2 lb. butter (if you use unsalted then add a
                pinch of salt)

1/2 cup sugar

2 cups flour

Mix the butter and sugar for about 15 minutes
until mixture is very light and fluffy resembling
whipped cream (the secret is in the long mixing).
Gradually fold in flour. Gather ball of dough
and place on lightly floured board. Flatten
and roll out to about 1/4" (about thickness of
finger). Cut with small cutter and when baking
tin is filled, prick each with the tines of fork
to release any air pockets. Bake at 350 only
until very light colored. Store in tightly
covered cookie tin (stays fresh forever).
Remember to use flour sparingly 'cause dough
may be slightly sticky.

Good luck - once you make these you'll get more Scottish by
each baking. Men love them to say nothing about the children.

DORO BANYON
HISTORICAL MYSTERY
SERIES

The Doro Banyon series has a cozier tone than the Arabella Stewart books. History and mystery still mesh as amateur sleuth Doro solves whodunits with a team of colorful characters in smalltown America during the 1920s. Travel back in time to a college campus and crack cases with them!

Prequel-The Lost Exam
Book 1-The Catalogued Corpse
Book 2-The Murdered Matron
Book 3-The Jammed Judges

The prequel is currently free to my newsletter subscribers, but it is being revised and lengthened. When that is finished, it will be for sale on various digital storefronts. Another free prequel will take its place.

You can sign up for my newsletter at: https://www.dslangbooks.com

Arabella Stewart Historical Mystery Series

The Arabella Stewart Historical Mystery series is set in small-town Ohio after the Great War. Bella returns home from serving as a U.S. Army Signal Corps operator to find her family resort and hometown in dire straits, and the murder of a neighbor adds to the trouble. Much to the dismay of Constable Jax Hastings, an Army veteran, Bella turns amateur sleuth to solve the case. As the series continues, Bella and Jax vanquish the shadows of the war, while solving a series of whodunits with a team of colorful characters. If you love history and mystery mixed with touches of humor and drama, this series is for you!

Book One-A Precarious Homecoming
Book Two-A Lingering Shadow
Book Three-A Lethal Arrogance

THE JAMMED JUDGES

www.ingramcontent.com/pod-product-compliance
Lightning Source LLC
Chambersburg PA
CBHW052028020726
47501CB00004B/1295